# Waiting for a Wedding

# ALSO BY CATHRYN BROWN

# Waiting for a Wedding

CATHRYN BROWN

Sienna Bay Press

PO Box 158582

Nashville, Tennessee 37215

www.cathrynbrown.com

Cover designed by Najla Qamber Designs

(www.najlaqamberdesigns.com)

Waiting for a Wedding/Cathryn Brown. - 1st ed.

ISBN: 978-1-945527-60-9

❀ Created with Vellum

# DEAR READER

When Simone entered the story in *Runaway to Romance*, I immediately liked her character. She loves baking, just like I do. And she's fun. She wants to see the joy in life.

Then chef Nick helped out his buddy Micah in *Married by Monday*. He also spends his day with food, so I thought they'd be a good fit.

But they didn't want to get together. A grandmother fixed that problem. I hope you love her as much as I do.

Before long, they're in a fake romance that gives way to genuine feelings, and where Simone and Nick discover that the recipe for love is sprinkled with unexpected surprises.

I hope you enjoy reading Nick and Simone's story!

# CHAPTER ONE

$S$ imone Mills checked the time on her SUV's dashboard. The country highway that led into tiny Two Hearts, Tennessee, rolled out before her. Instead of focusing on the beauty of the countryside, she saw the remaining miles ahead before she arrived at a wedding with the wedding cake that currently sat in the back of her vehicle.

At least, the January temperatures were kinder to cakes than summer had been. She didn't have to leave at the crack of dawn to avoid the heat. In July, she'd done that and still had to crank the air conditioning to its highest level. What a sight she must have been wearing this same hat, gloves, and winter coat then. But the cake had arrived intact. *Every* cake had arrived intact. On time. She'd never missed a wedding.

She resisted the urge to put her foot a little heavier on the gas pedal because she didn't have time for a ticket, and she certainly didn't want an accident.

Her phone rang, and Cassie's name came up on her SUV's system. Forcing enthusiasm into her voice, Simone answered, "Hello!" Maybe that would deflect her friend and the wedding planner for today's happy event.

"You aren't here. I know that's stating the obvious, but I'm at CJ and Paige's house and you aren't. I have to head over to the ceremony in about ten minutes. Then there's going to be a reception here where people will expect cake. And food," she added with a lower mutter. "Not that it's on you."

Ouch! Neither she nor the caterer had arrived. "I'm about a half hour out. Everything will be fine." She hoped. She really, really hoped. "My assistant went into labor a month early. She and the baby are doing great, but my workload doubled. I'd already planned for a lighter client schedule while she was off, but not for this surprise." Simone would be relieved when the new mother came back to work in a couple of months.

Back in wedding planner mode, Cassie said, "That makes sense. But you know who this wedding is for and how important it is."

Simone knew that all too well. "Don't worry. Mrs. Brantley will have the cake of her dreams."

Cassie sighed. "I know she will. I trust you."

Good thing this wedding planner knew her well. She had never cut it this close before. Everything on the cake was planned in detail, with the baking and assembly starting days in advance. She'd grown to trust her assistant and expected her to always be there. She might have to hire a second assistant or take fewer orders.

Cassie's voice interrupted her thoughts. "I'll see you when we come back after the ceremony." There was almost a pleading sound in her friend's voice. Simone hated to hear that. She'd let her down.

"I'll be there." At that moment, a warning light on her engine's dashboard popped on.

As Cassie ended the call with "See you *soon,*" Simone's anxiety ratcheted up about five hundred notches. The SUV was running okay. She just needed the vehicle to continue doing that for another half hour. These ninety-minute drives from

Nashville to Two Hearts were starting to wear her out. She loved her friends Cassie and Bella, and the townspeople she'd met, but she might have to stop working weddings there.

If she didn't get to the town, she'd have few choices for help today. Cassie would be at the wedding. So would Bella, because this was someone they both knew. In fact, the entire town would be at *this* wedding. Her options for people to contact narrowed. Cassie would at least check her messages in case something to do with the wedding had arisen, but she was the future daughter-in-law of the bride.

Simone wouldn't let down the bride and groom.

The SUV continued to drive smoothly. In another half hour, she'd be pulling into town. At least there, she knew people who could help her. Out here, not so much.

The seedy-looking motel that always gave her the creeps when she passed it came into view and she shuddered. At least she wouldn't be stuck there.

The vehicle chugged.

"Come on, Harriet. You've been a champ." Simone patted the dashboard. "Give me just a little more."

Her trustworthy girl rolled on for about twenty seconds, so Simone started to release the breath she'd been holding. Then it chugged again and her speed dropped.

"Please, please, please." As she patted the SUV's dashboard, Harriet slowed to a crawl. There was no way she was going to make it to Two Hearts. She would be stuck at the only establishment around—the no-tell motel on her left.

As Harriet limped into the motel's entrance, her vehicle suddenly shot sideways with a crunch, stopping at the side of the parking lot. She'd been hit.

Simone looked up to find a big, black SUV with tinted windows pulling in behind her. That must be the culprit. Her rearview mirror showed the vehicle's door opening.

The motel's parking lot had a few cars in it, none from law

enforcement, so this was a slow day crime-wise. She'd driven by more than once on her way home after an event when emergency lights lit the night sky.

Considering where she was, she'd rather leave than see who'd hit her. "Just one more time, Harriet?" Simone turned the key in the ignition, knowing in her heart nothing was going to happen, but also knowing she had to give it one more try, just in case. Silence greeted her.

When she looked up to find a man standing beside her vehicle, her mouth opened to scream. Then she realized it was Nick Barton from the Nashville restaurant Southern Somethings, and she felt like she'd won the lottery. Always easy on the eyes, the dark-haired, brown-eyed man made her heart skip every time she saw him. Hers and probably every woman's within range of his charm.

She didn't have time to date, so that was out, but she could look. He'd been kind every time she'd seen him at his restaurant or at one of the weddings he'd catered and she'd made a cake for, but they'd never spoken beyond a word or two.

He'd damaged Harriet. But he *could* help her get to the wedding. Simone jumped out of her door. "Nick!"

"Sorry about your SUV!" About her age, he looked older and strained today. He rubbed his hand over his face. "I swerved to avoid an alpaca."

Did she hear him wrong? "A what?"

"They're like a bigger llama."

"I know what one is, but—"

He interrupted by pointing across the highway, where, sure enough, a cream-colored alpaca ambled away from the road and toward a large field.

"It stepped into the road just as you pulled in here. I turned in what I thought was the right direction." He shrugged with obvious frustration. "Then you slowed down and went left too."

Simone walked to the back of her vehicle and rubbed her

hand over the damage. The rear panel behind the wheel had a scrape and dent. She'd just paid off Harriet. Now she had to repair the engine *and* body damage.

"It was either you or the alpaca. I'm sorry, but your SUV lost in the deal." Before she could argue that it would cost more than she wanted to spend to fix, Nick added, "I'll pay, of course, but why did you stop?"

"Harriet died."

He stared at her vehicle with a panic-stricken expression. "There's a dead woman in there?"

Simone giggled. "Harriet's my SUV."

As realization struck him, he laughed. Checking his watch, he said, "I need to get to Two Hearts. Can I give you a lift?"

So he was the late caterer. And she *would* get there in time.

"Thank you! If you could help me shift the cake to your truck, we can be on our way."

Nick frowned when he leaned forward and peered into the back of her SUV. "My vehicle's larger than yours, but it still may be a tight squeeze."

Simone gulped. "Um, cakes can't be squeezed."

He ran his hand over his head. "Yeah. Sorry. We'll make it work. Don't worry, Simone. I'll start moving things around." As he hurried away, he added, "But we need to hurry. Greg will never forgive me if I don't get this food to town in time for his mother's wedding reception."

Ten minutes later, they grunted as they hefted it out of the back of her vehicle, set it on the folding cart she always brought, and wheeled it over to his. When it rested in the space he'd cleared, she gasped. A giant gash tore through the bottom tier of the three-tier cake. Her heart stopped. Could you pass out from stress?

"Nick!" She pointed at the cake. Bits of pink cake mixed with the white frosting, telling her this damage went deep. "It's—"

"Whoa. Did we just do that?" He rubbed his eyes.

Had they? She went through their steps. "We didn't bump anything. This must have happened when—"

Nick finished her sentence again. "I hit you. I am so sorry."

They both leaned closer, and he asked, "Can this amount of damage be repaired?"

Probably. "I always bring extra frosting in what I call my Oh no! kit. With the accident, I might have forgotten it if we hadn't noticed this. It's usually beside the cake, but it must have shifted."

Nick folded the cart. "I'll put this on the roof rack. You need it, right?"

"Definitely." Simone crawled inside to get the toolbox that held filled piping bags for every color of frosting on the cake, extras of every decoration, and every tool that particular cake might need.

As she crawled out with it, her phone chimed with a message from Cassie.

*Where are you?*

Simone closed the back hatch and hit the lock button on her key fob. "Cassie's getting more anxious. We need to hurry." She gave Harriet a pat on the side as she walked away. When she'd climbed into his truck, she wished she was back in Harriet. "It's a good thing you're driving. I'm so short that I can barely get in here, let alone drive something this big."

As he started the vehicle, she noticed the alpaca making his or her way back toward the highway. "The fence must be broken. We need to tell someone, or it may not make it next time."

He checked his watch and focused on it for a moment. Now that they were seated, he seemed to be moving more slowly. "We don't have time to find the farmhouse that goes with this land. We don't have time for anything beyond driving to Two Hearts and barely that."

A sheriff's department car pulled into the motel's parking lot and stopped in front of the office.

"That's the answer!" Simone opened the door and hurried over to the officer. After she pointed to the animal and explained, the officer agreed to help. Back sitting beside Nick, she said, "He's going to take care of it. It's a good thing so many law enforcement vehicles stop here."

He laughed. "The neighbors may agree just this once." When they pulled onto the highway, she took out her phone to check the clock.

Nick spoke before she could. "We should make it in time."

She hoped so. He only needed to unload food. She had to repair a cake, and that could be delicate, time-consuming work.

Simone bit her lip to hold in the tears that threatened to spill down her cheeks.

# CHAPTER TWO

*N*ick jerked his head upright and forced his eyes open, squinting as he focused on the road ahead. Last night, he'd stayed at his restaurant until the last dish had been washed and everything had been set for the next day. Then he'd returned at dawn to begin preparing the food for Mrs. Brantley's wedding.

Catering in Two Hearts was wearing him out. Coming back home and seeing his family here was great, though. He'd been an absentee son before Cassie had suggested catering for her weddings. But running a restaurant well over an hour's drive from town and catering here couldn't work for the future.

That he'd made it this far today without a major accident was a miracle. The alpaca and Simone's SUV hadn't been his fault. Even with perfect reflexes, he wouldn't have seen the animal before it crested the side of the road. The accident could have been worse, though, and his slow reflexes could have caused more damage.

For everyone's safety, he'd have to make changes—and soon.

When farmland dotted with animals and the occasional

house morphed into houses on both sides of the highway, even his exhausted brain knew he'd almost arrived.

Simone sat next to him, with that pink toolbox of hers at her feet. She hadn't said a word to him in the last fifteen minutes. Just stared out her side window. But he hadn't responded beyond a grunt when she'd tried to make conversation earlier. He hadn't had enough functioning brain cells to talk and drive. Adrenaline from the accident had pushed him through the time it took to load the cake, but it had passed.

She sat up straighter when they passed the "Welcome to Two Hearts" sign.

Being so close to his destination gave him a surge of energy. Once he'd unloaded and set up the food, he'd be ready to head back to Nashville, arriving in plenty of time to prepare for tonight's dinner service.

When he ran into Simone again, he'd have to make up for ignoring her on the drive. Talking and lack of sleep didn't go together for him. Then again, maybe she hadn't noticed. She might be a quiet person.

"It looks like we made it on time." As Simone said those words, she turned toward him and smiled.

Nick glanced at her as she spoke. He had to admit the woman had a nice smile. Oh, she was easy on the eyes, anyway, with her shoulder-length blonde hair and blue eyes, but the smile made her even prettier. When the truck drifted to the right, he jerked the wheel to put them back on track.

Simone grabbed the door handle. Twisting in her seat to check their cargo, she said, "I hope everything in the back is okay."

"I'm sure it's fine. Everyone will be happy with the food, no matter what it looks like."

Her smile turned into a grimace. He hadn't meant that in a negative way, so he tried again. "I'm glad you were able to fit your cake in the back without too many problems."

Her grimace turned into something he couldn't read. She blinked rapidly and turned back toward the window. He wasn't sure what was going on, but he'd never been good at understanding women. He tried, but it often didn't go as he expected.

Nick turned off the highway and wound through side roads toward the lake, pulling up in front of CJ and Paige's grand Victorian house with minutes to spare. As they rolled to a stop, Simone opened the door. At the back, when he reached to lift the hatch, Simone put her hand on his arm and pointed up toward the rack. "If you could grab that first, please."

He tried for a happy-sounding "okay," but it came out more gruffly than he'd intended. She popped up the cart he brought down and, in a minute, she'd scooted the wedding cake onto it. Simone may be petite, but she was strong.

When he saw the backside of the cake again, he winced. "That doesn't look good."

She shook her head from side to side. "We'll just have to make it work." After giving him a tense smile, she wheeled the cake toward the gate.

"Let me help you." He started to follow her, but she held up a hand in a stop motion.

"I've got it." Simone struggled for a moment with the gate, but she pulled it open and wheeled up the sidewalk toward the front door.

CJ stepped out. "I'm glad you two are here. Cassie has called every five minutes." His phone rang. "Only three minutes since the last call." He answered. "They're here. Everything looks okay." CJ looked over at Nick.

He made an okay sign with his thumb and forefinger.

Simone only said, "Don't worry."

When CJ had ended the call, he lifted the cart onto the front porch, then over the stoop into the house.

"Thank you!" She gave him a brilliant smile before vanishing inside.

Nick could hear Paige's gleeful greeting when she spotted Simone.

CJ came over to him. "Do you need any help?"

"Definitely." When Nick lifted a tray, he stumbled as he took a step. Leaning against the side of his SUV, he waited to get his equilibrium back.

CJ took it from him. "Are you okay?"

"Exhausted."

CJ added another tray on top of the first one. "Go inside and make sure everything's correct there. I'll bring these in."

Nick nodded and, without any argument, walked toward the house. He would usually do the man thing and say he could take care of it, but he knew he might not be able to this time.

He'd always liked this house—in spite of the pale pink paint on the exterior. It had sat empty for decades, but even then, it had been one of the best old houses on the lake. He'd been glad that Paige and CJ had saved everything good inside—the wood floors, trim, and other period details.

Inside, he found Simone with her cake on a small table in the parlor to the right. She crouched next to the cake with the toolbox open beside her as she worked.

Paige waved him to the left and the dining room where decorated, cloth-covered tables stood. "I was told that all the food is cold. Is that correct, or do you need me to help you set up some sort of warming station?"

"Mrs. Brantley requested a cold meal because she knew people would be coming and going. She apparently invited the whole town?"

Paige sighed. "It isn't every day the mayor gets married. But then, people loved her long before she was the mayor and would have wanted to come." She adjusted a stack of napkins. "I'm ready with plates and everything else, just in case the whole town does stop by. Or I should say, Cassie made sure I would be ready. The church could only hold the number that would fit on the pews, so not everyone could be there for the ceremony."

They soon had the first batch of trays lined up and ready for guests. The food to replace this when it was gone waited on the kitchen counter.

Nick checked his watch. "Guests should be arriving soon, right?"

"Cassie has been giving me a countdown of when they would arrive. She is the most organized person I know. But in answer to your question, she just sent a text that the ceremony ended."

He heard a gasp from the parlor. Then Simone peered around the corner, her headband askew and frosting on her cheek. "Did I hear you correctly? The ceremony's over?"

When Paige answered, "Yes," the sound of Simone's footsteps as she hurried away told him she still had a problem.

Since he'd been the cause of the accident—well, he and an alpaca—he wished he could help. He went over to the parlor's entrance. With careful movements, she added details. "Were you able to save the cake?"

She paused for a second, then she bit her lip and went back to focusing on the job at hand. "It's better. But not what it should be."

He couldn't see the gash now. She just had to redo the rest of the decorative elements that surrounded it.

Nick went back to the kitchen to check on the food. The trays were all marked, so replacements should be simple. Satisfied that it was as it should be, he turned to walk away. Feeling wobbly, he gripped the countertop.

Paige spoke from beside him, but he hadn't heard her approach. "Nick, are you okay? You don't look good. No offense."

He *hated* to be needy. "It was a really late night last night at the restaurant. Then I was up early to prepare food for the wedding. Let's just say I didn't get much sleep. But I got here on time, and that's all that counts."

She led him to a chair at the kitchen table, where he sat down hard, leaned forward, and put his face in his hands.

"I need to rest long enough to get back in my SUV and head back into the city so I can do this all over again tonight." Nick sat up and focused on the evening's service. He'd be able to do it. He had to.

CJ came into the kitchen. "I just talked to Simone. She said she needs another five minutes, and the massive gash will be repaired. Her words to describe the damage, not mine." He looked from his wife to Nick. "What's up?"

"He's too tired to get back on the road."

"I'll be fine." Even as he spoke, Nick could feel his eyelids trying to close.

Paige and CJ looked at each other in that silent way that married people often do, then at him again.

Paige said, "You can't drive like this, Nick."

CJ said, "We have empty rooms upstairs. Why don't you go up there and take a rest? Then you can go."

Resting sounded heavenly. But he couldn't do that because he had to be back in Nashville for the dinner service. When his head jerked up, he realized he'd nodded off for a few seconds. "Maybe you're right." He could take a short nap. Then he'd be ready to go.

CJ directed him. "Go up the stairs to the third door on the left. If you're awake enough to count." He chuckled.

"Thanks for the vote of confidence." Nick trudged up the stairs and down the hall, counting the doors carefully because, as much as CJ was kidding, it was getting hard to do basic things like that. When he opened the door, he found a nice room decorated in masculine colors. But more than that, there was a big fluffy bed sitting in the middle of it.

Before he did anything else, he called his kitchen and front-of-house managers so they could take over the early evening portion. He should be back in his restaurant in a few hours.

Then he headed straight for that bed and stretched out on top. His eyes were already closed when he pulled the blanket Paige must have left there as a decoration up over himself.

# CHAPTER THREE

*S*imone jumped to her feet when she heard new voices as Paige greeted someone at the front door. Glancing around, she made sure she hadn't left any of her repair supplies out. With her foot, she scooted the Oh no! box out of sight under the tablecloth-covered table.

She'd made a quick trip to the bathroom a few minutes ago to freshen up. After removing frosting from her arm and face, she'd removed her headband, combed her hair, and put on fresh makeup. Her bright pink and white dress looked suitably wedding.

Now, inhaling and exhaling slowly, Simone tried to calm herself before she met the guests.

She smiled as two women her mother's age entered the parlor, one wearing a bold floral print dress, the other in a simple russet-colored one. Simone realized too late that she still wore the frosting-splatted smock. Maybe they would ignore her if she stayed quiet.

The woman in the floral dress clasped her hands as she saw the cake. "My goodness! That is gorgeous!"

The other woman moved forward for a closer examination. "Emmaline chose such a pretty color."

Simone had to agree. She'd loved creating a cake with white frosting and lots of bright pink flowers.

"Her new husband is a photographer, so he may have had some say in that, too." The first woman looked at the second with an expression Simone couldn't read. Then they both laughed.

"You're right. Emmaline would have been in charge of everything. And she'd have a list on her clipboard."

Simone grinned. That did seem to sum up the town's mayor. With the two women examining the cake, Simone chose that moment for her escape, moving swiftly toward the door.

Simone couldn't tell which of the two said, "Excuse me. Miss? Did you make this cake?"

Since she was wearing frosting-tinted clothes, she clearly had, but she wasn't dressed to engage the guests. Groaning inside, she stopped and turned to face them. "Yes, ma'am. I'm the wedding cake designer."

"This is brilliant." When the woman leaned closer to look at the decorations, Simone sucked in a breath. Would her hasty repair stand up to closer scrutiny?

"The details on this are amazing. My daughter is getting married in the spring. Are you open to doing other weddings?"

Simone let out her breath in a whoosh. Before she could answer, the second woman spoke. "What about a baby shower? My Sarah is having a baby in February. It's a girl," she added with a blissful expression. "I bet we could have the most adorable cake ever at the shower."

She loved making whimsical baby cakes. "I might be interested in both of those." She reached into the side of her box and pulled out a couple of business cards, handing one to each of the women.

They looked from the cake to her and smiled.

"I'm Betty. You'll definitely be hearing from me."

"Connie. Me too." As the two women left the room, Simone heard one say, "Two Hearts has changed so much. It's wonderful."

"I know. My Johnny has been working with CJ on remodeling projects. It isn't just weddings, anymore."

Simone wondered if Cassie even realized the impact she'd had by coming here early this year. When the women were gone, Simone made her escape, passing a few early arrivals in the dining room.

In the kitchen—where she'd expected to find Nick—she instead found Paige. Surprisingly, disappointment washed over her. Then she remembered their drive here. When she'd spent quality time with him, he hadn't been the man she'd expected.

He had been so grouchy. Simone pitied the woman who ended up with him. His future wife would likely never be able to get his toast just right in the morning.

An image of Nick walking down the aisle next to her popped into her head.

Her breath caught.

*Where in the world did that come from?* She immediately dismissed it. She'd be the first to admit that she did want her own wedding, longed for it really. After working with dozens of couples and attending many weddings, she knew what she wanted—first a wonderful man to marry—and had planned her own ceremony in quiet moments. But not with Mr. Grouchy.

She took off the smock and put her jacket back on, bringing her outfit up to a somewhat higher level. This small town had an informal dress code, so maybe she'd be okay.

Now that the cake was successfully delivered in one piece, and her job was done, Simone had every intention of leaving. Nick could drop her off in Nashville and she would arrange to have her SUV towed.

She turned to Paige. "Has Nick left already?"

Before Paige could reply, the bride and groom arrived. A commotion ensued as the guests who had already arrived greeted them with hugs and cheek kisses. The two of them watched from the kitchen doorway.

Her ride home seemed to have vanished. More people flowed into the house. "What can I do?" She could help while she waited for him to appear. Maybe he'd gone somewhere with CJ.

Paige stared at the people with a shocked expression. This would probably be the biggest gathering they'd held inside their house. Even so, she replied, "Oh, I couldn't—"

Simone held up a hand in protest. "Please do not consider me a guest. I'm the dessert part of the catering team. What can I do?"

Paige breathed a sigh of relief. "I know Cassie would normally be in the thick of things here, directing us and making sure everything goes smoothly, but I also know she's been busy with her future mother-in-law."

"Then we've got this." Simone peered out the kitchen door. "Your house is starting to fill up. Cassie isn't here yet. Is the food ready?"

"Yes, Nick set up it up before—"

Mrs. Brantley entered the room. "Thank you for sharing your lovely home!" Dressed in a knee-length lavender lace dress with a scoop neck, she made an elegant bride. Simone knew she'd carried a bouquet of roses in shades of purple and that Cassie had been her bridesmaid in a deep purple dress. With the pink on the cake, the colors were a bright combination, but apparently her favorites. Simone wished she'd been able to attend the ceremony, but she'd barely finished the cake in the time she had.

"You look beautiful today, Mrs. Brantley." Simone thought about it for a minute. "Or did your name just change?"

Mrs. Brantley giggled like a girl. "We talked about it, but I've been Emmaline Brantley for most of my life, so I'm going to keep my name. For now."

Simone had never given much thought to whether or not she would take a husband's last name. Simone Mills had a nice sound to it.

The afternoon passed in a blur. Guests came and went. They replaced trays of food when one was emptied. Cassie worked her usual magic, making sure everything flowed well.

Finally, when the last guests had filtered out, and Simone was alone in the dining room, she dropped into a chair. "Paige —" she called to her friend in the kitchen "—I thought making cakes was strenuous! I can't imagine how Cassie does this every week."

"I heard that." Cassie came around the corner from the parlor.

"I thought you'd left."

"I always stay until the end. I'm sorry I let you down and that you had to serve along with other duties today."

Simone waved away the comment. "Don't worry about it. I'm stuck here, anyway."

"Stuck?"

"My SUV broke down on the way. It's parked over at the no-tell motel a half hour out of town. Nick drove by and picked me up. But he seems to have vanished. I guess he abandoned me."

Paige entered the room. "Nick was so tired that we sent him upstairs to take a nap." She looked at the watch on her wrist. "And it looks like he slept longer than he'd intended. The reception was so hectic that I didn't notice. I do know he wanted to get back to his restaurant this afternoon."

They all turned toward the grand staircase.

Cassie asked, "Who wants to wake him up to tell him he overslept?"

Simone definitely didn't want to. Mr. Grouchy might be worse when he woke up.

Nick opened his eyes and took a moment to focus on his surroundings. Sitting up, he looked around. Then he remembered. He'd taken a short nap at Paige and CJ's house.

Stretching, he felt energized, like he could conquer whatever the rest of the day had in store for him. People were right about power napping.

He shifted his feet to the left and sat up, turning to get out of bed. One foot caught on the blanket. As he pulled again, he realized the momentum of sitting up had pushed him dangerously close to the edge of the bed.

He fell left, slid off the bed, and hit the floor with a thud.

Stunned, he lay there for a moment, grateful for the soft rug that buffered his landing. The good news was that no one else had seen him fall. *Out of the bed.* Really? He hadn't done that since he was five.

The bedroom door flew open. Paige, Simone, and Cassie burst into the room.

Simone leaned over him. "Nick, are you okay?"

"I'm fine," he told her, his face heating with embarrassment. He wished he was anywhere but here with this attractive woman watching his idiocy. "I couldn't free my foot from something on the bed."

Simone checked it out. She bit her lip and then coughed into her hand. "The blanket is tucked in, and your shoelace must have caught on the open weave."

He nodded, his head thumping against the floor.

Her words were, "I'm sure it could happen to anyone." Her expression said otherwise.

Now, he needed to save what little remained of his dignity. He was surprised none of the wedding guests had come up to see what had happened. Or Paige's husband. "Where's CJ?" If he wasn't here, maybe the guys wouldn't learn about his mishap.

Paige answered. "He went to get the dogs from the McDonald farm. CJ will bring home both our Daisy and Mrs. Brantley's Cookie, who's going to stay with us while the happy couple is on their honeymoon."

Good. He might be spared male harassment. His off-the-charts embarrassment wouldn't worsen.

A male voice asked, "What happened?"

Nick turned his head to see CJ standing in the open doorway. Daisy wandered over to him, apparently happy to have someone at her level, sniffed his cheek, and swiped her tongue across it.

"Never assume it can't get worse," Paige teased, her lip twitching as she tried not to laugh.

Grinning, CJ extended his hand to help him up. Back on his feet, Nick headed straight to the attached bathroom. "I hope you've all finished laughing before I return."

CJ chuckled. "Maybe."

Nick splashed water on his face in an effort to clear his head, then smoothed his hair in the mirror and took a deep breath as he prepared for the rest of his day. He had a full dinner service in front of him with another late night.

By the time he stepped out of the bathroom, the room had emptied. His phone buzzed, and he pulled it out to discover several texts—one from his father and the rest from his mother. His father told him to contact his mother, and his mother kept asking if he was in Two Hearts. The implication was she wanted him to take time to visit her before returning home. Unfortunately, he wouldn't have time before he went back to Nashville, but he'd be back soon.

Exiting the room, he moved to pocket his phone, and the time caught his attention.

2:02 p.m.

He'd slept for hours.

No! That meant he would barely be back before the dinner service began, and he'd miss most of the prep.

Nick leaned against the wall for support as the information sunk in.

His manager, Consuela, did an amazing job. Tonight, she was on her own. All because he'd overslept. Straightening, he went toward the stairs. After some coffee—because he dearly wanted coffee—he might as well head for his parents' house to see what his mother needed.

Maybe he'd stay the night there instead of driving home. He'd decided early on to only have the restaurant open Monday through Saturday. Working every day of the year would be hard to maintain.

At the bottom of the stairs, he heard voices coming from the kitchen. Should he go there and join the conversation or head out the door and send them a text? He popped into the kitchen, finding Paige and CJ. "Thank you for letting me stay. I seem to have overstayed my welcome."

Paige beamed. "I had wanted to turn this house into a bed-and-breakfast, so having people staying in our house makes me happy. You're welcome anytime, Nick." Paige had been a wonderful addition to Two Hearts earlier this year. Judging from the grin on his friend's face, he knew CJ agreed.

With a wave, Nick left and went out to his truck. Inside, he carefully reread his mother's texts. They seemed to have something to do with his grandmother.

A block into his drive, Nick realized he still needed coffee. He drove to Dinah's Place, hoping she hadn't closed down for the wedding. Thankfully, lights were on inside. He opened the restaurant's door and found a few customers in line at the counter.

Michelle waved to him, then called over the din, "Sit anywhere you'd like."

He took a table for two against the wall. When she came

over, he asked, "What's with the line?" Another person had come in and joined it.

"We closed during the wedding, but Dinah knew motel guests would need food for tomorrow. Since the town is shut down."

Right. No restaurant and no grocery store on Sunday.

"When I told Sam the motel was full with wedding guests, he had a brilliant idea. We could sell them box lunches and ready-made breakfasts today that they could store in the refrigerator there."

"That is smart. Are you enjoying married life?"

Michelle grinned so widely that he wondered if her cheeks hurt. "It's the best. How about you? Anyone special?"

He knew she was asking about his love life, but he ignored her and gave his order. He didn't have time for romance. "I want your biggest cup of coffee. Make that one for here and one to go."

Michelle had hurried to get her pen and order pad ready when he started speaking, but now she dropped them to her sides. "Anything to go with that? It looks like we'll end up with a few extra roast beef sandwiches. I can bring you one of those and some chips. Dinah roasted the beef herself."

When he thought about it for a moment, he knew he hadn't had a bite to eat today. "I will definitely take that." Now that food had been mentioned, he realized how hungry he was.

Michelle went away to fill his order, and Nick leaned back in his chair, feeling small-town relaxation seep into him. He loved his restaurant in Nashville. He'd thrown everything he had into that for years. First, he'd studied to learn how to make the food. Then he'd worked in restaurants to learn how to make a restaurant run successfully. And he'd succeeded beyond his expectations. Nashville had been good to him.

But days like this . . . he just wanted to be home in Two Hearts. The slower pace, friendly people—many he'd known

23

all his life—and nature right around the corner filled his heart.

You can take the boy out of the country, but you couldn't take the country out of the boy.

Michelle brought a coffee cup and filled it. "This is bottomless, so I'll be back with a refill." She added a small box with the various sugars and a small pitcher of creamer. He ignored those and took a long sip of his black coffee. The dark caffeine-filled liquid was nectar running through his veins.

When he had finished half of his cup, she brought his food and the promised refill. He dug in, enjoying the simple yet delicious meal. It wasn't just the meat that had been cooked by Dinah. This was also perfectly seasoned roast beef and homemade bread, with a special sauce he couldn't quite figure out.

Sometimes people got fancy with food. He was guilty of that occasionally in his restaurant, embellishing with something just because he could. But simple food that was high quality? That spoke to him.

When he finished his sandwich, Nick checked the texts again. All he could decipher was that his mother thought he was in town for a wedding today. And there was that mention of his grandmother. Since Nana could be a little cantankerous, mixed with a lot of sweet, his mother's concerns could be almost anything.

He went to the front and paid. "Dinah," he called to the kitchen, while Michelle took care of the other patrons. She stepped out, wiping her hands on her apron. "What's the fancy city chef doing here?"

"Enjoying the best roast beef sandwich east of the Mississippi."

She grinned. "Keep talking city boy."

"Hah! You know I'm from here."

She gestured toward his leather jacket and button-down shirt. "You look more city today."

After a quick goodbye, he was back out on the road. About five minutes into his drive, a small spot of bright pink on the floor mat caught his eye. Nick slammed on his brakes and pulled to the right side of the road, thankful no one was behind him when he made his sudden move.

Wedding cake frosting! He'd left the maker of that cake at Paige and CJ's house!

Glancing around carefully to make sure he didn't hit a car this time, he pulled back onto the highway, heading toward his parents. He'd send a text to CJ, explaining that he needed to take care of a family situation, and asked him to pass the message on to Cassie, who would, of course, tell Simone. It made him a chicken that he didn't try to contact her himself, but this way she could calm down before he talked to her again. Could he dare hope he'd skate by and everything would be okay?

He and Simone didn't seem to get along too well, anyway. She hadn't seemed happy after their drive. This would just be one more thing on a list that included hitting her vehicle, damaging to her cake, and all but ignoring her earlier. The good news was that he wouldn't see her again until the next wedding. And then he'd be sure to keep his distance.

# CHAPTER FOUR

*C*assie lifted a floral garland off the fireplace mantle, while Simone wrapped up the remains of the cake, about ten slices. "That was one of your prettiest cakes." Cassie set the garland in a box, then placed a flameless candle in another box. Simone knew she took flowers to nursing homes and that the candle would be returned to the rental company. "And I saw a couple of people come back for a second slice, so you nailed the flavor too."

Simone loudly sighed.

Cassie swung around to face her. "What was that ugly sound for? Didn't you think it was pretty?"

Simone left the cake where it was and plunked down on a small Victorian settee. "This cake *was* beautiful. An accident on the way here put a dent in it. I've never had that much damage in all the time I've been doing this. And that is a significant number of cakes that have arrived safely."

"What happened?"

Simone felt anger rising but tamped it down. "Nick happened." She sighed again. "But it wasn't completely his fault. And I might have been too upset about it."

Cassie's choking sound told her she was trying not to laugh. "You? No! That's not possible. You never let your true emotions shine through for everyone to see."

"Sarcasm can be so ugly." Simone chuckled. "He helped me put the cake into the back of his vehicle."

"That's nice."

"He did that after he swerved to avoid an alpaca and hit my SUV."

Cassie stared at her.

"Yes, that actually happened. Both Harriet and the cake were dented. I think I handled it well. But he ignored me after that. During the drive here, he didn't say a word. He wouldn't even reply to anything I said." She waved away the thought. "Let's just say that we had a tense drive into town."

Cassie frowned. "I've spent enough time with him to know that's unusual. He can be professional and formal, but he isn't rude."

Back on her feet, Simone grabbed the plastic-wrapped cake and started out of the room with it. "Rude sums up today perfectly. After our trip back to Nashville today, I won't see him much, so it doesn't matter."

Complete silence greeted her remark. That wasn't like Cassie. She turned around and found her friend with a pensive expression.

"About that ride—"

"I know. You don't have to remind me to be on my best behavior. I will be wonderful."

"That isn't it." When Cassie didn't say anything for a moment, Simone's heart rate ramped up. What now?

Simone spun on her heels and out of the room, calling, "Nick!"

Cassie raced behind her. "I'm afraid he's gone."

Simone gasped. "He's left and didn't tell me?" She took a

deep breath and continued toward the kitchen. "I've been abandoned here? Is that what you're telling me?"

Paige and CJ were in the kitchen. Paige said, "Abandon is a harsh word."

"So is rude," Simone muttered as she opened the fridge and moved things around to make space for the cake before saying anything else. She didn't want to make a hasty remark that she could come to regret. She carefully placed the leftovers inside and gently closed the refrigerator door.

Turning, she faced the three of them. The reality of her situation caught her off guard. "I don't have any other clothes. I don't even have a toothbrush. I'm not sure what to do. Not to mention the fact that my SUV is still parked at that nasty hotel. Even they would want it removed from their private property quickly. Although, I probably have a day or two before they realize it's not supposed to be there."

CJ said, "I know that George has a large trailer he uses to haul farm equipment around his property. I think we can get it and some of the guys together to go with him to rescue your vehicle."

"But what good does that do me? Is there even a garage in Two Hearts that I can take it to?" She normally went with the flow and was considered an upbeat person, but having everything pulled out from under her right now had her swallowing hard and wondering what to do next. For the first time, she truly understood what it must have been like when Cassie ran out of gas in Two Hearts.

"Leo works out of his home garage. But he's amazing. I can guarantee you he will get you back on the road. Just—"

Paige interrupted her husband. "Rip off the Band-Aid, CJ. Leo won't be working tomorrow. Like the rest of this town, he will be shut down on Sunday. And if he has to order a part . . ."

The picture became crystal clear. "Unless I can find someone to take me back to the city, I'm stuck here for a few days."

Cassie put her arm around Simone's shoulders. "Don't worry. You'll be fine. You can get stranded in much worse towns. I mean, look at how I did."

"You already got the sheriff. There isn't a sheriff for me to fall for." Everyone laughed.

"Good point. Hey, maybe somebody going back to the city will give you a ride."

Hope rose. "Good idea. Do you know anyone?"

"Everyone I know is staying at least tonight. Some of them decided to stay through Sunday night once they saw how cute it was here."

"So that's a maybe for tomorrow. Can I stay with you, Cassie?"

Cassie winced. "I'm sorry. I have some of Mrs. Brantley's relatives staying with me."

"That's okay. There's probably a room over at the motel."

Silence greeted her remark.

Simone realized what Cassie had implied a moment ago. "There's no room at the motel because the wedding guests are all staying there."

Cassie said, "That pretty much sums it up."

CJ spoke up. "On the other hand, you're welcome to stay here tonight."

Anxiety whooshed through her, catching her off guard. "That's lovely and generous of you, but I couldn't impose." She *really couldn't* impose. She'd hated it when her family had traveled and stayed with other people. She always felt like she was intruding and sharing bathrooms with strangers was terrible. Being an extroverted introvert had its downsides. People thought that she was a people person. But she needed time alone in her own space.

CJ added, "We would like you to stay with us. And remember that Paige planned to create a bed and breakfast. She bought this house partly because of the number of bedrooms and bathrooms. You get your own private space. And Paige decorated the rooms, so they're . . . cute."

Paige burst out laughing. "Cute is a good word, but not when I hear it from your mouth, CJ. Simone, I can give you the yellow room. It's pretty and it has an attached bathroom. Little by little, we—and by we, I mean CJ—have made it into the house that I envisioned when I first saw it. And someday . . ." She gave her husband a loving smile. "Someday, we may have little people staying in those rooms."

"You two are adorable," Cassie said.

Simone watched the sparks between her hosts. "They are. But you're all part of adorable couples. I'm the single one in the bunch now. But that's okay. And I gratefully accept your offer. I think I still have time to get to the grocery store, right? I need a few things."

Cassie snapped to attention. When there was something that needed to be done, she was on it. "I'll run you over there. I have a couple of hours before I need to get back to my guests. The good news is that Mrs. Brantley cooked all the food in advance, and it's either in my refrigerator or freezer."

"There wouldn't be any *extra* cookies, would there?" CJ asked.

Cassie grinned. "Of course. She made dozens of cookies. If you stop by later, I'll have an assortment ready."

Everyone knew that neither CJ nor Paige were great cooks. If they were going to eat well, most of the food had to come from outside.

Cassie grabbed her purse off the kitchen counter, where she must have left it earlier. "We'd better hurry. The store closes soon."

Simone tucked her purse under her arm. "Is it okay if I leave this box here?" She patted the top of her Oh no! kit.

"You brought us dessert. You can do anything." Paige grinned.

Simone said, "I can make you an awesome dessert later if you'd rather have something else."

CJ took a step closer. "What would we be talking about?"

Paige rolled her eyes. "If you didn't already know, he loves sweets."

Simone set her purse down. "Do you mind if I check supplies?"

Paige opened a cupboard. "Are you kidding? You're welcome to do anything you want in this kitchen."

Both CJ and Paige had happy expressions.

Simone checked the cupboard, finding mixes for a yellow cake and brownies. No flour, sugar, or other baking supplies. "I'll get a couple of things when I'm at the store." A quick check of the fridge didn't offer much, either, but she could pay her hosts back with a meal. "I see milk and eggs. Bacon. Those are good. I'll make something special tomorrow for breakfast."

CJ gave a sad sigh. "As much as I want to support your efforts, remember that we have to get up early for church."

Simone chuckled and picked up her purse again. "I am often up long before dawn to put the finishing touches on a cake. Believe me when I say fixing your breakfast at an early hour would be just as easy."

She and Cassie went out the door and across the yard to the road. Simone followed her when she turned left down the road. "Are we walking to your house?" She hoped not, because exhaustion didn't begin to describe how she felt right now.

"No. I arrived late, so I had to leave my car down the street by the lake park."

A few minutes later, they had driven across the small town, and Simone had essentials in her cart, including some makeup from the limited selection. When they wheeled up to the baking section, she rubbed her hands together with glee. "What should I make for them?"

Cassie said, "I wish I could come over to eat whatever it is, but I'm going to be with my houseguests. Especially now that Mrs. Brantley and James have left for their honeymoon."

"I don't want to make cake. I do that a lot. Maybe some chocolate chip cookies." She put a few needed ingredients in the cart. "That should do it."

"Don't you need to check a recipe on your phone?"

Simone turned the cart and wheeled it in the direction of the produce section. "I don't. I can bake just about anything without a recipe."

"Give me just a moment to marvel at that."

Simone chuckled. She grabbed some apples to snack on—as much as she'd like to, she knew she couldn't live on baked goods —and dropped them in the cart along with the flour, sugar, and other baking essentials she already had in there. "Don't tell anyone this—because I found that people look at me differently when it comes to food. They're afraid to cook for me."

"I feel that way about cooking for Nick. Greg invited him to dinner one night. I know my food is *okay* now. At least the few things that my future mother-in-law has helped me to learn to cook. Heaven knows that my mother wasn't any good in the kitchen or that she even knew where it was in the house. But cooking for a gourmet like Nick? That unnerves me."

"See, that's what I mean."

"But Nick's a chef."

Simone went over to the dairy section. She didn't remember seeing any butter in the fridge, but she wanted to make sure she had some for the cookies. Going down the dairy aisle, she paused to face Cassie, who had stopped to get a carton of milk. "I'm a chef."

Cassie stopped halfway down the dairy aisle, then hurried to catch up with her at the butter. "What do you mean you're *a chef*? You make cakes. Your cakes taste better than those of my other wedding cake vendors. Often miles ahead. But that's not the same thing as being a chef."

"You're right. And there are bakers who don't have any formal training who make delicious, beautiful wedding cakes. That isn't who I am. I went to culinary school in Paris. I've worked in high-end restaurants in Europe and the US."

"You're kidding!"

"Nope." Simone headed toward the front of the store. "I made a wedding cake for a friend's wedding, and I was hooked. I knew exactly what I wanted to do from then on."

They checked out, with Cassie remaining silent. Outside, her friend checked her watch. "Your bombshell announcement startled me, but I'll keep your secret. Would you like to stop by Bella's shop for a visit? I know she had a client meeting this afternoon. A bride who drove down from Kentucky and can't get away from her job for a weekday appointment. Bella fit her in this afternoon. I have an hour or so before I need to be home to do my hostess thing for dinner."

Simone knew she didn't have anywhere else to be at this point. She'd probably end up alone in the guest room with her phone as entertainment. *Phone.* "Hey, I just remembered I don't have a phone charger. Do you think they'd have one here?"

Cassie held one finger up in a pause motion. She returned to the store and came back with exactly what Simone needed. "I suggested stocking these to the owner because we have so many out-of-town visitors. He happily did because he knew he would make a good profit."

At Bella's Brides on Main Street, Cassie parked as a car with Kentucky license plates pulled away.

"Perfect timing." This felt like one of the few things to go well today.

Bella jumped to her feet when the door chime sounded, then dropped back down on her chair when she saw who it was. "Come sit and tell me all about the wedding."

Cassie slid into the chair next to Bella, and Simone sat across from them.

It seemed odd that Bella hadn't even made a brief appearance at an event the whole town had attended. "I was surprised you weren't there. Were you working on a rush job?"

Bella looked down at the floor and then up at them, her face bright red. "Mornings have been a bit of a challenge for me lately. But I'm told it should be ending in another week or so."

Cassie and Simone stared at Bella. Then Cassie jumped up first with Simone following and they leaned down to hug her. Bella would be the first of them to have a baby. A wave of envy swept over her, surprising Simone so much she struggled to keep smiling.

"You didn't tell anybody!" Cassie gave her another squeeze, then they sat again.

"I told Micah, of course. I just didn't want to share the news quite yet. For some reason, I wanted to hold on to my baby secret." Bella beamed with joy.

Cassie made a zipper motion on her lips. "Your secret is safe with me."

"Me too."

The mother-to-be put her hand on her belly. "My secret will make himself or herself known soon, so I think it's okay to start mentioning it. Maybe I will have Micah tell his grandmother. She's so plugged in to everybody in this town—even though she's moved away and is only visiting occasionally—that the news should be everywhere by tomorrow morning. That'll spare me from doing anything further."

Cassie chuckled. "I think you're right about that."

CJ opened the door and popped his head in. "Are you ready?"

Simone glanced over at Cassie and Bella.

Bella held up her hands. "Don't look at me. I don't know what's going on."

Cassie said, "I have an idea. You've been going back and forth between here and Nashville so much."

"True. But what does CJ have to do with that?" She glared at Cassie. "What have you done? And will I regret it?"

"I haven't *done* anything. He's going to show us some properties. Next door and across the street. Just in case you find them interesting."

She tried to be angry about it, but her friend was trying to help. Plus, Cassie wanted everyone she knew to move to Two Hearts. Simone stood. "Let's do this."

Cassie lit up. "You'll look?"

"Sure. Why not? I don't have to say yes. CJ's gone to all the trouble to come here. But I guess I'm sitting here in Bella's shop under false pretenses."

Cassie had the good graces to look embarrassed. "Everything I said was true. I just didn't mention this short field trip."

They all went outside where CJ said, "Which one do you want to look at first?"

Simone slowly scanned the buildings across the street, and then turned to face this side. All of them were brick, two-stories from the Victorian era. "You have keys to every place?"

"Paige has been looking at different buildings, so the owners gave me keys."

"She's going to open a photo studio?" Cassie smiled widely.

"She is. Over there." He pointed to a building that Simone knew had accidentally pushed Bella and Micah together. She'd heard the story at their wedding reception.

Bella said, "That's the one that started me off on my path with Micah. I got sprayed with the fire hose."

Simone considered the buildings. "So, if I set up shop in one of these, the right man for me will walk in the door?"

CJ laughed. "I don't think we can guarantee that, even in a town named Two Hearts. But we'll see what we can do."

She'd driven past here many times and had sometimes stopped to visit Bella in her shop. A narrow brick building across the street had caught her eye a time or two. "Let's try that one." She pointed to it.

They started on their way across the traffic-free street.

"Why did you choose the small one?" Cassie asked.

"I make cakes. I don't need much space." She didn't mention that it reminded her of a dollhouse her grandmother had given her when she was little. Hours had been spent playing with the Victorian-style house with a bow window and a door exactly like this one.

They arrived, and CJ unlocked the old-fashioned door with glass on the top half and wood on the bottom. Pushing it open, he waved his hand for her to enter before him.

When she stepped inside, she was surprised to discover wonderfully worn-with-age wood floors. The others followed behind her, commenting as they did, but she didn't say anything as she took in the beautiful architectural elements.

The walls—even though covered in what must be decades of dust and cobwebs—had pretty wallpaper. She probably couldn't save the wall covering, but the pattern gave her ideas. When she got to the back of the building, she could already see where her ovens and workstation would go. Storage shelves could reach up to the high ceilings. There would be plenty of room for another person to work with her, too. And a back door to the alley would help with supply deliveries.

The building seemed impossibly narrow from the street, but much larger inside. It must just be small in comparison to the other stores on the street. She looked up at the white-painted wood ceiling. Or what had once been white.

Cassie, Bella, and CJ were off to the side, watching her.

They'd brought her to a great place. "This is pretty awesome."

"Does that mean you're moving to Two Hearts?" Bella asked tentatively. "Because I'd love to have you working across the street."

Was she? And then the bubble burst. "I have an apartment in the city with a lease that won't end for more than a year. I pay month-to-month for my worksite, so that wouldn't be a problem, but no. It looks like I'm not going anywhere."

And that reminded her that she should probably send a text or call her roommate to let her know that she wouldn't be coming home tonight. Not that she would notice because her boyfriend would be over there.

Simone remembered last night when she'd been tired after work and had longed for peace and quiet. She could hear the sound of a television and then laughter as she entered the two-bedroom unit.

In the living room, she'd loudly said her roommate's name. When Simone hadn't been heard over the noise, she'd grabbed the remote off the end of the couch and hit pause on the movie. Chrissy and her boyfriend Arnold spun around with shocked expressions. Chrissy had said, "Oh my goodness! You almost gave me a heart attack. You should have said you were here."

They'd been down this road before. "I tried, but you didn't hear me over the TV. Anyway, I'm home. I've already had dinner, so I think I'll head to my room. I'm going to make a few customer calls, so if you could keep the TV down, that would be great." When her roommate reached for the remote, she added, "Any luck finding your newlywed home?"

Happiness evaporated from Chrissy's face. "We have looked so hard, Simone. Even with the two of us, the rent is crazy. Or it's just a place that we don't like as well as this one. It's too bad nothing has come up in this building. If it was at the same price you have, we'd grab it in a heartbeat."

"Well, I hope your search is better tomorrow." She meant that because she liked Chrissy and because she needed her home back. "And remember that if you think of anyone who might make a good roommate, send them my way. They just can't be a night owl with my schedule."

When Simone went into her bedroom, she'd closed the door and leaned back against it. Out of a good-sized unit, this is what she was left with most evenings.

Pushing that memory away, she focused on the cute place she now stood in. She could picture herself decorating a cake at the worktable, light filtering in from the front window. When she had an appointment, the customer would enter her shop and sit down with her at an antique desk she'd put up front.

A business here felt so real that she couldn't believe it didn't already exist. She *almost* wanted to run away to Two Hearts, but that dream was just out of reach. Simone headed for the front door, all the while feeling the tug of this place. There was something almost magical about it. When she neared the front, she could see the door painted a pretty pink.

*No.* Why dwell on something that simply couldn't be?

She pushed the impossible dream out of her mind and went back outside.

# CHAPTER FIVE

*T*en minutes later, Nick pulled onto the long drive that led off the highway to his parents' farmhouse. He passed through the familiar forest of fruit trees—peach, apple, cherry, and probably others knowing his mother—emerging from the surrounding acres at the family home. A cluster of buildings included the white wood clapboard farmhouse, a chicken coop, a goat barn, and the prized smokehouse his father had insisted on building years ago. A couple of cars he didn't recognize were parked out front.

As he eased his vehicle's door open, two furiously barking dogs raced toward him. By the time he'd stepped out, their tails were wagging so hard their rear ends were shaking back and forth. Willie and Caramel.

"How are you boys?" The two border collies bounded around his legs. As he petted them, he spotted his father coming out of the barn. When he waved to him and started toward him, his father pointed to the house, so Nick swung back in that direction, his concern rising. What was going on?

His mother ran over to him as soon as she saw him. "Nicky! It's your grandmother."

His heart dropped to his stomach. "Something's wrong with Nana?"

His mother hesitated. "I'm honestly not sure. She was outside working in the garden yesterday, perfectly healthy. Today this happened."

He glanced toward his old bedroom, the one his grandmother had occupied since she moved in a year ago. "What happened?"

"She said she didn't want to get out of bed. I want to take her to a doctor in Nashville to make sure there's nothing serious. But she reminded me that her last physical showed her as healthy as someone ten or twenty years younger."

"Then what's going on?"

She lifted her hands in frustration. "I don't know." His mother leaned closer. "I do know she's gotten a lot of extra attention. Your cousins have stopped by. Rick and Jenna are still here." She motioned toward the kitchen table where several people sat. "The preacher was here yesterday and today. You know she enjoys his company."

That was true. Nana always stayed after church to speak to him, and she was on several church committees.

"Do you really think your own mother would fool you for that?"

His mother gave a strangled laugh. "I don't know what to think. I'm more than a little concerned."

His mother was right. His grandmother had done all sorts of things, especially since his grandfather had passed away fifteen years ago. One time, she was concerned about getting old and decided she needed to explore the Himalayas.

He'd dismissed the idea because he couldn't see how she would manage that financially. The next thing he knew, he was getting postcards from Tibet. He still wasn't sure how that had come to pass, but it had something to do with her volunteering to lead a tour group.

And then there was the bungee jumping. He worried she'd break her neck, but she was better at it than some younger people.

"I'll talk to her, Mom."

"Nicky?" a weak voice called from the bedroom. "Is that you? Come see your old grandmother."

She patted his arm. "Be good to your Nana."

He went toward the bedroom, hesitating outside the door because he wasn't sure what he'd find. When he did enter, he found a very healthy-looking woman in her late seventies stretched out in bed with a book beside her. She appeared quite comfortable.

Nana waved him over. "Come sit beside me, Nicky." She raised a hand weakly and put it on her chest. "Tell your grandmother what's going on in your life."

He glanced back at the doorway where his mother stood watching. "Nothing very interesting, Nana. Everything's the same." His morning came to mind—including his time with Simone. Once again, he felt a pang of guilt. It wasn't like him to be unpleasant to be around.

"Nicky?"

His grandmother's voice pulled him to the present. "Sorry, Nana. I was thinking about something else. This morning, I drove in from Nashville. And I stopped for coffee on the way here."

"You mean you stopped at Dinah's? She's a good cook. Oh, nothing like your fancy food, of course—but good."

He couldn't argue that point. Being here next to Nana told him he needed to spend more time in Two Hearts, not less. How? He wasn't sure. But maybe . . . An idea came to him, and he couldn't shake it. "I haven't decided on which one, but I'm going to lease one of those old stores on Main Street for a catering kitchen." Nick swallowed hard. If he went through with it, he'd just committed himself to a *big* project.

His mother and grandmother said, "Ooh! That's great!" in unison.

His grandmother asked, "You're moving back to Two Hearts?" She seemed to hold her breath, waiting for the answer. They went through this almost every time he saw her. It was one of the reasons he hesitated before he turned up the driveway. He felt like he disappointed her every time he got in his vehicle to leave.

He put his hand on hers. "No, Nana. I own a restaurant in Nashville. You know that. You've been there. When you're feeling better, Mom can bring you to the city, and I'll make you whatever you want."

"That's lovely, Nicky, but I'm not sure—" she sighed deeply "—if I'll be able to do that again."

Panicking, he pulled away from her and turned toward the doorway, but his mother was gone. "I'm sure you'll get better, Nana."

"Before I go, I would like to see my grandchildren happy."

"I am happy, Nana. I have a good life that I've worked hard to build."

"I know you have, but you haven't built a life beyond work. This worries me, Nicky. I worry day and night about you."

Here they went again. He opened his mouth to give the standard answer, when she sighed again, this time sounding weaker, and said, "I just want to know you're happy before I leave . . . this world. I'm not getting any younger and neither are you. Men can father children even as they age, but things aren't the same for women. Unless you plan on marrying a much younger woman, you're going to have to get going on those babies so I can have great-grandchildren."

Nick groaned inside.

He was not having a fertility discussion with his grandmother. He opened his mouth to speak again when she said—after an even deeper and feebler sigh— "Just remember,

Nicky, that I'd like to hold your child in my arms. But if that's not possible in the time I have left, I would at least like to be at your wedding. I saw a dress the other day in a catalog and I thought, 'That would be perfect for me to wear to Nicky's engagement party or wedding.' Are you dating anyone, Nicky?" Nana's eyelids fluttered closed as she rested back on her pillow.

He wanted to tell her no, which was the truth. Simone's face popped into his mind, surprising him. It was probably because he'd spent time with her today.

His crazy life had gotten busier when he'd added catering in Two Hearts, so he didn't have time to date. He now had to figure out how to make his business work, which may soon include a catering kitchen in Two Hearts. But seeing his hometown come to life gave him hope about life in general.

His grandmother barely opened her eyes. "You haven't answered me, sweetheart. Are you seeing anyone?"

He wanted to make her happy. Words slipped out before he could stop them. "A very nice woman."

His grandmother's eyes opened wider. "You say you have a girlfriend? Tell me about her. Are you proposing to her soon? Or have you already?"

What had he done? He'd just lied to his grandmother.

"What did you say her name was?"

"I didn't." And he wouldn't. He'd make a date with someone today, so his small lie would be short lived.

"What?" She put her hand behind her ear as though she needed him to speak louder. Was failing hearing caused by her current problem?

He leaned closer. "I hadn't given a name."

She blinked quickly as though fighting tears. "You won't share her name with your grandmother?"

His lips moved, but no sound came out. He couldn't compound one lie with another.

"I'm sorry, Nicky, but I can't hear you." She slowly breathed in and out as though it were a struggle.

"Simone!" He blurted out the first name that popped into his mind. She'd definitely left a strong impression this morning.

"Did you say you were engaged to her?" She put her hand on her chest, and her eyes closed.

Nana was not long for this world. "Yes! I'm engaged to Simone!" he shouted as loudly as he could.

Her eyes lit up, and a wide smile flashed across a strong and vibrant face. Then it was gone, and she looked feeble again. Had he wanted her healthy so much that he'd imagined that?

He kissed his grandmother on her cheek. "I have to go now, Nana. I'll visit again soon." Then he made a hasty exit.

His mother's stunned expression as he passed through the kitchen made him consider slowing down to explain, but his feet didn't want to.

*What had he done?*

He'd have to come back later to tell his parents about his little white lie.

Nick climbed into his truck and rested his head on the steering wheel. He actually felt like banging his head on it, but he knew that wouldn't help.

What now? He'd told a lie to his *grandmother*. One that he hoped wouldn't have long-term repercussions. Why couldn't he have said Randi or another woman in town? She was a single woman. Inoffensive. Kind. Attractive. No. He'd chosen a woman who disliked him. Simone.

He put the key in the ignition and headed down the long drive to the highway. Maybe Micah would have words of advice because, right now, he needed some. His good friend had been through a lot this year by marrying a woman that Nick had later learned he hadn't wanted to marry. He'd done it to please his grandfather. Now, he and his wife were in love, would probably have at least five kids, and planned to spend their lives in the house Micah's grandmother gave him.

Micah had married Bella, the wedding dress designer. *And a close friend of Simone's.* Nick slowed his SUV to a crawl as he neared the road to town. Creeping forward, he rethought the idea of going to Micah. But his friend was an attorney and used to sorting out conflicts. If anything had ever needed his wisdom, this was it. He just hoped he was in his office on a Saturday because he couldn't talk about this with Bella nearby.

With his decision made, Nick turned right onto the highway and sped up, driving straight to his friend's downtown office. Well, as downtown as the tiny town of Two Hearts ever got. He popped the door open and hesitated again for a minute.

Was he being a fool for thinking his friend could help get him out of the hole he'd dug? No. He needed to talk to someone about this, and that had to be in Two Hearts. He hadn't had time to make friends back in Nashville. He only knew his employees and other people in the industry who worked equally long hours.

Nick pushed the door to the old building open and went upstairs, the old building with its wood stairs in strong contrast to everything around him in Nashville. He hurried down the hall to Micah's office, glad to find the door unlocked today. As expected, he found the secretary's desk vacant. Through Micah's open door, he spotted CJ in one of the chairs facing the desk.

Nick held up his hands in apology. "Sorry. I didn't realize you'd be busy. I'll see you another time."

Micah stood. "Come on in. We're just chatting. It's so rare that I see you in Two Hearts that I won't let you get away that easy."

CJ said, "I can leave if you two need to talk."

Would it be better if he talked to Micah alone? "You know, it might be good to have both of your opinions. Not that you aren't a genius, Micah."

His friend chuckled. Then he seemed to notice the seriousness in Nick's tone. Micah waved him inside. "Take a chair and tell us what's going on. And don't say you're just here to shoot the breeze because your expression tells me otherwise."

"I was just at my family's house. My grandmother was in bed talking about dying."

"Nick, I'm so sorry. I know you've always been close." To CJ, he said, "Nick has had her wrapped around his finger since the day he was born. He'd do anything for her too."

"Well, that's the problem. When she asked who I was dating and said she needed to know I was settled before she left this earth—"

Micah's expression showed shock. "It's that serious? I hadn't heard anything about this in town."

"This illness seemed to come on her suddenly. Mom said it started this morning. Anyway, she wanted to know who I was dating, and she kept pressing me. So, I gave her a name."

CJ frowned. "You don't have a girlfriend—unless I missed something big."

Nick looked at CJ. "Exactly! You see my problem." To both men, he said, "I wanted to take away Nana's concern, so I— without thinking—gave her the first name that came into my head." He closed his eyes and rubbed his hand over his face.

Micah shrugged. "Surely it can't be that bad. Who'd you say you were dating?"

"*Simone*. I said Simone. She must have been on my mind because of what happened this morning."

CJ chuckled.

Micah looked between the two men. "I'm apparently missing something here."

CJ said, "Simone's truck broke down on the way. Nick hit it

as she pulled off the road and damaged Mrs. Brantley's wedding cake. Then I guess he ignored her the whole way to town. She wasn't happy. The word 'rude' was used."

Micah grinned. "So she's the least likely person to ever want to go on a date with this guy." He pointed at Nick. "You sure painted yourself in a corner. These things always seem to work out, though. I mean, Simone's nice."

Nick could feel his panic level rising. "Don't go there. The problem is not dating Simone. The problem is what I'm going to do about what I told my grandmother."

Both men shrugged, confused.

"I don't see the problem. Your grandmother isn't going to know if you stop dating her. Or even if you never date her." CJ's brow furrowed. "You know what I mean."

Nick rested his forehead on both hands. "It gets worse." He looked up at the other men and they leaned forward.

Micah raised an eyebrow. "How?"

"Nana kept pushing. It wasn't good enough that I was seeing Simone. She kept telling me that she needed to see me married. That she wanted great-grandchildren. And, oh my goodness, she started talking about female fertility waning with age."

CJ and Micah winced.

"Awkward." Micah leaned back in his chair.

"You have no idea."

CJ started to smile, and it grew wider and wider. "You didn't?"

Nick nodded vigorously.

Micah said, "What am I missing?"

CJ said, "I recognize this because Paige and I said we were engaged when we wanted to call off the matchmakers. He just told his grandmother he's engaged to Simone."

Micah's head swiveled back to Nick. "You did what?!"

"You know my grandmother! You know how she can be! She

seemed so upset and so feeble. I shouted that, yes, I was engaged to Simone."

Both men grinned.

Always a mediator and fixer, Micah said, "I can't believe you did that. But maybe it's fixable. CJ, was it really bad between Nick and Simone this morning?"

"Oh, yeah. It was bad. She's not going to date him, and she's definitely not going to marry him." CJ laughed.

"I don't want to marry the woman. Or anyone right now." Nick groaned.

"Well, as long as this little tale is contained to your grandmother, it will be fine."

Nick pictured his exit from the house. Who had been there at that time? He'd been so upset that he hadn't paid attention. He couldn't even guess at the ownership of the cars parked near his.

Yes, his mother had heard. She'd probably be so frustrated about the lack of information about Simone and his love life that he hoped she'd wait until he called her to explain. She'd never been a gossiper.

Nick's phone buzzed. He took it out of his pocket and groaned. "Mom's texting me."

*Who is Simone?*

Micah said, "I don't know how to help you. You seem to have dug quite a hole for yourself."

"I just wanted to make her happy. I can't believe I lied to her."

Micah laughed. "That isn't the first time. Remember when she caught us out with the McGillicuddy twins?"

Nick chuckled. "That *was* funny. I'm still not sure why either of us took them out that day."

CJ looked between them. "There's a story here."

"The story is that these two women asked us if we would like to take them to the movie. They were twenty-one and pretty. We were nineteen and stupid."

CJ gestured forward with his hands.

"They asked us to stop and get a bite to eat before the movie. That sounded harmless. Before we knew it, the tab was run up to two or three times what the movie was going to cost. It took everything we had at the time—we were poor students home for the summer—so we brought them home with no movie."

"They were Two Hearts's girls?"

"No. They were visiting an aunt or something."

"They were visiting Mrs. Brantley. Greg had gotten a summer job in another state. They were daughters of an old friend of hers. We never told her what happened. I'm not sure where those girls ended up, but we never saw them again."

"But when we were leaving the restaurant and your grandmother saw us and then noticed how trashy the girls dressed, you told her we were helping two poor women to their car."

By now, CJ was grinning too.

Nick had forgotten his own situation until his phone buzzed again.

*If you're going to marry her, I want to know more.*

"Guys, I am in trouble here. Suggestions? Ideas? Plans?"

Micah tapped his fingers on the edge of his desk. After a long silence, he said, "Tell your grandmother you lied."

Nick shook his head. "I can't do that."

"Maybe she'd believe she imagined it?"

He pondered that for a moment. "That would be a lie on a lie. Of course, saying I'm engaged is a lie too." And there were the other people at the house. "And I'm still not sure who else overheard me. My parents often have family and others stopping by."

CJ offered, "Then you have to take Simone to meet her."

Nick swallowed hard. "I came up with the idea of telling Nana I'm sorry for lying. It didn't occur to me to bring Simone over there." He hesitated before adding, "I may have been a little harsh with her this morning."

"She wasn't happy with you when she arrived at our house. I don't know what happened, but you really got under her skin."

Micah raised his hands in the air like a scale with his right higher than his left. "Apologize to grandma." Then he dropped the right and the other rose. "Or apologize to Simone. They kind of balance each other out." He brought the hands level.

"No. They don't. Telling my grandmother that I lied to her on her deathbed is far worse."

"You're right. Forget what I just said."

"I wonder if Simone's still in town."

"She doesn't have a car, so she's probably with Bella and Cassie." Micah picked up his phone. "Hey Sweetie, I'm just checking to see how your day's going. Are Cassie and Simone with you? Okay. But you'll be home for dinner?" Micah grinned broadly. "I like the way you think."

Still grinning after he ended the call, he said, "Simone is with them at Bella's shop on Main Street. But she's hoping for a ride to the city. I usually wouldn't hold out much hope for that, but it's possible that a wedding guest will be going there."

"So, I need to hurry. And my plan is to apologize to Simone and take her to meet my grandmother. Does that make sense to everyone in the room?" He glanced at each man.

Micah said, "I agree that's your only plan. But you probably want to talk to your mom first. Do you want to tell her what's really going on, or do you want to continue with the lie there too?"

"I'll call Mom on the way to Main Street."

One of the men, he thought CJ, hummed the wedding march as Nick left the room. Laughter from the open office followed him down the hallway. The good thing about having friends was that they understood you. That you had someone to talk to. The bad thing was that they understood you and made sure you knew that.

# CHAPTER SIX

*N*ick sat in his truck and tried to list his options. Then he realized his friends were right. He didn't have any. He had to confess to his grandmother—on her deathbed—that he had lied and there wasn't a woman in his life.

Or he needed to talk to Simone—whom he had been rude to and ignored during their drive after hitting her SUV and damaging her cake. As much as it pained him to admit it, he might have been able to hit the brakes in time to avoid both the alpaca and her vehicle if he'd been more alert. At the very least, he should have replied when she tried to have a conversation.

Maybe if he explained that he'd been tired. That's it! He'd logically explain what had happened, and she would understand.

He reached to start his truck and stopped.

But he'd also abandoned her. Completely forgotten that he was supposed to drive her back to the city today. It's true he ended up staying here, though. *Also,* because he'd been tired.

CJ left the building, got in his pickup, and drove off a few minutes later. Micah also left, going in the opposite direction, probably toward his house.

After fifteen minutes of going nowhere with his thoughts, Nick started driving. He had never been a coward. If he had, he wouldn't even have his business. Risks had to be taken all the time. When he'd first gone out on his own, that had been a risk. When he'd moved into this much larger place from the hole-in-the-wall space he started in, that had been a massive risk. They'd always paid off, so he just needed to move forward and . . .

He drew closer to Bella's Brides. *What? Get down on his knees and beg?* When he pictured his grandmother lying in bed, he knew he would actually do that. He would beg for her. He just hoped he didn't have to.

He found CJ walking out of one of the smaller storefronts on Main Street. Nick pulled into a parking space there. It was probably better that he wasn't right in front of the wedding dress store, anyway.

Nick got out of his truck, relieved to have a short reprieve before he had to talk to Simone. "Is someone moving in?"

"My wife." CJ turned and looked at the building with pride in his eyes. "She's opening her wedding studio here. I told her I'd work on it in my spare time. That's why you found both Micah and me in his office today. We were reviewing some of the final documents, and Paige had just left. She ran over quickly after all the wedding guests had left to sign the papers." He stared at the entryway. "She says her store should have a turquoise door. What do you think?"

Nick laughed. "That is far out of my range of expertise." He looked around at Main Street with fresh eyes. He'd always seen it as a derelict reminder of a town that had lost its way. Having an abandoned shopping district had told him Two Hearts had nothing to offer and had been a big reason why he'd left. But new life was being breathed into Main Street with Bella's Brides across the street and the photo studio going in.

He knew in his mind that the town had been coming back to life this year through weddings. He'd been part of that process. But it didn't feel real and tangible until he saw vacant buildings being converted back into usable spaces.

The house Paige had bought and fixed up had made a huge difference in that area. It no longer felt like a forgotten wasteland.

But Main Street? That was huge. These buildings had been abandoned as long as he had been alive, probably longer. Tiny pieces of an idea came to mind and started to grow. What if . . .?

Could he have a commercial kitchen in Two Hearts, a place to prepare food for weddings? That would solve a lot of problems. The logistics of bringing out food and keeping it safe had been a big issue.

"CJ, do you know who owns all these buildings?"

"Paige has looked at every one of them. She wanted to make sure she had chosen right. That means I know who owns every one of them." He rolled his eyes. "This was the first one she went into, and it was the one she ended up loving." He reached into his pocket and pulled out a wad of keys with tags on the key rings. "I have access to all of them."

"I'd like to look into a few of them. Do you have a moment?"

"If you're thinking of putting a business on Main Street, I have all afternoon and into the night. If the town prospers, so do Paige and I. I was ready to move on to the next town when I arrived here, because that's what I had been doing, but now that I've decided to make it my home, I want to see it come to life again."

He checked both directions to make sure no traffic was coming, letting one car pass before he stepped into the middle of the street to check out the buildings on the side they were already on. There was a large building that appealed to him.

"Let's check that one out first. I want to see what it looks like inside, space-wise."

CJ started in that direction, picking through the keys he was holding to find the correct one. He inserted it into the lock when they arrived.

When Nick opened the door, a stale smell floated out. Stepping inside, he found it dark and dingy. But the place was enormous. Did he need this much room? He walked around, though, to truly get a sense of this building and the space.

He liked it. The floors were wood, but badly chipped, so he would probably need to replace them. That was fine because he needed flooring that could be easily cleaned to keep the kitchen sanitary. He found a large bathroom—at least large for a business—at the back. That would save money. But he'd probably have to completely redo the plumbing considering the age of this building and the last time it was inhabited.

"I think this may be too big. Let's try another one."

The two men went outside, and Nick pointed to the one just to the left of this. "That's a lot smaller. Maybe that would be better for my purposes."

CJ rocked back on his heels. "There is a lot to choose from. Are you sure about that one?"

It felt like there was a subtext and meaning that he wasn't catching. "Should I ignore that one for some reason?"

CJ shrugged. "It's just that Simone looked at it a little while ago, and I think she's interested. I probably shouldn't say anything, but on the other hand, I probably should."

Nick wanted to see the size of the second building so he could compare them. "I want to take a quick look, anyway." Considering that he wanted to ask a huge favor of her, he should stay a mile away from anything Simone had even a slight interest in. But he wanted to see it, anyway.

"Okaaay," CJ dragged the word out. They went inside, and Nick immediately liked the space. Maybe this *would* be enough.

Female voices had him turn around.

Cassie asked, "Are you buying this building, Nick?"

Simone didn't say a word, but she also didn't look happy.

"I'm thinking about putting a commercial kitchen in town. A place to do the wedding catering." He may as well share that idea with them to see what they thought of it. Cassie was his only client in the area.

She didn't even look around the room before she said, "I think that's a great idea. But you need more space."

Simone nodded. "Definitely more space."

Before he could stop himself—before he contained the stupidity that rushed out of his mouth past his lips—he said, "What does a wedding cake maker know about running a restaurant?"

The women gasped.

CJ grinned and leaned against the wall with his arms crossed, a position that said he was settling in to watch the show.

"We know what you meant to say, Nick." Simone advanced on him, so angry steam probably rose from her. "But I believe you need more space than this for a full catering operation. How many servings have you needed for an event?"

Cassie stepped in. "I can answer that. The largest wedding I've done out here has been five hundred people. Nick catered it out at Cherry and Levi's flower farm."

"So you're often cooking for a group of hundreds and you need to have all the setup and all the prep?"

He saw the room with new eyes. He hated to admit it, but she was 100 percent correct.

She opened her mouth to say something else, but he held up his hand to stop her. "I concede. I see your point. This would work for a kitchen where I was making a normal number of meals for a restaurant, but might not be best for full-on catering for a crowd."

Out of the corner of his eye, he saw CJ stand. "Do you want to see the one next door again or perhaps one of the others? Maybe one across the street?"

"Are you working with Randi selling real estate?" Bella asked.

CJ chuckled. "No. But as the main carpenter in Two Hearts, I know that if someone moves into one of the spaces, I have work for a while."

He had a good point. "Let me go look at the one next door again. I've always liked this side of the street better for some reason." They went back in there, and Nick looked around. It was still bigger than he needed, but it made more sense to have extra space than not.

"You could put tables in the front and have a big kitchen in the back." Simone pointed to the various places as she spoke. "Are you thinking of opening a restaurant in Two Hearts or just a kitchen?"

"We don't have a restaurant that serves dinner," Bella said. "There are times when I get off work, and I don't want to have to do anything. It would be nice to be able to go out to eat."

The excitement of the idea grew in him. Always practical, though, he slammed on the brakes. "Your idea sounds great." He made a point of acknowledging Simone as he said that. When he noticed a slight smile, he smiled back.

"Nick?" Cassie asked.

He'd lost his train of thought. Right. "I have a growing restaurant in Nashville. I don't know how I would make this happen. It's going to be a struggle to continue catering. I almost drove my SUV into the ditch today because I was so exhausted."

He thought he heard one of the women mutter "coward" as they passed him on the way to the door, but he was probably wrong. Then the word "alpaca" floated by, telling him his hearing was fine and they were talking about him. Through the grimy window, he watched them cross the street and go into Bella's shop.

"That went well," CJ said with a grin.

"I messed up, didn't I?"

"Only if you want Simone to talk to you again."

Yes, he did want that. His blood pressure shot up. Nick somehow managed to leave the building and appear calm. Collected. Not revealing the panic that stormed through his body.

CJ asked, "You look like you're going to walk in front of a firing squad."

Or not.

Truer words had never been spoken. "I need to ask Simone for help with my grandmother situation."

CJ chuckled. Then he realized Nick wasn't laughing with him. "You're serious? I thought you must have found a different answer." Shaking his head, CJ walked away.

Maybe his grandmother would forget the name he'd given? Her sharp mind wouldn't usually do that, but she hadn't been normal today. He could get someone else to pretend to be his fiancée.

His text alert sounded.

*Your grandmother asked when she'd be meeting Simone.*

He couldn't put this off. He started across the street.

A horn sounded and brakes squealed.

Nick jumped back on the sidewalk, and the car passed by with the driver shaking his head. Fortunately, the car had out-of-state plates, so no one in town would know.

After checking both directions, he crossed the street. At Bella's Brides, Nick cupped his hands on the shop's glass door to see inside. He'd never been in a wedding-anything store and didn't want to change that now. But he had no choice. What could he say to repair the situation between him and Simone?

"Simone, I'm sorry I was so grouchy that I seemed to be a

complete and utter jerk. I hope you can forgive me. Oh, and I need you to meet my grandmother and pretend to be my fiancée," he whispered, trying out the words.

With a smile—one he hoped was charming and not crazed—he reached for the door handle and pulled it open. There was very little chance of this working, but he had to give this a shot.

As soon as he stepped through, all conversation stopped. The three women stared at him.

Cassie, always the gracious wedding planner and businesswoman, said, "Can I help you with something, Nick?"

He swallowed. "Um, I wonder if I could speak with Simone. Alone."

Cassie and Bella turned to Simone.

"I don't believe we have anything private to say to each other."

"Please hear me out."

Simone crossed her arms. "Anything you want to say can be said in front of my friends." She glared at him.

This was going to be even worse than expected. "I went to my family's home after I left here, and my grandmother was in bed acting like she was dying."

Bella said, "I'm so sorry, Nick! We saw her in town not long ago. Didn't we, Cassie? I think we were together."

Cassie nodded. "She looked great. That's so sad that she went downhill so quickly." To Simone, she added, "His grandmother is a little spitfire. I've only met her a few times, but she always left me smiling."

Okay, this was a good setup for helping him. "Well, she was breathing raggedly and asking me as she always does about the women in my life. I might quite possibly have said the dumbest thing I have in my entire life. She wanted to know if I was dating anyone. It's her fondest wish that I'm settled before she . . . passes away."

Nick paused to get a grip on emotions that were running

wild. "So I blurted out the first name that came to mind, one that was fresh in my mind because—" he winced "—of our time together."

# CHAPTER SEVEN

Simone watched Nick squirm. The last thing she wanted to do was help this man, even if she did appreciate his apology. But did he really mean it? He'd only said it under duress.

Cassie and Bella remained silent and watched her.

"Okay, I will go with you to see your grandmother. But I'm not going to lie to her. You're going to have to find a plausible solution to this. I want to tell her the truth."

Nick sighed. "If you have a gentle way to tell her that I haven't thought of, please share."

Simone stood. "Maybe we'll come up with something together on the way."

Cassie glared at him. "Simone, are you sure you want to do this?"

"I know that Nick made an error earlier today." Bella leveled her gaze at him. "But if he's genuinely sorry . . ."

He nodded vigorously up and down. "I am. I am."

"What are you sorry for?" Simone still didn't trust the man.

If ever a man had the appearance of wanting the Earth to

open and swallow him at that moment, it was Nick Barton. "For being rude?"

She'd have to take that. He had been rude. If he realized that, at least they were on the right track.

Bella added, "And, Simone, he is one of Micah's closest friends, so he must have some redeeming qualities."

Simone heard him mutter, "High praise," and bit her lip to hide a smile. She clapped her hands together once. "Then let's do this. You owe me dinner at your restaurant." She paused. "I think for a group of six." Turning to her friends, she asked, "Does that sound good to you?"

Before they could answer, Nick said, between gritted teeth, "It would be my pleasure."

Laughter bubbled up inside her at his discomfort, but she tamped it down. He was too much fun to mess with.

A couple of minutes later, they were heading north on Main Street, which became the highway.

She kept thinking about the situation. Every time, telling the truth felt like the only option.

They drove in silence out of town and into the countryside, then down a slightly narrower road, and finally left on what turned out to be a gravel driveway. Fruit trees passed by on both sides of the drive, probably peach in this part of the country.

Nick stopped in front of a charming, older, white farmhouse.

He turned toward her. "Any ideas?"

She shook her head. "None."

He rubbed his hand over his face. "Then we'll tell her the truth."

Two dogs raced out, barking furiously. As soon as Nick greeted them, they wagged their hind ends. She stepped out and came around his truck.

"They're friendly."

Simone fought rolling her eyes. Growing up with cats and dogs had given her opportunities to find out when an animal of almost any variety was in a good mood. They went toward the house with the dogs at their heels. When they were ten feet from it, the door opened. A fifty-something woman Nick strongly resembled stood in the opening.

"This is her?" she asked in a low voice.

"Yes, Mom. This is Simone."

"The actual Simone or someone you found to play her?"

What was going on here? She felt like she was either part of a bad comedy movie or at the beginning of a suspense, possibly a horror one.

"Mom, this is Simone Mills. She's a friend of Cassie's and Bella's. You probably know them."

"Of course, I do. I helped clean Cassie's house before she moved in, and I was on the painting crew for Bella's Brides before it opened." His mother waved them inside. "I hope you've got this figured out, Nick."

They walked through a kitchen, past the opening to a living room—all charming farmhouse-style—and into a bedroom where an elderly woman lay in bed with her feeble face the only thing sticking out of the covers and her breathing labored. Her plan to tell her the truth went up in a puff of smoke. If this woman wanted a fiancée, she was going to get one.

Before Nick could say anything that would mess that up, Simone stepped forward. "Nick has told me so much about you, Mrs.—" She quickly glanced at him when she realized she didn't know the woman's name.

"West."

"Mrs. West, it's an honor to meet you." She looked up at Nick with what she hoped were stars in her eyes. "I'm sorry I didn't meet you sooner. Our romance happened so quickly that we didn't have time."

Nick sputtered next to her.

His grandmother reached out a hand, and Nick took it in his. "Is there a problem, Nicky?" The endearment was sweet.

"No, Nana. Everything's okay. It's just new having Simone in my life."

Simone leaned closer to him. "Nice save."

The old woman took a deep, labored breath. "I'm so glad you were able to come here while there was still time."

Simone looked up at Nick. His pained expression said he really did love this old lady. His grandmother didn't look like she would survive the week, months, or even year it could take to plan their imaginary wedding. "We need to have you get well so you can be at our wedding."

Nick sucked in a lungful of air. She hoped his grandmother hadn't heard him. This man was the worst actor ever.

"Tell me what you do for work." His grandmother opened her eyes again, putting a strong gaze on Simone. And then it was gone. She must feel better at times.

"I create wedding cakes. I do it all from the initial idea to delivering a decorated cake—everything I can to help a couple have a wonderful reception and start their life out on a happy note."

She pictured the wounded cake from earlier today and glared at Nick. When she turned back to his grandmother, the older woman had a shrewd expression. Then it disappeared again.

"So you're both in the food business? Isn't that nice, Nicky. You can work side by side in the kitchen."

"I think we cook different kinds of food, Nana. There isn't much call for wedding cake in restaurants." Seeming to wonder if he'd insulted her again, he turned to her. "Isn't that right, Simone? Wedding cake is best served . . . at a wedding." He laughed nervously.

*Do not try for a second career or even a hobby on the stage.*

Nick took one step forward. She could feel his presence

right behind her. Then he put his hand on her shoulder. With a gentle squeeze, he said, "I think we need to leave Nana to rest now. We'll share the rest of our plans when we know more. Isn't that right, Simone?"

"Are you sure, Nick? I wouldn't mind staying and visiting a few minutes more." She did like his grandmother.

Nick slipped his hand in hers, and she almost leaped away from him but caught herself in time. Then his warmth seeped into her. She caught herself just before a sigh drifted out. With a gulp, she focused on the scene in front of her, not the man who now stood beside her.

Still holding Simone's hand firmly, he said to his grandmother, "I'll be back soon, Nana. I'm going to be in town more often because I'm planning to have a kitchen for my catering in one of those old buildings on Main Street."

Simone whipped around to face him. When had he decided that?

He seemed as startled by his words as she was.

The old lady's eyes lit up, and she clapped her hands with glee. "Oh, Nicky, that's wonderful! And you, Simone, when will I see you again?"

She didn't want to commit to anything. "Soon. I often deliver cakes to weddings in Two Hearts."

"I'll have to make a special trip out here to talk to CJ more about renovating my building. I'll see you soon."

His grandmother's expression looked hopeful, but something more. "So you can both visit me soon?"

Simone patted Mrs. West's hand. "Don't worry. We'll be here again."

Her gaze sharpened. "I'm looking forward to getting to know you, my Nicky's sweet bride-to-be."

She felt Nick's entire body go still beside her.

"I'm sure that will be—" he choked a little on the next word "—lovely, Nana." Nick checked his watch. "Time to go."

She reached down and touched the woman's shoulder through the covers. "I'll see you soon. I hope you're much better the next time we meet."

Nick kissed his grandmother's cheek and whispered something in her ear before turning and leading them out of the room. He motioned for his mother to follow them outside.

His mother stood wringing her hands on the front steps outside the closed front door. "You did such a good job, Nick and Simone. If I didn't know better, I would have believed every second of your story." She wiped a tear from her eye. "I can't tell you how much I appreciate that you, Simone, a stranger, would do this for my mother. Just last week, she was so healthy.

"She took to her bed . . . when I told her Nick would be in town today. Are you sure nothing happened between you and your grandmother?" She narrowed her gaze and Simone could see the family resemblance in that moment. "You didn't say something to hurt her feelings, did you, Nick?"

"Of course not! I hadn't talked to her for weeks. I came to town, and the next thing I know, you're telling me Nana's not doing well."

His mother cocked her head to the side and studied the house. "I wonder . . ."

Nick followed his mother's gaze. "About?"

His mother stared at the house for another few seconds, then turned toward her son again. "Nothing. It's nothing. I hope you can both make it out here next Saturday. She's not the only one looking forward to it."

As they drove away, Nick said, "Why? That's all I want to know."

She didn't pretend not to understand what he meant. "I like her."

With a sigh, he added, "I can understand that. But the truth would have gotten us out of this. Now my grandmother will expect to see us together for a while."

"I can put up with you."

He laughed and the happy sound wove through her, making her heart beat faster.

"I love Nana, so I appreciate your time with her."

This was the Nick others knew. She'd seen that he could be a sweet guy around family, but, until now, not with her.

"As long as we can get along together well enough that she buys into it, this will work. I know spending time together is a struggle."

Ba-boom. What was it about her that made him always come back with a line that upped the nasty ante? The thing was that his comments were starting to make her feel like laughing because of the ridiculousness of them. If Nick wanted to be like that, she'd let him. But she'd find some way to let him know how she felt about the situation. He might not be happy with the results.

The man could most definitely cook. She had to admit that everything that came out of Southern Something's kitchen was wonderful. It was too bad that the chef and owner had an attitude when it came to her. But she'd enjoy spending time with Mrs. West. And she looked forward to the expensive dinner he would give her and her friends.

# CHAPTER EIGHT

$S$imone called Cassie after they left Nick's childhood home, partly because she wanted to talk to her friend and partly so she and Mr. Nick Barton wouldn't have to talk, something that at this point was quite uncomfortable.

*Her fiancé.* This would be one of those things to tell her grandchildren about decades from now. The chef who didn't like her and who had to pretend to be engaged to her.

After Cassie answered, Simone asked, "I'm just checking in to see if you can do anything later." She knew Cassie couldn't, but again . . . filling time.

"Things have changed. I opened up the food Mrs. Brantley left for us for tonight. We're a group of six, and we have enough roast beef and vegetables to feed twenty people."

Cassie chuckled and Simone joined in. "I guess you shouldn't be surprised. She's the ultimate hostess."

"You're right. But this also means that I can have you join us. I know you're staying with Paige and CJ, but I don't remember hearing anything about dinner."

Simone thought over the conversation they'd had. She had said she'd bake something sweet tonight and promised to make breakfast. Cassie was right. She was on her own for this meal. Even though she knew they wouldn't let her go hungry.

"I guess I'm happy to join you."

When her friend didn't reply right away, Simone checked her phone to see if it was still connected. "Cassie?"

"I wondered if you'd like to invite Nick. He's in town too, isn't he?"

A quick glance at Nick showed him staring straight ahead as he drove down the road. That seemed to be how he did everything. Focused and unwavering.

Except when his grandmother got in the middle of things.

Simone grinned. "Can I just have him drop me at your house?" The underlying meaning was that Nick wouldn't be staying.

"I thought you'd say something like that, but I had to ask." A muffled moment later, Simone heard, "We'll go outside later, Romeo." Then Cassie came back on in a normal voice. "Sorry, Romeo kept meowing at the back door. He loves being outside!" Her friend had rescued an adorable gray and white kitten.

"Anyway," Cassie continued, "I'm sure Nick's mother will feed him. See you soon." And the call ended.

They'd reached the edge of Two Hearts. "Nick, can you drop me off at Cassie's house?"

He slowed and pulled in front of Dinah's Place. Leaving the engine running, he turned to her. "I don't know if we can pull off this pretend engagement, even just in front of my grandmother, if we don't have at least one conversation together." He gave a nod toward the restaurant. "Can I buy you a cup of coffee?"

She opened her mouth to say "no," then she remembered the sweet old lady who'd started this. "Do I get pie too?"

He turned off his vehicle. "You can have two slices."

"Careful what you agree to. I may be slightly addicted to Dinah's pie."

Chuckling, he opened his door and stepped out. She met him in front of his SUV, and they entered the restaurant together. Something they both should have thought about more carefully before they did it.

Heads turned their direction and more than one set of eyes rose in surprise. Small-town gossip would probably have them planning their wedding by nightfall—if they didn't diffuse it.

When Michelle arrived to take their order, Nick surprised Simone by doing just that. "We'll just have coffee and pie today. After working the wedding today, we both needed a break."

Michelle nodded. "It certainly was a busy morning! Cassie and Bella were in here a little while ago. They seemed happy with how it all went."

Simone relaxed. The two of them were simply wedding workers in her eyes. "I'm just glad I got the cake here on time." She realized Nick might see that as a dig at him, but Michelle spoke before she could say more.

"I've heard over and over again today that the cake was so pretty! And the food, Nick! Everyone loved the food." She eyed them. "Are you sure you want to eat something?"

"Definitely. What are today's pie flavors?"

Michelle rattled them off. Nick chose sweet potato pie, and she went with strawberry.

Coffee arrived first, quickly followed by their pie.

Simone closed her eyes as she took the first bite. "Delicious." She opened her eyes and went in for another forkful.

"Why did you close your eyes?"

"Take a bite of your pie."

He shrugged then did as she'd asked.

"What do you see as you eat that?"

"Michelle is serving coffee. A couple is on their way to the front to pay. The former mayor is doing his best to stay awake."

She grinned at his last words. "Now, do that again and close your eyes."

As soon as he put the pie in his mouth, he said, "Wow. I'm focused on the pie." A moment later, he added, "I'll do this in the future. Probably not when I'm in public, though." He laughed.

"I don't always close my eyes, but this pie—"

"Definitely worth it."

Then the awkward moments began.

"I guess that when we talk to your grandmother, we can call this a date."

Nick choked on his coffee at the word "date." "Let's avoid that word. I'm going to consider this a conversation." He checked his watch. "We got here just before closing. I guess we'd better get this chat going." Then he looked like he didn't know what to say.

She couldn't blame him because she didn't either.

He really was cute when he got flustered. Too bad he had zero interest in her or apparently in dating. But was he her type anyway? Probably not. She'd always preferred men who were as open as she was to adventure and living in the moment. Nick planned every moment of his structured day.

After a few bites of the melt-in-your-mouth pie, Simone decided to take pity on him by starting the conversation. "What was it like growing up in Two Hearts?"

"Probably like most small towns in America, but without some of the charming things small towns are known for. I'm glad the two parks have been revived. They're even talking about music in the city park every Saturday night this summer." He took a bite of pie before continuing. "And thank you for figuring out what to say."

His smile after those words touched her heart. She'd have to be on guard around him. Maybe hang a sign saying "pretend" on her wall to remind her constantly that everything about their relationship was fake. In case her thoughts drifted to Nick, which, of course, they wouldn't.

"What about where you're from? Small town or big city?"

"Smallish. Much larger than Two Hearts, but nothing like the size of Nashville. And much colder in the winter." Simone took a sip of coffee and looked down at the single bite of pie she had left. He'd agreed to two. Should she take him up on that?

"It's obvious why I'm in Tennessee. Where are you from and why are you here?"

"Texas. I worked in Florida for a while, but wanted to have four seasons again. I applied for and got a job in Nashville as a pastry chef. I started baking wedding cakes, the restaurant folded about a year later, and here I am."

Michelle cleared tables and Dinah came out to help. Their time together was coming to an end. That was probably a good thing.

Dinah took Simone's now empty plate. "I baked more pies than I should have for a few hours open in the afternoon. I know Cassie's taking care of Emmaline's guests tonight. If I send leftover pie home with you, will you be able to get it to her?"

"If you give me the recipe, I could make a pie for them." Simone had asked before.

Dinah grinned. "That crust recipe is stored right here." She tapped the side of her head with her free hand.

"Can't blame a chef for trying. My vehicle's in the shop, but I was about to ask Nick if he'd drop me off at Cassie's house."

Nick answered. "I would be happy to. I'm staying with CJ and Paige—"

"I'll box up a few pieces for you to take there too."

"Maybe Paige is making something for dessert." Nick ate his last bite of pie.

Dinah laughed. "Honey, that isn't going to happen. That Paige. Poor girl tries." She shook her head as she walked away. She soon returned with several boxes. "The two on top are for Cassie. The one on the bottom is for you, Nick."

When she left, Simone realized they were the last ones there.

"I guess this is our cue that it's time to leave." She picked up the boxes.

When they arrived at Cassie's house, Simone said, "I'm glad you suggested Dinah's."

"Me too." He seemed surprised by his words. "And thank you again for helping me with Nana."

She pushed thoughts of Nick Barton out of her head as she headed from his truck to her friend's back door. Small towns *were* appealing. The simple things like going to back doors instead of the more formal front.

And it would probably be easier to meet neighbors. She didn't know a single person who lived in her apartment building in Nashville. Other than her roommate and her roommate's boyfriend. Maybe that was on her, though. She could bake something and knock on doors to introduce herself.

She thought about the people she passed to and from her unit. They were so focused on their own lives, would they even open when she knocked?

Cassie met her at the door.

"Great news! The guys got the car over to Leo. If you want to go over there now, he said he can take a quick look at it."

"I'm without wheels. How far is it?"

Cassie pointed to the right. "Two blocks that way. It is getting dark, though. Hang on. Let me run you over."

A few minutes later, they pulled up at Leo's house. An oversized two-bay garage that took up most of what would have been a large yard had one door open, with a man in overalls and about her age standing in front.

Cassie said, "This is Leo. I've come to think of him as Two Hearts's car whisperer."

Leo grinned. He wore sturdy glasses, had his hair askew, and oil stains down the front of his shirt, evidence of time spent with engines.

Her vehicle would be in good hands. "If you know repair, I'm very happy."

"Ma'am, I don't think there's much about cars I don't know. Tell me what happened."

Simone recounted the trouble. "It chugged then sounded good for a moment. Then it chugged more, and that was it. I had to cruise into a parking lot."

He gave a single nod. "Fuel pump."

"Don't you need to check?" Now she was starting to wonder about his skills.

"I can check. And I will do that first thing on Monday morning. But I'm certain that's what it is."

Simone only caught hints of the words that came after "Monday morning." She lifted her eyebrows. "It won't get fixed till Monday?"

"I'll call the auto parts supplier then. If they've got what I need in stock—which they probably do—it's just a matter of getting the part to me."

"That should be easy, right?"

He turned to Cassie with a puzzled expression. "She new here?"

"She's visiting from Nashville."

"Oh! Now I understand." To Simone, he said, "Ma'am, this is a small town. The parts place isn't here. It has to be delivered. I believe that will happen on Monday. Then I need to install it. Best case . . . I think you'll be out of here that afternoon." He added, "I hope."

They drove away after profusely thanking Leo for his help. He'd even mentioned a friend in a neighboring town who did quality body work, but she had too many things going on right now to be in a hurry to fix the damage from the accident.

The clothes Simone wore suddenly felt like they were sticking to her and dirty. They'd been fine thirty seconds earlier, but now she was overwhelmed with the fact that she didn't have anything else to wear.

Cassie offered her a sympathetic look. "Don't worry. You can borrow jeans and sweaters from me."

Simone turned to her friend. "How did you know I was thinking about clothes?"

"Remember? I rode into town in a wedding dress. I wore strangers' clothing until you and Bella brought my things."

"I appreciate your offer, but you and I aren't the same size." Simone patted her hip. "I have ten pounds more." *On each hip.*

Cassie pursed her lips as she thought. "You know, you're about Mrs. Brantley's size. I'm sure she'd be happy to loan you something."

Simone pictured the older woman. "I think you're right about the size. It would feel very strange, though, to take someone's clothes when they weren't around to agree to it."

"Are you going to spend money in Two Hearts while you're here? Are you helping to make Two Hearts a more prosperous place by delivering cakes for weddings?"

Simone leaned back in her seat. "I guess so and yes."

"Then she'd be thrilled. Remember, she's the mayor. She's trying to do everything she can to help this town come back to life."

With that situation settled, Simone remembered the clothes she'd seen the mayor wear, and that made her nervous. She pushed that thought away. Old-fashioned but clean would be better than her current option.

It looked like she was settling in for a few days. Not by choice, but here just the same. Nick would be heading back to town, so she didn't have to figure out how to work with him in their sort-of relationship.

At least it was a secret. The only ones who knew were his grandmother, who was too feeble to share the information, and his mother, who wouldn't dare because she knew the truth.

~

Simone stretched and yawned as she opened her eyes to a pitch-dark room. She fumbled to her right and, instead of finding her phone, discovered a lamp on a nightstand.

With it on, she remembered where she was. She'd spent the night at the McIntosh's house—after what had become the longest day of her life. She'd barely glanced at her surroundings before dropping into bed at eight o'clock.

The pale-yellow walls and the floral coverings on the bed and windows—which didn't match each other but somehow went together anyway—had shades of yellow, pink, and other pastels. When she pushed the covers aside to get up, her hand landed on her phone. She must have fallen into bed clutching it. Sitting up, she put her feet on the soft green rug beside the bed.

The good news about going to sleep so early was that she felt refreshed and ready for her day. The bad news was that she'd woken up so early that she'd have to be quiet, so she didn't disturb anyone.

After a shower, she crept downstairs. The corgi Daisy didn't appear, so she must spend nights in her owner's room. Simone had called last night to apologize for not making cookies but promised instead to make something extra for breakfast. CJ and Paige had quickly agreed to her proposal.

With cinnamon rolls in mind, she rooted around in the kitchen cupboards now, finding a pan for those and a soufflé dish. Cinnamon rolls and a soufflé were an unusual combination—one hearty American and the other delicate French—but she'd go with it because she had everything she needed for both.

Using a simple recipe she knew had excellent results, Simone soon had the sweet treat rising as it waited to be baked. Then she made coffee and had a short break before starting on the soufflé. Timing had to be perfect between the two parts of the meal.

As she took the cinnamon rolls out of the oven, CJ entered the kitchen with Paige right behind him. "Good timing. Breakfast will be ready in about fifteen minutes."

"That is one of the most heavenly scents I have ever woken up to," Paige said as she walked around her husband, who smiled blissfully in the entrance to the kitchen. "You baked those this morning?"

Simone laughed. "You forget what my profession is."

Paige stared at her, dumbfounded. "Something tells me you didn't make the cinnamon rolls out of the frozen bread dough I bought at the grocery store."

"No, but I do have to ask, why do you have so many cooking pans, and why did you have yeast and two kinds of flour if nobody here cooks much?"

CJ chuckled. "That's easy. The food is there because Paige has a relentless desire to figure out how to cook. It has thus far ended in three cases of food poisoning for me."

Paige nudged his arm. "Nonsense. Just because something tasted bad didn't mean you were poisoned."

"Perhaps. But those times were incredibly unpleasant no matter what."

Simone didn't know if she should say anything.

Paige must be used to her husband's banter because she didn't reply to him. "As to the baking pans, I bought a box filled to overflowing with kitchen bakeware and tools at an auction. The whole thing cost me almost nothing. I didn't even know what half of it was used for, but I washed it all up and put it in the cupboard, anyway."

CJ stared longingly at the food. "Are you sure we can't eat those now?"

Simone grinned. "I am. I want them to cool for a few

minutes. I'm about to add a glaze on top." She pulled out a package of powdered sugar and poured some into a bowl.

Another set of footsteps sounded like they were coming down the stairs, and they were too heavy for a small dog. "Where's Daisy this morning?"

Paige answered. "I let her out the front door as soon as I got up. She's currently trying to catch butterflies. She never does. I'm grateful for that, but she's like me with cooking—she hasn't given up trying."

The footsteps grew closer. "Then who—?"

Nick came around the corner, walking around Paige and stopping in the middle of the kitchen, his eyes widening when he spotted her.

Simone dropped the bag of powdered sugar she'd been holding onto the kitchen counter, the white powder flying up and covering her chest.

When neither she nor Nick said a word, CJ cleared his throat. "Both of you needed a place to spend the night. With his grandmother in his old room, Nick would have had to spend an uncomfortable night on a couch at his parents' house. I invited him, and Paige invited Simone. Neither of us knew what the other had done."

Nick seemed to realize he was staring at her, so he turned to CJ and said, "Thank you. I'm glad I didn't have to drive back to the city last night." He gestured toward the nearly ready food. "I thought you said that Paige didn't cook much."

CJ's grin warned Paige. "No, I said she didn't cook *well*. She tries to cook more often than she should."

Paige gave him a gentle punch on the arm. "That would be insulting if it weren't true. I'd give up if it wasn't for the fact that we have one restaurant in town, and it closes midafternoon. There's nowhere to go at dinnertime or on 'Sunday. And sandwiches get old quickly."

Nick frowned. "So who—?"

Simone shook the sugar dust into the sink. "I'm making breakfast."

He leaned closer. "They smell great. I guess they've come a long way with ready-made foods."

Paige gasped.

Simone wavered between anger and amusement, deciding to go with the humor in the situation. "They're from scratch. I only cook from scratch."

Nick shrugged. "I guess making cinnamon rolls is still baking, so it's like a cake." He sniffed the air. "But I smell more than that. Something cheesy."

Simone checked the timer. "Soufflé."

Paige beamed. "Soufflé? You made that too? My kitchen has never seen a breakfast this wonderful! Or anything, for that matter."

Nick knelt and peered through the oven's window. "It seems to be rising well."

Simone told herself that Nick didn't know about her background. "Of course it is." Every time he said these things, though, he annoyed her just a little more.

"Soufflés can be challenging."

Simone closed her eyes and counted to ten.

Paige and CJ backed out of the kitchen. She didn't blame them for wanting to step away from the rest of this conversation.

She drizzled the glaze over the still-warm cinnamon rolls. "Many great meals are created in home kitchens around the world. Not all great food comes from restaurants." She wanted to add *with hoity-toity chefs*, but she reined herself in at the last minute.

Nick had the good grace to turn red and stammer for a moment. "I'm sorry. I didn't mean to insult home cooks. You make great cakes, and those look good." He pointed at the cinnamon rolls.

CATHRYN BROWN

She set the now-empty icing bowl in the sink and turned to face him. His look of complete innocence at the insult set off her funny bone. A grin turned into laughter.

"What's funny?"

His confusion set her off even more. Holding her stomach, she slid to the floor. "You are so pompous!" She gasped for air between words.

"I'm not!" he said firmly.

"Yes. You. Are. Have you been to Paris, France?"

He shrugged. "Many times. I like to study the food there. The French have such a way with the classics."

Her laughter subsiding, she straightened, but couldn't shake her grin. "I went to school there. And I worked there."

"So you're a trained chef?"

She nodded.

"And I truly am pompous?"

She nodded again.

He grinned. "You're right. Truce?" He extended his hand toward her.

"Truce." When she put her hand in his, warmth oozed through her. She stared into his eyes. If only he weren't so driven by work—

The timer on the soufflé sounded.

She pulled her hand back and busied herself with the oven.

Nick spoke from right behind her, closer than she'd expected. "That is a first-class soufflé." His breath ruffled her hair.

She closed her eyes and drank in the moment, surprised at how close he was . . . and how much she liked it.

*He's not the one for you, Simone.*

Daisy raced into the room, the little corgi sniffing the air as she skidded to a stop beside them. Simone was grateful for the interruption.

Nick reached down to pet the dog. "Even she thinks it smells good. Did you train in soufflés over there?"

She blew out a breath. "I did. I also worked in a restaurant that specialized in them, where it was my job as the newcomer to make soufflés all day long." She named the restaurant, knowing he would immediately recognize the name. She directed her gaze at him and smiled with innocence. "Have you heard of it?"

Simone held back a giggle as she spotted Paige peering around the corner. Without waiting for Nick to respond—from his dumbfounded expression she thought it might be a long wait—she stepped aside.

"Let's get some plates and start serving our food. If family style from the stove is okay, let's do that."

Paige glanced between them, apparently deciding it was safe to return to the room. "I put plates from the butler's pantry on the table. Let's eat! We don't want to be late to church, do we?"

# CHAPTER NINE

*A*fter a contentious start to the day, the rest of the morning went fairly well. Simone and Nick regaled their hosts with horror stories from cooking school. Laughter and good food were the best things in the world, as far as she was concerned.

They had found peace between them. That would be helpful as they pretended to be engaged. At least that would just mean a visit now and then to his grandmother.

Nick drove his truck to church, Paige and CJ drove together, and Simone opted to walk, something she couldn't do in Nashville because of the distances between her house and most destinations.

Besides, the mid-January temperatures had been amazing. She knew the pleasant weather could all come to a halt, and there could be six inches of snow on the ground before you even knew what was happening. That was the good and bad, the ups and downs of winter in Tennessee.

When she neared the church, Simone noticed a group clustered around someone or something. Drawing closer, she realized they'd surrounded Bella. Her baby news had flown around town, and these were the excited well-wishers.

Bella's wide-eyed expression said she was overwhelmed by all the attention, so Simone swooped in to try to help.

"Bella! It's so good to see you here. Could you walk me inside while I talk to you about an upcoming wedding?"

Bella stared at her, unfocused.

Simone tucked her arm around Bella's. Smiling at the group, she said, "You can talk to her after church, ladies. She and I will get this sorted out." With a firm hand, she led Bella away from them, and the conversation quickly picked up as they left.

At the top of the church stairs, Bella stopped. "Thank you." She shook her head. "I have never experienced anything like that before. We got married with little notice, so we had a small amount of fanfare on the day of the wedding and right after. But this . . . She glanced over her shoulder at the ladies and quickly back toward the church. "I've got *six months* of this to look forward to."

"It's news right now. But your announcement will be replaced by something else pretty quickly." Simone hoped she was right. She was just glad the news wouldn't be her "engagement."

Inside, they found Cassie, Greg, and Micah.

Bella marched over to her husband. "You just kept going. You didn't save me!"

Micah's eyes grew wide. "From what?"

Bella stabbed her arm in the women's direction. "All the well-wishers."

Micah slowly turned in the direction she pointed, then back at her. "Is it bad when people say good things?"

Bella huffed. "When one person does, it's fine. Two people, okay. Three, we're still in the decent range. When ten or twelve people come upon you and start talking to you about something, you've got a . . . mob. A *baby* mob."

He put his arm around her shoulders. "I didn't know that. I will rescue you from now on."

Bella scooted closer to him and leaned her head on his shoulder. "Thank you."

Greg said, "We have a few minutes before the service starts, so we'd better take our seats." He gestured forward for Simone to lead the way, probably because she was the guest.

She'd been here enough times that she knew the general area they sat in. She slid into the pew and over to the middle, with Greg and Cassie to her right. Bella and Micah tended to sit in the row in front of them, and that's what they did this time too.

Movement to her left made her turn to see if she knew the person who'd sat next to her. Her heart beat faster when she found herself staring into Nick Barton's brown eyes.

Nick stepped into a pew and took a few steps, realizing as soon as he looked forward—and right into Simone's blue eyes—that he'd made a mistake and would be sitting next to her. That was bad. The last thing he needed was for anyone in this town to start saying they were a couple. They'd have to stage a fake breakup to end their fake engagement.

He'd never hear the end of it. They still brought up his breakup with Terri Scott in high school. Now, his grandmother was pushing him and Simone together. He didn't want the entire population putting pressure on them.

Nick turned to leave but found that Dinah and Michelle were right on his heels. Unless he wanted to make a spectacle of himself by stepping around them, he was stuck here.

Accepting his fate, he sat down.

Simone leaned over to him. "This isn't good, Nick. People are going to connect the two of us as a couple." He nodded and patted her hand. As he did so, Dinah glanced over. Her immediate grin went from ear to ear. He'd gone and made things worse.

Before the minister could speak, Nick said just loud enough for everyone around them to hear, "You and your boyfriend will have to stop in Southern Somethings for dinner."

Shock registered on her face. Then realization. All she said was, "Thank you." He hoped that was enough to get Dinah and the gossip squad off their backs permanently.

As he sat there, Nick glanced over at Simone. He had no idea if she was dating someone. He should probably know. And it wasn't personal. Not at all. He didn't care if she was dating half the town. But how did one ask about her love life?

He went over options. *Excuse me, I don't want to date you myself, but I just want to make sure there's no one in your life.* Straight to the point and only mildly awkward. That would probably have to do.

When everyone stood to leave, he went out the same direction he had come in, hoping to find her outside and with her friends so he'd simply be one addition to the group and not a romantic pursuit.

This time, he got what he hoped for. As he approached the group that included Cassie, Bella, and Simone, he wondered if what he hoped for had been foolish. He went in, anyway. The lone male.

He greeted Simone. "I never asked this, but I probably need to know for the Nana situation. Are you dating anyone? I'm not asking for myself, of course."

Simone rolled her eyes.

He hadn't spoken low enough because Bella chimed in. "Smooth. I'm glad you aren't interested, because you wouldn't win any woman with that line."

Simone leaned in closer to her friends. "It's that situation he asked about at Bella's?"

The two women stood straighter and all nodded.

"Okay, we understand. We thought there was a real romance brewing."

Both Nick and Simone waved their hands in front of them.

She said, "No, definitely not."

"Not for me." No one could mistake his negative tone for interest in her.

Simone turned to him and raised an eyebrow.

Maybe he'd put too much passion in his words.

When Simone seemed about to speak, Cassie said, "Don't go there."

"You're right. Both Nick and I knew the rules. It's just for his grandmother. Right?"

He and Simone shrugged at the same time.

As he walked away, he heard Simone ask them, "But what's *wrong* with me?"

He wanted to turn back and say *absolutely nothing*. But then he remembered all the reasons why they were a bad fit. Not the least of which was his putting his foot in his mouth and insulting her every chance he got. And that seemed to happen frequently.

Now, he could return to Nashville and try to forget everything that had happened this weekend. Life could get back to normal. And he wouldn't even need to see Simone next weekend. She'd visit Nana on her own.

When he started his vehicle, he knew he couldn't return to Nashville yet. Not with Nana not doing well. He headed toward his parents' house, calling his mom on the way. "How is she today?"

"Fine. She slept in this morning. We didn't come to church because I didn't want to leave her."

Nick felt his heart squeeze. He couldn't imagine his life without Nana. "Please tell her I'm on my way."

At his parents' house, he found his mother in the kitchen.

"I'm glad you came by. Your Nana perked up when I said you were almost here."

He walked into the bedroom. Nana was still in bed, but she seemed healthier and stronger than yesterday.

"Nicky! I'm so glad to see you." She leaned over to look through the doorway. "And where's your sweet girl?"

"She was busy this morning. But I came over after church. How are you?" He scooted a chair beside the bed and sat down.

*Cough.* Then she took a deep, wheezing breath. "I'm okay. Don't worry about me." Now appearing drained and pathetic, she asked, "I realized something after you were here last time. I didn't see a ring on Simone's hand. What's going on here, Nicky?" When her gaze turned shrewd, he wondered if she'd figured out the entire engagement was a fake.

He hoped not because he didn't want to disappoint his grandmother.

The answer came to him! "We just got engaged. It's a funny story, Nana. We'd seen each other for a while, but we hadn't made any commitment." All true. He had known Simone for months. And they would see each other at weddings. This was going well.

"And then, yesterday morning, her SUV broke down while bringing a wedding cake out here. I came upon her right after her engine quit. We transferred the cake over to my vehicle and brought everything to town. There was something so romantic about being there—the two of us and the wedding." So much for the truth. He'd never teared up at a wedding.

She reached out from under the covers and patted his hand. "Nicky, you're a romantic, just like your grandfather was. He was constantly surprising me with sweet little gifts. We couldn't afford much, but we were happy." She shook her finger at him. "Don't forget to do that for her."

A moment later, her eyes started to close as she fell asleep.

Then they popped open again. "I want to see the ring next time, Nicky. I'm curious about the style you bought that suits her. And we can talk about all of your wedding plans. Because I—" her breath hitched "—may not be here much longer." She closed her eyes and immediately fell asleep.

Nick stood and quietly pushed the chair back. He trudged out of the room and found his mother listening near the door. "Mom, what are we going to do?"

Nick's mother turned and stared at the door. "I don't want you to worry about this, Nick. I don't think the situation is as dire as it appears."

He looked back through the open doorway. "She really wants me settled."

His mother nodded. "That she does. Are you going to get a ring?"

Was he? A ring would be a huge expense, possibly thousands. And for what? A piece of jewelry he'd store in a drawer soon.

His grandmother's chest rose and fell evenly as she slept. "Yes. The next time she sees Simone, there's going to be a ring on her finger."

Of course, anything she wore would be paired with those sneakers of hers that had splotches of frosting colors all over them. This time, the image made him smile. Maybe they would become friends because of all this.

Nick walked to his truck in a daze. His grandmother had been having that effect on him lately. Every time he left her, he felt as if his world had been turned upside down.

Saying he was engaged and introducing Nana to Simone would not be enough. They would have to *look* engaged. A ring would solidify the appearance of their relationship and should make his grandmother happy. He could certainly do that for her.

Now he just had to explain this to Simone. All he had to do was go to a jewelry store, pick the least expensive ring, and give it to her. She could put the ring on her finger when she visited his grandmother and all would be well.

He pulled onto the highway and cruised back to town.

Then his grandmother's words about the ring being Simone's style came back to him. They hadn't seemed important at that moment, but maybe they were. "No!" he shouted.

Not just any ring would do. To sell the idea to his grandmother, the ring had to be one Simone would choose for *herself* or one he would choose if he knew her so well he wanted to marry her. But he didn't know her well.

A handful of miles ticked by, then he reached the outskirts of Two Hearts. He passed the diner and the church, slowing when he reached Main Street.

His promise to his grandmother about moving his catering business here came to mind. At least he saw that as a promise. He had told her he would be getting the space on Main Street. That meant he would.

Nick ignored the little voice asking if the engagement lie was actually a promise to his grandmother that he would marry Simone. Marrying her or anyone else right now would be one of the last things he wanted to do.

He pulled into a parking spot beside the buildings he was considering. Getting out, he stood a few feet from the smaller unit and tried to picture his business inside. Would this one work? He'd spend less money both to buy or lease and probably to renovate too.

But Simone wanted this one. At least she seemed to. He moved to the larger storefront. This building had plenty of space for today *and* room to grow.

The window in front of him caught a reflection. Either he'd conjured her up from his imagination or she was here. Either way, Simone appeared to be crossing the street toward him.

Without turning, he said, "What brings you here?"

She paused a few feet behind him, and then gave a low chuckle, a sound he enjoyed. "The window. Anyway, I was walking home after church. I love how everything's so close together that I can easily walk everywhere. I stopped to look at that building again. You?"

He nodded. "Same. I wanted to picture my business inside."

She looked up at him, concern furrowing her forehead. "I also saw you looking at the small one."

"I keep thinking that less square footage would be less costly. This project is expensive, especially considering that I'm only catering here." He turned to face her. "Do you want the narrow one?"

She said without hesitation, "Absolutely."

"Okay, then. That one's off the table for me."

A broad smile brought her to life. "Thank you. But wanting something and having it are two very different things. I earn a good income from making cakes. But I'm not sure that money is enough to uproot everything I've built in Nashville *and* remodel an old building with who-knows-what construction horrors hiding in the walls."

She had succinctly expressed what he'd been feeling about the risks. "I've been saving money for a while. When you spend every waking moment at work, you don't need much of a place to live. And I don't take extravagant vacations."

Her smile widened. "That I can understand. Maybe you don't need a Two Hearts kitchen."

He turned back to the storefront. "The problem is, I told my grandmother I was fixing this up. I don't have a choice."

"You can be thrifty with your choices. Not be too extravagant with flooring, lighting, and everything else."

He hoped that would be possible. "*If* construction doesn't reveal those horrors you mentioned." He kept staring at the brick building, now imagining the entire place renovated. "My life would be so much easier if I had a catering kitchen in town. I'll need to convince at least one if not two of my employees to move out here, though. I'd have to fund their moves. That's even more expense."

"If they're just assisting you, Nick, you could hire people from Two Hearts. That's all you need right now."

She was right. "I can train someone who's competent in the kitchen to help with prep. Slicing, dicing, and generally getting everything ready." His mind went over the possibilities, and he slowly nodded. "The idea is so obvious that I wonder why I didn't think of it on my own."

She shrugged. "Two Hearts is your hometown. You still can't see the town as having potential. You only see it as dead."

He glanced around the mostly dead area he was standing in. "You're right. But there's a glimmer of hope that wasn't there a year ago. With Bella—"

"And don't forget about Paige on this side of the street. Now you."

"And you. If you want this, you'll find a way."

This time the smile lit her eyes too. She cupped her hands on the window of the building she was interested in and sighed. When she brought her hands down, he remembered . . . the ring.

Nick cleared his throat. "Nana has made another request."

She looked up at him. "She's okay, isn't she?"

"As far as I know. But she said we didn't look engaged because you didn't have—"

"A ring." Simone held up her ringless left hand. "I can solve that problem. My dad gave me one with my birthstone when I was fifteen."

"Unless that's a diamond—and even then, the design would

have to look like an engagement ring—I don't think that's going to work."

"The stone is amethyst, so it's purple. But you're right that nothing about the style says bridal."

"I wish that could work." He couldn't find any solutions other than the obvious one. "I need to buy a ring. And I don't know the first thing about doing that."

"Just get whatever you want."

He sighed. "If only that were possible. Nana was clear that the ring had to look like something you would wear. That the style suited you. She only met you once, but you're going to spend more time together. She's so perceptive—at least she was when she was healthy—that I think she'd eventually realize I'd bought it on my own."

She glanced down at her clothes. "Yikes! Don't base your choice on what I have on now. For a minute, I forgot that I'm wearing someone else's clothing. This—" she motioned up and down "—isn't my style."

"Not your clothes?" That didn't make sense.

"Remember that I wasn't supposed to stay here. And, unlike you, who probably has a stash of clothing at your family home, I was stuck with nothing. These belong to the mayor." She didn't look happy about her wardrobe choices.

He shouldn't have laughed, but a chuckle snuck out before he could stop it.

She narrowed her gaze. "Be careful about laughing at a woman's distress."

He bit his lip.

She changed the subject. "As to the ring, I can try to explain my style—or I can go with you to the jewelry store, and we can choose a ring together."

An image of the two of them walking into a jewelry store scared him to his core. "That would look to the world like we were really—"

"Engaged. I know. If you don't want this situation spread far and wide, I understand."

He didn't. He really didn't. But how would he describe her style to a salesperson in a way that made his grandmother happy with the final results? Shopping had never been his highest skill.

"An interior designer created Southern Something's interior design because I knew the result would be much better than if I'd tried. I'm not good at these things, Simone. As much as I don't want to do this, let's go shopping."

"You're warned. I enjoy shopping. I may have to try on a few —or ten—rings before I find the right one."

"I loathe shopping for anything but food and kitchen items. When can you do this?"

"If everything goes well, I should be home Tuesday morning."

Nick thought over his Tuesday. Nothing stood out. "Southern Somethings has a lull midafternoon. Would you be available at 2:30 or 3:00?"

She pulled out her phone and checked her calendar, something he probably should have done. "That works. Do you want me to meet you somewhere?"

Since he didn't know any jewelers, he didn't have an answer for her. "Any ideas of where to go?"

"I'm not much of a jewelry person, but I know someone who will have the answer. She has the answer to all wedding questions, and this falls into that category." Simone paused and pursed her lips as she thought. "Although, everyone who comes to a wedding planner would already have a ring on their finger, wouldn't they?"

Cassie? He would normally say *no, don't mention this to her*, but Cassie had been there when he'd first talked to Simone about the fake engagement. Why shouldn't she get a laugh out of this too?

"Please tell her to keep it quiet. The last thing I want is for the people in this town to think I'm really engaged. Not that you aren't a wonderful woman, but I am years away from actually wanting to get married."

Simone shrugged. "I agree. And Cassie can keep a secret. In the wedding business, we have to keep a lot of them." She made a note in the calendar then put her phone away. "I'll see you Tuesday afternoon." She held up her hand and turned it in the light as though she were admiring a ring. "I wonder how I would feel if the engagement was real. We make a beautiful couple."

He gulped.

She nudged his arm. "Just kidding. See you then, Mr. Barton." She walked away.

That woman would certainly keep her real fiancé on his toes.

Nick wasn't sure what he would find when he returned to Southern Somethings. He'd left them alone before, but only once, and that was when he'd had a virus that was going around and had been out two weeks. Otherwise, he had been there every single night and day since his restaurant had opened three years ago.

He tried to steer the truck from Two Hearts to his home—a sterile condo in Nashville—but the vehicle had other ideas. Thinking about Simone must have taken his mind off driving because when he started paying attention to his surroundings again, he was about a block away from his restaurant. He might as well check so that he didn't worry about what he'd find the next morning.

He parked and went inside, where he found everything exactly done correctly. The kitchen was spotless. He opened the door to the walk-in refrigerator and found food neatly stored and marked with dates and contents. When he went to the seating area, everything was clean and set up for the next service.

He pulled out a chair and sat down, realizing now that he almost wanted to find something wrong, so he would feel needed. Instead, his head chef and other staff in the restaurant kitchen, along with his front-of-house manager, had done an outstanding job.

Maybe he could spend more time in Two Hearts. He'd gone and committed to the kitchen out there with a vague notion of finding someone to run operations. Simone had flat out turned him down. He didn't blame her, though. She wanted to bake cakes, so that's what she did. He actually envied her a little.

He made his way back through the restaurant and locked up the door, setting the alarm again as he did so. As soon as he was in his SUV, he dialed his friend Stan, who owned three restaurants in L.A. How did he manage more than one?

"Stan? This is Nick Barton."

"Nick! It's good to hear you, man. What have you been up to? I bet you have a chain of five restaurants by now." His friend chuckled.

Should he have expanded by now? "Still just the one, but I've been doing a lot of catering in my hometown. It's about an hour and a half out of Nashville. I decided to build a catering kitchen out there."

"I do catering out of my restaurants, but that sounds like an intriguing idea. Why not an actual restaurant? Then you'd get business all the time."

Nick thumped his fingers on the steering wheel. "But I don't want business all the time. I still need to run this place in Nashville. This driving back and forth ninety minutes each way is wearing on me already."

"You don't have chefs in place under you that can run the restaurant?"

"Actually, I do. I was just gone for a Saturday dinner service, and they did an amazing job."

"Oh! I understand the problem."

"I'm glad you do. Someone needs to. Please share."

"You're holding on too tightly. You can't expand if you do that. You needed to be there all the time when your restaurant was new, but now that you have people in place that can run day-to-day operations without you, it's time to expand your horizons. You could even sell that restaurant if you wanted to."

Nick's heart fell into his stomach. "Stan, I don't think I could ever sell Southern Somethings."

He sighed. "She's your first child. They're hard to let go of. But you don't have to sell your restaurant. The catering kitchen might be a good idea, though. You'd have something else to think about. Aren't you getting bored going to the same place every single day?"

Was he bored? He had enjoyed going out to Two Hearts every once in a while to make something different. "I see what you're telling me. I'll have to think about this."

"Don't think about expanding for too long, Nick. I think you're like me. You like a challenge. That shows in your food and in the care you give to your restaurant. Grab a hold of a new challenge."

Why did Simone's face pop into his mind when he heard the word *challenge*? "I appreciate this. I knew you would be able to set me straight. And how are your restaurants doing?"

"I sold one to my front-of-house manager, and she's done an excellent job. And then I opened a new place. Just to keep things interesting." Nick heard a timer of some sort going off. "That's telling me that I have to pick my son up for his soccer game. I'd better go."

"Thank you again!" Nick started up his truck and began his

short drive home. With his grandmother's situation, maybe he did need to spend more time in Two Hearts. He could test the idea with one day a week. If there wasn't a wedding that week, he could just choose a day to hang out with his family. *And Simone*, a little voice added. She tended to spend the day there when she worked a wedding.

# CHAPTER TEN

*M*onday morning, Simone stepped into Cassie's kitchen carrying a paper bag filled with clothing belonging to Mrs. Brantley, along with the toiletries she'd purchased on Saturday. "I'm glad to be back over here. Paige and CJ were awesome, but I don't know them as well as you. Staying here is more like hanging out with a sister or cousin. A little less awkward. I really wanted to pay them for letting me use the room, but they wouldn't let me."

Cassie laughed. "The way I've heard the story, they want to pay you." Cassie counted off on her fingers. "One: as Paige told me, and in great detail, you made homemade cinnamon rolls and a soufflé yesterday morning for breakfast. Two: lunch included Monte Cristo sandwiches and homemade French fries. Three: dinner was chicken paprikash." She stared at Simone for a moment. "That one threw me off a bit. But no matter what, they felt like they'd had a gourmet dining experience and were very happy."

"The chicken dish is one my mom used to make. It's her Hungarian grandmother's recipe."

"Well, they loved that and everything else you made. CJ

hinted that you could rent the room for as long as you needed it." She chuckled. When Simone didn't laugh, Cassie said, "Something else seems to be wrong."

Simone sighed. "I like it here."

"Here as in Two Hearts or my house?"

"Two Hearts."

Cassie stared at her for a moment, not saying anything.

Simone wasn't sure how to express the level of enjoyment she'd had in Two Hearts the last few days. Even with the frustration of some of the Nick stuff.

When she didn't add to her sentence, Cassie asked, "Is liking this town a problem? You know *I* do."

"No, I just wonder where I want to be. My life is in Nashville. But my work is now almost all in Two Hearts. My friends are mostly here too."

"Does that mean you're thinking of moving to Two Hearts? Because that would be great!" With a gleam in her eyes, Cassie asked, "Couldn't that be a problem with your fiancé? He'd be in a different location?" Then she started grinning.

Simone put her hands on her hips and stared at Cassie. "Don't even think that, let alone say it out loud. Someone might hear you."

Cassie chuckled. "But seriously, we'd love to have you out here. I had the lure of Greg and Bella had Micah, so the decision was easier for us. Moving Bella's Brides was the hardest part for her. Would changing business locations be difficult for you? You'd have a smaller customer pool, but little competition here. With rent less, there's the possibility your actual income will increase."

She'd never considered that before. "I rented the commercial kitchen I use for the cakes, and that's month-to-month, so that location is easy to let go of. My apartment, though, is another story. To get a great deal on the rent, I signed a two-year lease."

"And?"

"And I did that seven months ago."

"Yikes! You seem so in love with Two Hearts and that store downtown. I really hope you can move."

She did too. And that thought startled her.

"I grew up in a fairly small town. Much larger than Two Hearts, but still small. I knew I never wanted to go back to another one. I like having the accessibility of everything in a city. You want a salad on a Sunday afternoon? No problem. Coffee at midnight? Sure! Here? No. But the people are nice. And you know who your neighbors are."

"All true. But with the apartment problem, none of this matters, does it?"

Simone pushed those thoughts out of her head. "There actually is a situation with Nick that I need to talk about."

Cassie got up and walked toward the coffee pot. "This sounds like I'm going to need a refill. I have cookies. Want any?"

Simone patted her hip. "Need you ask? You know I love sweets. I probably should have stayed a savory chef instead of spending all day with baked goods."

"You look great, and you know that." Cassie set her cookie jar in the middle of the table and filled both of their mugs with coffee. "So, what's the situation? And how can I help?"

"Nick's grandmother said we didn't look engaged because I didn't have a ring."

Cassie cocked her head to the side, looking up as she thought about it. "Maybe just wear something you've got. Or I can dig something up here. My parents gave me jewelry for gifts, even though I didn't really wear much."

"That's the problem." Simone leaned forward, resting her chin on her steepled hands. "His grandmother wanted the ring to be something that looks like *me*, that suits my personality."

"That's interesting. A wily move if I've ever heard one. She's trying to push the two of you together even more."

"I know. None of this makes sense. But then she's not well. I guess if it makes an old lady who's not well happy, then we're going to buy a ring."

"If you're sure. Then what's the question for me?"

"I don't know how I forgot. Do you know any jewelers?"

"The best one in Nashville. Carly told me where Jake bought her ring—one that's absolutely gorgeous and perfect for her. Every once in a while, I get a couple who plans to get married but hasn't done anything toward that, including buying that all-important piece of jewelry. Everyone who has gone there has been thrilled." She picked up her phone and flipped through her contacts. "Here it is. Music City Gems. I'll text the information right over."

Simone's phone chimed in her pocket. "Thanks. As much as I don't want to think the words, much less say them out loud, we're going to buy a ring tomorrow."

Cassie looked down at her left hand and smiled. "My heart has a warm and fuzzy feeling every time I look at my ring."

Simone laughed. "I don't think that's going to happen with this purchase."

"Let's pretend you're in love with Nick, that you want to wear a symbol of your love."

Simone's heart stopped beating with the words "your love." She hadn't fallen for him, had she? No. Absolutely not.

"Simone?"

"Huh?" She looked up. "Sorry. What did you say?"

"I asked if you had any ideas about your ring. Maybe shopping would be easier if we figured that out before you got there."

Good plan. Focus on the ring and not the meaning. "I know I like things that are quirky. And I'm not into giant diamonds or anything like that."

"Carly's ring had a lot of different stones. That would probably be over-the-top for you, though, if you want something on the simple side. She is a country music star, so she's worn a lot of flashy designs over the years."

"Definitely not looking for flashy." She sighed. "I just don't know what I want." No matter what she did, she couldn't picture an engagement ring on her finger. "I may have a mental block."

"I'm sure you'll figure it out once you're there."

Did she want to? "I'm not ready to have a ring on my finger. And Nick was freaking out about the whole thing."

"I'm not surprised." Cassie leaned back in her chair. "I am surprised, though, that he isn't married. He is handsome, don't you think?"

Simone snorted. "You have to be blind not to think that man was handsome."

"And nice."

Simone hesitated over that one. "I didn't think so for a while, but seeing him with his grandmother changed my mind. I think you're right. He's handsome and nice."

"And he has a thriving business. If I'm not mistaken, Bella mentioned that he made the ten most eligible in Nashville list last year."

Simone grinned. "I've spent enough time with that man to know that's the last thing he'd want."

"I know. I guess he was fielding proposals from eligible women both on the phone and in his restaurant, some subtle and some not so subtle. And now, you're *engaged* to him."

"You know this isn't real."

A knock at the back door was followed by the sound of it opening and Bella's voice.

Simone continued the conversation. "We don't have a relationship. This is an agreement to help an old lady. That's all. Don't you dare go making this anything more."

Bella headed for the cupboard and took out a mug. "Making what more? Did I miss something good?"

"Cassie told me all the wonderful qualities of the man I'm engaged to. But I'm *not* engaged."

Bella filled the mug with water and put it in the microwave. Turning back to face them, she said, "Just like I wasn't married."

Simone frowned. "But you *were* married."

"Not in the true sense of the word. I had a license, but we were roommates. That was all."

Simone's phone buzzed with a text. She pulled and checked the screen. "Leo has the part. My SUV will be ready first thing in the morning." A weight lifted off her shoulders. She would be free to go whenever she wanted.

Then her phone rang. She answered, expecting to find Leo calling with more information about her vehicle. Instead, it was her assistant. Simone hit the mute button on her phone.

"It's my assistant. Is it okay if I talk to her in your living room?"

"Of course."

Simone spoke as she walked. "I hope you and your baby are doing well."

"I love being a mother. Even more than I thought I would." She paused. "Simone, you're the best boss ever . . ."

Whew! Simone had wondered if the woman would come back after having her baby.

"But I want to stay home with my little guy. He's so cute. I don't want to miss a moment. My husband and I have talked about the money side of things, and we'll make it work."

Simone took a deep breath and let it out slowly before replying. "I understand. Keep in touch."

They ended the call with her assistant giddy about the idea of staying home with her baby and Simone shocked at the loss of someone she'd trained and worked with for a year. Simone went back in the kitchen and told the women what had happened.

"That's too bad, Simone," Bella said as she reached for

another cookie. "I know it takes a while to train someone. I'm so glad April came back to work after maternity leave."

"Her skills grew until I could give her almost any task. She was great. Oh well. I'll just add hiring someone to my list of things to do." She sat down again and took a sip of her coffee.

"Speaking of being busy, how is your life feeling, Cassie, now that your guests have all left?" Bella asked as she dropped a tea bag into her mug.

"Much more peaceful. You know I love my job, making all the pieces of a wedding work. There are often a lot of people, but the event only lasts for a few hours. This went on for close to a week."

Simone stood. "I hadn't thought about that. You're ready for quiet. I can go back over to Paige and CJ's."

Cassie pointed at the chair. "Sit. I'm not trying to feed you and take care of you and be the perfect host. You can take care of yourself. I felt like I was always on duty with them. Not in a bad way, because they were nice people, but there was constant pressure to not let down my future mother-in-law."

Bella reached into the cookie jar and came out with three cookies. "I'm eating for two now." She bit into one of them. "Mmm. I know what you mean, Cassie. Our house was packed over the holidays."

Simone needed something to do to take her mind off of . . . everything. "Can I cook dinner? That would make me feel better about staying."

Cassie looked over at Bella, who nodded, then shoved another cookie in her mouth. "Can you make the eight of us dinner, Simone?"

Bella put her hand on her barely rounded stomach. "We would be thrilled. We've been fond of Italian food lately."

Simone grinned. "I can make that. Anything in particular, or just cheese and pasta?

"Cheese and pasta would be lovely. Anything covered in tomato sauce."

"I'll go by the store and pick some things up." Then she realized she still didn't have a SUV and needed to bring her purchases here. "Cassie?"

"I'm happy to be your wheels. Let's get you settled in first, and then we can do that."

# CHAPTER ELEVEN

*N*ick checked in at his restaurant bright and early Monday morning to make sure everything was under control before he took off for his long drive to Two Hearts.

His team had done an excellent job Saturday while he'd been in Two Hearts, surprising him with the fact that maybe he didn't have to be there every second of every day. His kitchen manager had surprised him even more. He may not be using his staff to their full potential. Mondays were slow, so there would be less risk but another opportunity for them to surprise him.

He hadn't been back in the city a day, but he'd made the decision about the building on Main Street.

Driving into Two Hearts, he had the same feeling he always did—home. He may have lived in many places, first to study and then to work, traveled even more places—he'd eaten his way through Italy on one month-long trip when he was still a student—but nothing said home like this place. He'd come as close as he could in Nashville, where he could have the type of restaurant he wanted, to make the food he enjoyed making.

He passed the sign that said, "Welcome to Two Hearts," the one that had been falling down before Cassie had ridden into town.

Cassie and her friends. He sighed. Every time he saw Simone, he said the wrong thing to her.

But he didn't want to upset her.

He'd buy the larger building on Main Street. Once he decided to move forward with something, he didn't hesitate. This branch of his business would give him both a local kitchen *and* get him closer to his family more often.

When he'd called to tell CJ and book him for the renovation, CJ had talked to Paige and then put the phone on speaker when they'd offered him a room for the night. That would be better than sleeping on his parents' couch, but he didn't want to be a disruptive guest.

"I'm a night owl. I don't want to keep you guys up. It's a fact of the business I work in. I'm usually awake until well after midnight because, so many nights of the week, I have to close the restaurant." Or did he anymore? His employees were doing an excellent job. He'd find out how necessary he was if he spent more time in Two Hearts.

Paige spoke. "No problem. You can sit in the front parlor—I love saying that. It sounds so Victorian. Or your room. CJ and I can go to our suite and leave you alone."

"That's nice of you. But I think what I'll do is spend some more time with my family. If my grandmother is that sick . . ."

CJ nodded. "I am sorry to hear that about her. I've only met her a few times, but she always seemed to be full of life."

"She always has been. Anyway, I think I'll just go sit at her bedside and get to your place at about ten o'clock." Nick couldn't imagine his life without Nana. He shook that feeling off. "But first, I'll meet you at the building for one last walkthrough."

A couple of hours later, he'd pulled into a parking space on Main Street. This time, pride surged through him when he visualized the completed project.

He met CJ inside. Nick pictured the eight-burner commercial stove, stainless steel work surfaces, vinyl flooring, and painted and tiled walls. This would be a much nicer kitchen than the one in his first location.

CJ pointed to the front door. "If you buy this, do you want to keep the front of the building as is?"

"Yes. I want to retain the character. And it's not a maybe on this building. I am absolutely doing this. We just need to get the building permits in for the design."

CJ chuckled. "I can tell that you've been in Nashville a while. Many of the outlying counties don't have building permits and codes and rules like that. This county is one of those. Once you have the agreement with the owner, we can start work."

"Do you think we could get papers signed today? I happen to have an in with a lawyer here in town."

CJ grinned. "If you can get Micah to draw up the agreement, you could go over to Charlie Scott's house to get the papers signed. I know he's ready to roll and will accept almost anything you offer. He's had to pay taxes on the place for years, so not having to do that anymore would be huge for him."

They waved goodbye as Nick climbed into his vehicle. As he started the engine, CJ ran over and tapped on the window. Nick rolled it down.

CJ said, "There's a key under the flowerpot. If you get home and the door is locked, just use the key."

Nick agreed. "And to thank you for this, I can make breakfast tomorrow."

CJ grinned. "We would both love that. Paige desperately wants to master cooking, but the skills have evaded her thus far." With a laugh, Nick drove over to Micah's house, relieved when he found a car in the driveway.

Before knocking on the door, Nick took out his phone and called. "Micah, I have a favor to ask."

"Anything."

"Would you be able to draw up a contract for me to purchase a building on Main Street?"

Silence greeted him. "As in you're buying one of the buildings on Main Street in Two Hearts, Tennessee? I just want to be clear about this."

Nick laughed. "Exactly."

"You're moving home?" He spoke so loudly that Nick jerked the phone away from his ear.

"Don't get too excited. This is just for a kitchen for the catering I've been doing. I've been driving with cooked food for ninety minutes, and that isn't the best option."

"It's at least a start. Sure. I can draw up a contract."

"How long would it take to do something like that?"

"This would be a fairly simple contract. Probably an hour or so. When did you need it?"

"Would now be too soon? I'm on your front porch." With those words, Nick heard footsteps coming through the phone line, and then the front door opened. "Why didn't you just say you were in front of my house?" Laughing, Micah waved him in.

Nick found Micah but no Bella in the living room. When he asked, Micah gestured with his thumb toward the kitchen. "She's making dinner. I know you're a good cook, but Bella's cooking lasagna, and her grandmother's recipe is the best I have ever eaten."

Nick grinned. "I love lasagna."

Micah walked over to the kitchen door and pushed it open. "Bella, there's plenty for Nick to stay for dinner, isn't there?"

Nick heard laughter coming from the kitchen. Then Bella stepped out, wiping her hands on an apron. "It's great to see you, Nick. Micah doesn't realize I make lasagna in a giant pan. I love all the leftovers for lunches. But I am happy to share some with you." She fidgeted with her hands. "I have to say, though, I'm more than a little nervous to serve my lasagna to a well-known and respected chef."

"This is your grandmother's recipe, right?"

"It is."

"Nothing I make can compete with a handed-down recipe from grandma. Is there anything I can do to help?"

She glanced over at Micah with a curious expression. He seemed to understand what she wanted to know.

"I'm drawing up a real estate contract for him to purchase one of the places on Main Street."

Bella smiled. "The one we were in with Cassie and . . . Simone?"

Nick noticed the hesitation. "I chose the larger one."

Bella raised an eyebrow. "I guess that means Simone was right that you needed a little more room?"

He hated to admit the truth. "She was. The more I thought about the space, the more I realized she was correct." And he hadn't wanted to disappoint Simone by taking the one she wanted, but he wasn't going to tell them that.

Seeming to fight laughter, she returned to the kitchen. "Dinner will be ready in about forty-five minutes. Will you guys be done by then?"

Micah pulled a laptop computer from a business bag next to the door. "I'll make sure we are. Nothing is getting between me and your lasagna."

When Bella was in the kitchen and Nick could hear the sounds of pans and clanking, Micah leaned forward and said, "How's everything going with your bride-to-be?"

"Don't go there. We're getting by. At least I don't see my *fiancée* too often." Nick all but choked on the word. It had become easier and easier to pretend they were engaged, and that may be the most disturbing thing of all.

Micah focused on Nick, seeming to be about to say something, and then looked away with a smile.

"What?"

"Excuse me?" Micah worked at his computer.

Nick pulled the laptop away from him. "Please tell me what's going on."

Micah glanced at the door again. In a lowered voice he said, "Simone hasn't told you, and it probably isn't my place to say anything, but . . . she's thinking about moving to Two Hearts."

Nick stared at him, waiting for the punch line. When Micah just shrugged, Nick realized he wasn't kidding. Simone in Two Hearts with him spending more time here would add complications.

Micah slid the computer away from Nick. "I'd better get to work on this."

Nick gave his friend the information he needed, and he started drawing up the papers. "I almost forgot, I need a first right of refusal on the place next-door, too. He also owns that."

Micah winced. "I'm not sure I can get both of those done before dinner. Can you stay after dinner, and I'll do that once we finish dessert?"

"There's lasagna *and* dessert?"

"Both are her grandmother's recipes. We're having a grandmother night."

"With ice cream or whipped cream?"

Micah grinned. "Ice cream."

"Count me in. And thank you, Micah. I'm looking forward to getting this deal sealed. I'm going to go outside and call the owner. CJ gave me his information."

Standing on the front step, he dialed Charlie Scott and made arrangements to stop by later tonight for the signatures. Nick had brought his business checkbook, just in case.

Normally, he wouldn't pay outright for an entire building. He'd get a loan his company paid for over time, but prices were so cheap in Two Hearts that this was not a hard decision to make. He just hoped the renovation cost was what he expected.

But he wasn't looking for anything fancy. Everything needed to be easily cleaned because he knew he did have to meet state health department codes for a restaurant, even if the county didn't have any.

# CHAPTER TWELVE

*S*imone walked into Southern Somethings, finding only a couple of tables occupied, just as Nick had said. Instead of hoping to get a table at noon or dinnertime, she'd need to remember this time.

Nick came from the kitchen, a look of sheer panic on his face.

"Ready?" Simone asked him.

He glanced around furtively as though people would hear that one word and figure out his life story.

When he reached her, she said, "Nick, I'm just a woman meeting you. We could be talking about draperies. Don't assume everyone thinks we're having a grand romance. We don't look like a couple." She shrugged. "We're in the same room, but you didn't hug or kiss me, and you're six feet away."

He took a deep breath and released the air slowly. "You're right. This whole situation is laughable, but isn't. Does that make sense?"

"I couldn't have said it better."

"I want to be able to walk away from," he dropped his voice, "*our relationship* with no one asking about *us* later. It's already bigger than I'd like with three couples, my grandmother, and my parents. We have to keep it contained."

"I don't see why we can't manage that. I'll ask again. Ready?" Simone cocked her head to the side and watched him.

He surveyed the room in a professional manner, this time clearly checking on his business and customers. "Everything seems fine. I'm ready." They started toward the door. "We can drive or walk. It's about six blocks from here."

"Walk! I've had so much fun walking in Two Hearts, not having to get in a car for everything."

"This will be the city version of that. With the charming additions of lots of cars, honking, and exhaust fumes."

"I have my walking shoes on. I'm good." Simone slipped her arm through his once they were on the sidewalk, just to see how he reacted. They did have to look engaged. *Right*, the little voice in her head said. *You're enjoying this more than you're willing to admit.* She released his arm and continued on.

When they arrived at the jewelry store, she went up to the glass door, but Nick was no longer beside her. She turned to find him about a dozen steps back and frozen in place.

"Nick?"

He stared at the store's glass door.

"I think our experience should be fairly painless." Still no response. "Well, maybe not to your wallet."

His eyes widened as he seemed to realize that this could get very expensive. At least he was paying attention.

She grinned. "Don't worry, Nick. I'm an inexpensive fiancée. I'm not into big diamonds."

He snapped out of his stupor and walked toward her. "Let's do this. It will be practice for when I actually get engaged, I guess."

Inside, the store was empty except for one man behind the counter. Jewelry stores must also have midafternoon lulls. They walked over to him.

"Welcome. What can I help you with today?" The man looked from one of them to the other, his smile growing. They must have "engagement ring" and "ready to buy" written all over them.

"I'm looking for a ring for my fiancée."

The man smoothly offered suggestions with no comments about their engagement. "What do you have in mind? A traditional single diamond in a band? Something a little more modern? Or a vintage style?" With each suggestion, he pointed to one in the case that fit his description.

Everything felt too fussy. "Can an engagement ring be just gold? No gemstones?"

"Certainly. Your ring can be anything you want it to be. But are you sure you don't want even a small stone or two? You're going to wear this for a long time, so I want to make sure that you choose something you'll also enjoy in the future too."

She studied the rings in the jewelry case. "I'm a baker, so my hands are in the middle of frosting and all kinds of things all the time."

He considered her words, Nick remaining silent through the discussion. "What type of cakes do you make?"

"I specialize in wedding cakes, but I make others too."

He smiled. "I thought you looked familiar. I think you made the cake for my eldest daughter's wedding last year. I'd never had a wedding cake taste that good before."

"I'm Simone Mills, owner of Delicious Weddings."

The man stabbed his finger in the air as he said, "That's it! I'm Victor Hawkins. My daughter is Sylvia."

"Blush, sage green, and cream. That was a pretty cake."

"Sylvia was so happy that we've already booked you for my middle daughter's April wedding. She's getting married in a small town in the country called Two Hearts."

Nick glanced over at Simone. This was getting a little close to home.

Simone wanted to move the conversation away from her work. "I do take cakes out there since my good friends moved their operations out there. Cassie, the wedding planner, and Bella, the wedding dressmaker. Maybe your daughter is using those businesses too."

"I believe so." He rubbed his hands together. "How can I help you find your perfect engagement ring?" He reached into the case and pulled out several.

She slipped on one ring, but the heavy gold band felt bulky and overdone for her. The petite design of the next one felt too much like a youthful promise ring. Then she spotted another one in the tray.

When she picked that one up, he said, "That's one of the pieces I made. You won't see it anywhere else. The ring is 14 karat gold, which is harder than 18 karat and a good choice for anyone who works with their hands a lot. There are diamonds, though."

She may not have wanted gemstones, but the small diamonds tucked into the curves of gold twisting around the narrow band added a beautiful touch. The ring appeared delicate, but had a presence.

Nick stayed silently at her side. She held up the ring to show him. "What do you think, honey?"

She saw him jerk back ever so slightly, but the salesman didn't seem to notice.

"It's just as beautiful as you are." When he looked into her eyes, she almost believed his words were true. Maybe she'd sold him short with her earlier assessment of his acting abilities. When he took the piece of jewelry from her hand and slid it on her finger, she knew she had. This felt so *real*.

The man quoted the price, and Nick said, "I was expecting more. Are you sure that's the one you want, sweetheart?"

She nodded, unable to speak around the emotions that had rushed in. She blinked her eyes to stop the tears that threatened.

With a sniff, she said, "It's perfect." And she meant those words. When she did get married, she'd want a ring exactly like this one. Maybe she'd be able to come here.

The ring wiggled on her finger when she raised her hand. "It's a little too big, though."

The salesman checked the fit. "If you have a half hour, I can resize this. You can walk away from here today truly engaged with the ring on your finger. Would you like that?"

He turned to her.

Momentary excitement changed to disappointment. "I'd love that, but I don't have time before an appointment."

Nick surprised her with his next words. "I can stay. Are you okay walking back alone?"

"I am." She tilted the ring on her finger, enjoying the sparkle as the diamonds caught the store's overhead lights.

After Nick paid for her dream ring—too bad she couldn't keep it forever—he walked her to the door. She slid her hand in his as they went. His barely noticeable jolt at her gesture passed quickly.

She leaned over and whispered to him, "This man is a customer. I need him to think we are a love match. For him and his family, I'm going to have a real breakup later."

Nick sighed. "Life is getting more and more complicated."

"You couldn't have said it better." Standing on her toes, she kissed him on the cheek. This time, he didn't jump. Maybe he was getting used to being a fake fiancé.

He said, "Stop by the restaurant later. I'll have the ring waiting for you."

She loved the idea for about fifteen seconds. "I wish I could, but I have a birthday party tonight."

"Tomorrow then. But you don't have family here, and your best friends are in Two Hearts, right? Is the party for a friend?"

Was he fishing to see if she had a boyfriend? "Business. I bake cakes for children's parties and also do the entertainment."

She put on a silly grin. "Meet the clown." When he stared at her as though trying to picture that, she pulled out the clown nose she had in her purse. With that red ball on, she asked, "Does the nose suit me?"

"Everything about my life is strange right now."

She left with him shaking his head.

If he thought he was fake engaged to someone quirky before, he was certain of that now.

# CHAPTER THIRTEEN

wo hours of being a clown, serving cake and ice cream, and the general wrangling of ten six-year-old boys had taken its toll. Simone popped off her red nose as she went out the front door and fought the urge to run to her truck, instead moving at a fast walk so she didn't reveal through her actions that she would never be back.

Stress lifted as she drove away from the birthday party. She kept doing these because she liked the extra income, but the money may not be worth the anxiety they caused.

Crossing the city toward her apartment, she hoped she wouldn't find more tension there. Chrissy had been a great roommate until recently. Their hours at home had crossed little in the past because Simone worked days and Chrissy had worked nights at a hotel's front desk.

Then she'd met Arnold and switched to a day job. Now she was home every night. Along with her fiancé Arnold.

Simone parked and walked into the five-story building, taking the elevator to the third floor. As she reached the door to her unit, she listened for a moment. The walls in this 1970s-era building were paper thin, probably because of less stringent building codes at the time of construction. When she didn't hear anything, she opened the door slowly and found . . . Quiet bliss. Maybe they'd gone to dinner or a movie.

Shaking tension out of her shoulders, she came inside and locked the door behind her. Thankfully, Chrissy and Arnold weren't here. After the day she'd had, she didn't think she could take much noise, and the pair of them didn't seem to do anything but make a racket lately.

She fixed a cup of chamomile tea, a relaxation trick she'd learned from Bella, the ultimate tea lover. As she sipped, the warm brew soothed her. Leaning against the kitchen counter, she realized she could do something she hadn't been able to for a while because of the ever-present duo: take a hot bath. Sinking into hot water sounded heavenly.

A few minutes later, she sighed as lavender-scented water enveloped her and the flicker of candlelight lit the room. She'd debated bringing a book in to read, but since she'd started in Two Hearts, bought an engagement ring in Nashville, and attended a wild party for children, she didn't have enough energy left.

Leaning back on the small pillow behind her head, she closed her eyes. "This feels so good!" The day replayed in her mind, especially the moments with Nick. He had to be a good guy because he'd do anything for his grandmother. That showed character in her book.

A noise had her pry open her tired eyes. Arnold stood in the now-open doorway and shouted, "Hey Chrissy, get the next episode of our show queued up!" His eyes locked on Simone, and he took a step back.

"Please leave." She said the words quietly, even though she wanted to shout at him. She did shout her roommate's name at the top of her lungs after that.

"What's going on, Arnold? That sounds like Simone."

When Chrissy rounded the corner, she said, "Oh no," with a quiet tone that said she understood the situation better than he did. She nudged him out of the door. "I guess you didn't lock the door." Chrissy stood, wringing her hands.

"I was home alone in my own apartment. Why would I lock the door? In case a man decided to walk in here while I was taking a bath?" This hit a new low for her on the embarrassment meter.

Simone jumped when a loud program came on the TV.

Chrissy bit her lip, clearly knowing this would not go over well.

"How's the apartment search going?" Simone tried to keep her voice even and free of the anger building inside. "You must have seen ten of them."

"Sixteen. The problem is our price range. They tend to not be well cared for and some of the people hanging around don't look like they're going to get Model Citizen of the Year awards. Yesterday, one smelled like mold. Even Arnold picked up on the strong odor, and he doesn't have that great of a sense of smell. I love cats, but another one smelled like cat urine. Not a little like maybe there was a cat box in there. More like a giant thousand-pound cat had used the carpet in the whole place."

Simone grimaced. "That's a nasty visual you've put in my head. I hope everything works out. It's too bad there isn't anything in this building. The units are older, but they're well maintained."

"That seems to be why everybody stays put. I'm a little concerned because we're running out of time before the wedding."

"What about his place? Isn't moving there an option?"

Chrissy groaned. "You think the situation in our apartment is a problem? He has four other roommates in a house. There isn't a quiet moment. If we can't find something that we like soon, we're going to have to take one of those places that look iffy. Because I don't want to go from our wedding to sharing this place with you. Not that you haven't been an awesome roommate, but you know what I mean."

"That isn't an option, anyway. I wouldn't be comfortable sharing this small apartment with a married couple. This space isn't big enough, and we would all be sharing one bathroom." The one she was still in and having a conversation with the door open.

Chrissy's head fell forward. "I know what you're saying. Until this minute, though, I always thought of this place as the backup plan. I guess there really isn't a backup plan unless it's moving in with him and the frat boys." She left and turned toward the living room.

Simone got out of the tub and closed the door, then dried off, and went to her bedroom, leaning against the door with a sigh. Her life had been chaotic for the last few days.

She'd traveled the world, and that had taught her that having a quiet place to sleep made all the difference to your day. She could have adventures all day long, as long as she came home to that.

She picked up her phone and started to call Bella, then remembered she and Micah were in Nashville at an event Micah's grandfather had requested they attend. Instead, she called Cassie.

After small talk about what Simone had done since she'd returned to Nashville—leaving out today's jewelry shopping trip because she wasn't ready to talk about the ring she'd pick up tomorrow—words came out of her mouth that startled even her. "I'm ready to give Two Hearts a try, but I'm locked in here."

Cassie's swift intake of breath followed those words. "Are you serious? Remember that the impossible can become possible if you think it is. Stop believing you can't."

Simone thought about those words. "How could I move?"

"You mentioned your apartment lease before. What about changing the lease somehow?"

Could she get out of that agreement? That seemed unlikely. "This apartment keeps coming back as a stumbling block. Another problem, of course, is that I would need a commercial kitchen to cook in. The cakes I make with buttercream frosting and fillings with perishables like cream can't be made and sold from a home kitchen."

"I remember you did a vegan cake for a client a few months ago. Even without butter and other dairy, the cake and frosting were fabulous."

"I used a special dairy-free margarine and made the filling with coconut cream and strawberries."

"Everyone raved about it."

She could do a lot of variations using nonperishable ingredients. "That might work for a while." At least until she figured out a way to get the building on Main Street. Or a better idea appeared.

"And you could stay—"

"Before you say *at your house*, please know that isn't going to happen. I think I've run out of patience with roommates. I'm not fussy. My home doesn't need to be a fancy place, but after this experience, I want a quiet space, and I need to control all four walls."

"I'm sure we'd find you something in Two Hearts. You know how many places are empty. That's the benefit of a formerly dying town. It's only been brought back to life in small ways, so everything is still inexpensive. If you're interested."

Simone yawned, covering her mouth with her hand to muffle the sound. "It's a lot to think about. I'd better get to bed before I fall over."

Cassie laughed. "I hope to see you soon. In person and holding a suitcase."

They ended the call. Simone's mind was so full of thoughts about moving that she didn't expect to fall asleep, but even the occasional boom from the living room couldn't keep her awake.

Simone entered Southern Somethings with even less confidence than she'd had yesterday. If that were possible. The vague idea of going to a jewelry store had been replaced with the certainty that she would have an engagement ring on her finger. Today.

Like yesterday, a handful of diners sat scattered about the large area. The hostess stood halfway across the room, handing a guest his menu. Nick had said to stop by, but not when, so he wouldn't know to meet her. And she'd been too caught up in the idea of the ring to think to send a message.

Instead of waiting for the hostess to return—and having to explain she was there to see Nick—Simone made her way to the kitchen. A server returned to the kitchen with an empty plate as she approached.

"Can I help you?"

"I'm here to see Nick Barton."

The man's smirk at her words told her this may not be the first time a woman had said something like that.

"He's expecting me."

His demeanor changed. "I'll tell him . . ." He dragged out the last word.

"Simone."

"I'll tell him Simone is here. Would you like to have a seat?" He gestured toward the closest table.

Simone shook her head. "I'll wait here." She pointed to the side of the room, an area in shadows that wouldn't highlight her presence. Maybe she'd be able to sneak in and out of here without drawing attention to herself. She didn't want his employees to see their boss give her an engagement ring. Even though they weren't engaged in anyone's eyes but his grandmother's.

Sometimes life threw you surprises you didn't see coming.

Nick stepped through the kitchen door, so she went over to meet him. He grabbed her hand and pulled her back through the doorway before she could say a word.

"I need your opinion." He stopped in front of a workstation, glancing down at their locked hands as he did. Dropping her hand like it was on fire, he moved a foot away from her. He cleared his throat and then picked up a piece of fruit from the stainless steel worktop. "We were having a discussion. Cinnamon or ginger with poached pears?"

Startled, she turned to see the woman who was the other half of the discussion. "Neve! I haven't seen you in a while." Years ago, she had worked with Neve at a restaurant in New York. They'd both been fairly new to the business, but she'd known her friend would move up.

"It's great to see you, Simone! I recently had a slice of wedding cake you'd made." She kissed the joined tips of her fingers, then spread them out. "Delicious!"

Simone grinned. "Thank you. Now, what's this about ginger versus cinnamon? I know firsthand that your seasoning instincts are spot on."

Neve pointed to Nick and shrugged.

Simone laughed. "I'm not getting in the middle of this. But Neve's the best. Roll with whatever she says."

Nick raised his hands in defeat. "I'm stepping away and will let you do the job I hired you to do." To Simone, he added, "Have you had lunch?"

Had she? She went through her day. Toast and coffee for breakfast and another cup of coffee as she worked on a cake. "I haven't had time."

"Then let me put together something for us. I spent the morning testing a new recipe, so I'll pack up some of that."

When Nick left to do that, Neve whispered, "You and Nick?"

He'd set up a problem when he'd made them appear to be a couple. "We're friends. We both work weddings, him with the food and me with the cake."

Neve cocked her head to the side and raised her eyebrows.

"Okay, so I may be interested. But I don't think he returns the feeling."

The pastry chef grinned. "I've been here six months. I've never seen him make lunch for himself and a woman."

"Never?" Simone watched as he loaded a container with food.

"Not once. That makes you special."

Nick returned with a large, filled paper bag. "I'd offer a picnic, but today is too cold. We can eat in the private dining room. It's empty right now."

"And you have a pear dish to create," he said as he passed his sous chef.

Neve turned back to her workstation with a wink toward Simone. "Yes, boss."

They walked through the part of the restaurant Simone knew well, then through a set of double doors to a private area that could hold about fifty diners. The overall decor was different but complimented the rest of his restaurant—the Nashville style of rustic meets industrial. Rough-hewn, stained wood paneling covered one wall, and black and white photos of the city decorated the other walls. Tables had stained wood tops with steel legs and chairs.

Nick set the bag on a table near the far wall and started pulling out containers. "I probably should have just made plates for us, but I thought this would be more fun."

Fun? Nick Barton wanted to have fun? She was here for an engagement ring she didn't want. Zero fun there. But a picnic lunch might be fun. And since she was dining with a handsome, nice guy . . .

When he'd opened several containers, Nick pulled out a chair for her. "Ready?" Once they were seated, her host spooned food onto plates, explaining his plans for each as he did.

Simone put a spoonful of soup in her mouth and sighed. "On the menu. And I'd like a to-go container, please."

He grinned. "I thought I had a winner. And the pasta?"

The pasta dish appeared unconventional, with veggies, fruit, and cheese. The first bite surprised her. "Also a winner." She kept eating. "I may not need that to-go container of soup because I'll be too full to eat dinner."

They ate side by side in silence, but it was the pleasant silence of friends. That surprised her even more than this impromptu picnic.

"How's your grandmother?" She wanted to take the words back as soon as she said them.

Nick's smile disappeared. "I talked to her yesterday. She sounds strong and healthy at first, then her energy fades quickly."

"I'm sorry. My grandmother is back in my small Texas hometown. She's going strong. Mom said she was out shoveling snow the other day."

"That's how Nana usually is. Minus the snow because we get very little of that here."

Simone leaped on the subject of the weather. That always seemed safe. "Maybe not often, but I've seen it snow a lot more than I expected for the South."

"And ice. That's even worse." He stared at his plate, then set down his fork, as he halfheartedly added, "At least the frozen stuff melts quickly." He looked up at her. "I can't pretend any longer. Not that I didn't enjoy our lunch. But we're both ignoring the inevitable."

Simone swallowed hard.

He reached into his pocket and pulled out a box. After opening it, he set it on the table and pushed it over to her.

The design caught her eye now as much as yesterday.

A gasp came from the entrance.

Nick and Simone turned toward the sound.

Neve stood with her eyes wide and her hand over her mouth. "I'm sorry to interrupt. I had no idea." She stepped back.

"Wait!" Simone cried out. "Come in here, so we can explain."

The other woman hesitated but glanced over her shoulder as if she wondered about the chance of making a graceful escape. With a sigh, she came toward them.

Nick stood. "This is a fake engagement. We're not really engaged."

Neve looked at Simone.

"It's true."

"So I didn't interrupt the most important moment of your life?"

Simone grinned. "Not even close."

"My grandmother isn't well. Her greatest wish is for me to be settled before she . . ."

"I'm so sorry, Mr. Barton."

He continued. "Simone offered to help."

"But she looked at the ring like she loved it."

Simone motioned her over. "You will too. It's gorgeous!"

Neve picked up the small box. "You're right about that. I wouldn't mind a ring like that. If you're offering, Mr. Barton."

He laughed and Simone was glad to see his humor restored.

"I think one fiancée is all I can handle." He put his arm around Simone and pulled her to his side. When she started to enjoy the closeness, he added, "Could you take a photo of us for my grandmother?" He reached into his pocket with his other hand and pulled out his phone.

Neve framed the shot. "You need to be wearing your ring, Simone."

Nick glanced at Simone. "She's right."

She slipped the ring on and smiled for the camera. Once

Neve had left with a promise for the two of them to get together soon, Simone said, "I hope this photo doesn't get out to anyone else."

"Nana is barely able to use the phone now." He took a breath. "I'm sure Mom won't do anything with it."

# CHAPTER FOURTEEN

$\mathcal{T}$he next few days were remarkably peaceful. She went to work, came home, and spent the evening in her room. With earplugs, she was able to pretend she had a quiet home.

Until it wasn't. Chrissy had her fiancé's parents over for dinner. The extra set of voices and activity couldn't be muffled as easily. Then she discovered that the love of loud movies had been inherited from Arnold's parents when a boom sounded.

Chrissy would move after her wedding, but then a new, and most likely, total stranger, would move in to take her place. Living here could be wonderful or worse than now. What if her new roommate burned everything she cooked? The chef's side of Simone couldn't take that, not to mention the wear and tear on smoke detectors.

The next morning, Simone sat on a stool at the large table that served as the cake decorating station in her bakery and called Bella to see if she had any ideas. Her friend said, "I have an idea. I've seen this in movies, but don't know if it's just a big screen thing and not real."

"Hurry and explain!"

Bella huffed. "I've been stitching on tiny crystals this morning. I guess my mind has slowed down to make that tolerable. Anyway, I meant that in the movies, renters sublet apartments. They have a lease and transfer the contract to someone else. Or maybe the new renter is put on the same lease? I'm sure Micah would know. Do you think subletting yours is possible?"

Would it be? She scrolled through the numbers on her phone to find the contact information for the building manager. "I'll call you back as soon as I know more."

A few minutes later—and grinning from ear to ear—she had her answer.

But then she wondered if she'd found the answer she really wanted. She'd have to give up everything she'd built here. She'd seen Cassie and Bella succeed, and Paige was starting from scratch in Two Hearts with a new career. Those three women were surviving on the income they earned from weddings while living in Two Hearts.

She'd have to think about it because this was a huge decision.

Then she went to work baking a cake. As she did that, she realized she did have some obligations, small projects and even a few weddings in the next six to twelve months. But if she'd been driving to Two Hearts with cakes, she could certainly drive a cake to Nashville, if she needed to. Practice makes perfect, after all.

After more baking and preparation, she worked on decorating.

After covering the cake with white frosting, Simone added details. Squeezing the frosting bag, she put on crisscross rows of pale blue and pink piping. Then she put alternating pink and blue dots in the center of each box that had been created.

Gender reveal cakes were her favorites after wedding cakes. She'd tinted the cake batter pink to denote the baby's female gender, something only she knew outside of the couple's medical professionals. The addition of strawberry cream filling removed any question when you sliced into this three-layer cake.

A message on her phone chimed. She found a text from Chrissy.

*We viewed apartments 19, 20, and 21.*

Simone wiped off her hands so she could pick up the phone and see the rest of the message. Did they have good news?

*Each one worse than the next. Then we upped how much we were willing to spend. Going to see 22 soon.*

Simone stared at the text. Should she give them the apartment and move to Two Hearts? It wasn't just a matter of having a different place to live and work. She'd have a completely different lifestyle.

Growing up in a town of forty thousand, she'd had multiple restaurants and things to do. Not a lot but enough. Even that would be out of her life. But she had to remember that she had a vehicle, so she had a way to access everything she needed or wanted. This wouldn't be the same as being stuck there with her SUV being repaired.

Cassie had mentioned a pizza place that wasn't too far from Two Hearts, so she could get a pizza fix there. Moving needed more consideration. She'd give herself the rest of this week, maybe next. There had been enough upheaval in her life with her fake engagement.

That made her want to roll her eyes every time. The fact that she'd ended up in a fake engagement to Nick Barton? How did these things happen? Certainly not in her life.

She put the cake into the refrigerator and started on a birthday cake she'd also baked earlier. This one was much simpler. Just chocolate ganache icing with "Happy Birthday, Larry" across the top. Larry would be getting a great cake because this was her favorite out of all she made. Of course, he had to be a chocolate lover too, but she'd confirmed that with his wife when the order had been placed.

As she made the filling and then the ganache, she thought about life in Two Hearts. Here she did everything she could to pay for the high rent. She needed a roommate to make the rent reasonable. But she loved her work and wouldn't trade that for anything. She could make more as a chef in a restaurant, but that would mean walking away from her sweet piece of the food industry.

She pulled up to the baby gender reveal location and brought the cake to the door.

"Simone! I am so glad to see you." The grandmother-to-be looked down at the box in Simone's hands. "You received the paperwork?"

Simone knew that the unspoken words were, *would you please, please, please tell me the baby's gender?*

"I did. And unless you're willing to scrape off the piping that crisscrosses the cake and somehow re-frost—you'll have to wait like everybody else." Simone said the words with a wide smile. She'd had a grandmother-to-be cut into a cake and replace simpler frosting when she'd first started making these. The woman had blurted out the baby's gender as the couple began to slice, so Simone had added security measures.

"We had planned to wait until after dinner. A cake is *dessert*. But we realized no one would be able to sit still. We're going to cut into it in a few minutes if you'd like to come inside."

Did she? She had an apartment to go home to, probably with her roommate and Arnold inside. "Sure. I'd love that." Cindy stepped back and ushered her inside.

"Everyone! This is Simone. She made the cake, and *she knows the secret,*" the woman said with a mysterious air.

Simone laughed. "I hope you enjoy it. I have to start with white cake for all of them, but I try to give you some lusciousness."

After introductions, she remembered the immediate family, but not the rest. The expecting couple was Madison and Jose. Her sister and boyfriend were Alyssa and Gavin.

What turned out to be a half hour later, the lights dimmed, with only the light over the cake shining like a spotlight. The couple both put their hands on the knife as often is done with a wedding cake, slicing down. Simone noticed that Madison's hand was shaking.

With the slice cut, they slid the server underneath and pulled the piece out.

The grandmother shouted, "It's a girl!"

Jose hugged Madison as tears ran down her face.

They started passing out slices, including one to her. After sampling all day to make sure her products were good, she usually resisted sweets at night, but she dutifully took a piece. As they ate, the room became silent, only broken by sounds like "yum" and "delicious."

When she was ready to leave after a wonderful dinner of salmon, rice pilaf, and roasted winter vegetables, the mother-to-be's sister loudly cleared her throat. "Ahem."

Everyone looked at her.

"Gavin and I have an announcement to make."

Alyssa reached into her pocket, pulled out a ring, and slid it on her finger. "We're engaged!"

The room erupted in joyous sounds as people came in for hugs. That's what an engagement should look like. The purse next to Simone contained her never-to-be-revealed ring.

At least in Two Hearts, she would have a good excuse for not seeing Nick very often. It wasn't that she didn't like him. It was that she might like him a little too much.

The couple waved them over. "Simone, one reason we mentioned this now was because we'd like for you to make the cake for us."

Simone always felt honored when someone chose her for

their big day. "I would be happy to do that. When are you getting married?"

"We don't see any reason to wait. Maybe May?"

Her new fiancé shrugged. "Whatever she wants is fine with me."

Simone knew from her time in the wedding industry that four months were a very short timeline for almost everything. She was standing in a gorgeous home, so she knew that budget probably wasn't a big concern. "Have you chosen and scheduled a place to get married or one for the reception?"

The woman, still with stars in her eyes, shook her head. "No, we just decided."

She didn't want to dampen their joy, but before they got too carried away and started sending out invitations via email to everyone they knew for a date that was just four months away, she said, "It's probably too late to book something here in the city. Nashville fills up early."

The joy level decreased. Should she offer Two Hearts? The odds were pretty good that sometime in May would be available.

"If you look and you don't find a solution, I have one for you."

The mother of the bride said, "Do you own something that works for this?"

"I'm good friends with a wedding planner and a wedding dress designer. They do the best quality work, often working for singers and other performers."

"And you can get us into them on short notice?"

"I believe so, but the tricky part about this is that they moved to a small town last year about an hour and a half from Nashville. Two Hearts, Tennessee. That location may be available for your wedding. Even though four months doesn't seem like short notice, in this business, it is."

The bride-to-be started researching Simone's suggestion on

her phone. "The place sounds familiar. And the town has such a cute name." A minute later, she squealed. "Oh, my goodness! Two Hearts is where Carly Daniels got married." She kept flipping through her phone. "And Nikki Lane?" She looked up at Simone.

"Yes, to both. And I made their cakes. They got married in the small chapel in Two Hearts and had receptions outside. One was in a park on the lake and another was at a farm."

Cindy asked again, "And you think we can book this on such short notice?"

"The reason you can is that Cassie and Bella are still growing their business. Two Hearts was a dying town that's being brought back to life by weddings. And a very cute place."

The woman said, "This might work."

"It's much easier to have the reception at that time of year because the weather will allow outdoor settings."

The young woman nodded with stars in her eyes. "Everything sounds wonderful. Gavin? Does all of that work for you?"

He leaned over and kissed her. "I'm a guy, Alyssa. I just show up in whatever you tell me to wear and say I love you in front of a bunch of strangers."

Everyone laughed.

Simone said, "I will give you the contact information for both of them. And I'll put you on my schedule for May fourteenth. We'll talk later about the kind of cake you'd like."

Alyssa pointed at the crumbs that were left from the reveal cake. "That was fabulous. You're going to have to work hard to top it."

Simone grinned. "Challenge accepted." With that, she left and drove home, her heart full. As she parked at the apartment complex, she realized she had just booked yet one more wedding in Two Hearts.

# CHAPTER FIFTEEN

*S*imone got up Friday morning after a wonderfully refreshing night of sleep. She'd been blissfully silent the evening before and for the last few days. Maybe her conversation with Chrissy had helped and she would be able to keep living here, like always.

But that wasn't the only thing influencing a possible move to Two Hearts. She would find a new roommate when Chrissy eventually did move out, but that woman would probably be another stranger, someone who may or may not become a friend. And they might cook fish every night of the week, something she enjoyed eating but didn't enjoy in her home when she wasn't the one cooking it. There was something about the lingering odor of fish . . .

She put on a pot of coffee and then hopped in the shower, enjoying the peace and quiet of her morning. If she paid for this place all on her own, though, she wouldn't have much left for anything fun, including an occasional meal at Southern Somethings.

With her hair wet and her robe on, she went to grab some

coffee. As she filled her cup, the door to the apartment opened and Arnold waltzed in without knocking.

"Is Chrissy around?"

Simone stopped and stared at the male who apparently had a key to her home. A male she was not well acquainted with—other than the fact that he liked movies with loud sounds. "She must be in her room."

He headed in that direction, and in a few minutes, she heard Chrissy's voice as they walked down the hall toward her.

"Chrissy, may I have a word with you?" Simone did her best to have a civil tone to her voice, even though she was seething. She went down the hall toward her room, and her roommate followed. When they were inside, Simone closed the door and turned to face her.

"Arnold has a key."

Chrissy stared at her, dumbfounded. "He's over here so much that I thought it made sense to give him one."

"You gave him a key to the place *I* live. This isn't just the place *you* live. And you did it without asking me. That's the worst part of this."

"I don't know what you're getting so worked up about, Simone. He's a nice guy. I'm marrying him."

"I don't know him. I was standing in my kitchen with wet hair and a robe on when a man walked in the front door."

Chrissy looked at the floor. "I didn't consider that. I'm sorry." She looked up at Simone. "I don't know what else to say."

Without wasting another moment—and knowing she really should give things like this more thought—Simone made a decision. "I do."

Chrissy held up her hands in a stop motion. "Please don't throw me out right now. Please! I'm trying really hard to find a new place to live."

"I'm not throwing you out." She looked around the place

she'd called home for two, going on three years. "I talked to the landlord yesterday."

Chrissy gasped, probably wondering what ill fate awaited her.

"I discovered that the lease I signed for this apartment has a clause that allows me to sublet my apartment. That means that I can have you and Arnold take over the lease."

Chrissy put one hand on her hip and stared at her. "Where are you going to live? You already told me you don't want three people living here."

Exactly. "I'm moving to Two Hearts, Tennessee." Instead of nervousness when she said the words, Simone felt joy and peace. She knew she'd made the right choice.

Chrissy started to smile. "You're giving us the apartment?"

"Well, you two have to pay the rent. But if he can pay half the rent just like I did—"

"He can. And the lower rent here will help us save up more for the wedding and honeymoon and eventually buying a house. If we moved into one of the more expensive places, we were never going to be able to get our own home."

Just what Simone had been thinking a little while ago.

"I won't have everything out of here for a week or two, but I'm going to sleep in Two Hearts tonight and every night after this. I just have to arrange for someone to come and get my things. Is that okay?"

Giggling, Chrissy swept Simone up in a hug and squeezed her tightly. "Okay? You've given me the best gift for my wedding that I could ever ask for." Then she stepped back and tilted her head, chewing her lip. "I just thought of something. What about the gift of the wedding cake? I won't be your roommate anymore." The pleading expression in her eyes would melt the hardest heart.

"Of course. I've got you on the calendar. But you may have

to come out to Two Hearts now for your cake tasting. You might even fall in love with the place."

"Anything is possible. But we have jobs here." Grinning, Chrissy left.

Simone packed a bag for a week. Then she gathered her baking supplies and put them in another bag. She wanted to be able to get by until everything had been moved to her new home. Whatever that would be.

She heard a shout from the living room and then another squeal. Arnold must be as excited as his bride-to-be.

When Simone came down the hall with her two bags rolling behind her, Arnold said, "Thank you so much. Trying to find a place to live was one of the hardest things I had ever done. And I really didn't want to have to bring Chrissy back to what she calls the frat house." He looked at Chrissy. "But they are a great bunch of guys."

Chrissy snorted. "They leave the kitchen sink piled high with dishes and dirty laundry strewn around. No, thank you."

As Simone drove to work, possibly for one of the last times in this location, she realized the monumental step she had just taken. The advice was always not to burn your bridges behind you. To have a way to come back in case you changed your mind or things didn't work out.

She'd just lit the bridge on fire and maybe even added an explosion or two to make sure she'd destroyed every piece. Not that she couldn't rent another place in Nashville, if she wanted to. But knowing the hassle that would be after watching Chrissy and her beau left her unenthusiastic about the option.

She made a call. "Cassie? I know I just left your house, but could I use the room for a couple of days?"

"Always. But what's going on that you have to come back here so soon? I don't have any weddings on the books for the next couple of days."

This was the moment she expected to clench in panic, but

the words flowed out. "I just gave my roommate and her fiancé my apartment, and I'm moving to Two Hearts."

"What? Seriously? This is fabulous news! I'm going to be so happy having you out here too. And I have a couple of places for you to look at to rent. I've come up with five good options since we last talked, but there's one I'm particularly interested in showing you."

"And they're in that price range we discussed?" Simone's budget was tight, especially since she was going to lose some of her Nashville business.

Cassie laughed. "Less than that. Remember, it's Two Hearts. Some places have been empty for decades."

Bella had mentioned cobwebs and bugs after she'd toured her business's building. She hoped the condition wouldn't be worse than that. "That doesn't conjure up a good image."

"Don't worry. I wouldn't stick you with something scary. These will look more like something from a 1930s or 1940s movie than they will from a horror show."

"I'm going to pack up some things from my workspace— everything that fits in my vehicle—and head out. But I'm going to need someone to help me move the big things. Do you think any of the men from Two Hearts would be willing to help me load a rented moving truck?"

"I've learned that living in a small town is different. People *want* to help their neighbors. You won't have to rent anything. Someone or multiple someones from here will come to Nashville with a truck to help you move. Since they know you can cook, though, you may owe them a meal."

Simone could hear the smile in her friend's voice.

"Perfect." Her move to Two Hearts should go smoothly.

# CHAPTER SIXTEEN

*S*imone's tension grew with every mile added to the counter on the SUV's dashboard. Had she done the right thing? Or had she let her soft heart influence her to the point that she made a life-altering, incredibly bad decision?

She could have simply asked Chrissy to move out, and her roommate would have gone to live with the frat boys. That wouldn't have been ideal for her, but she would have survived.

But this decision hadn't come from out of the blue, had it? Her friends had been trying to get her to Two Hearts for a while.

Before long, she passed the motel where her vehicle had broken down. Patting the car's dashboard, she said, "You're doing well now, Harriet." Leo and his genius had brought her back to life. A glance to the right showed an intact fence with alpacas on the other side.

By the time she reached the *Welcome to Two Hearts* sign, her blood pressure had hit an all-time high. She pulled into the grocery store's parking lot and off to the side, taking deep breaths and letting each out slowly to calm herself.

She had survived Hong Kong, Shanghai, Machu Picchu,

Madrid, Paris, and London by herself. She'd met people on the way, and eaten things she couldn't identify on her trip but she had survived. She would survive and thrive in little Two Hearts, Tennessee.

Simone directed the car back onto the road and, a couple of minutes later, pulled into Cassie's driveway. She found her friend sitting in the backyard with her cat racing around like the crazy cat he could be.

"Chasing butterflies?"

Cassie jumped. She put her hand on her chest. "I didn't hear you coming."

"Must be a good book." Cassie flipped the paperback over so Simone could see the title on the cover. "It is. As to the butterflies, Romeo will chase anything that moves. A fly, a flower in the breeze or," she winced "—a bee. I try to discourage him from anything that can hurt him."

"How's that going?"

She looked over at her little gray and white cat. "Actually, I think he's learning that giant-sized flying things should be avoided." Cassie looked up at Simone. "That's best for a cat, but how about you? Are you attacking big problems or are you running away from them?" She closed the book and set it on her lap.

Her friend had a way of getting right to the heart of the matter.

Cassie gestured toward the empty chair beside her. "Have a seat. Bella will be here in a few minutes with pie and coffee from Dinah's."

"That sounds heavenly." Simone sank into the seat. "Should I explain the situation to you or wait until she's here?"

Cassie focused on her, chewing on her lip. "Since I'm certain you'd have to repeat the story, I'm going to be a good friend and say 'wait.' Let's switch subjects to take my mind off of what has to be a juicy story." The glint in her eye said she was on the edge of asking for a preview. "Let's talk about cakes. Do you have anything interesting scheduled?"

"I had one for this weekend, but the couple eloped to Hawaii two weeks ago."

Cassie nodded. "The Carter-Fetterman wedding. I must say, I didn't see that one coming. I should have, though, because people were pushing the bride to do things she didn't want to do. There were going to be hundreds of people attending, and she'd wanted a smaller event."

"The bride sent me a photo of them saying their vows in front of a stunning tropical waterfall."

"I received the picture too. They looked so happy that I felt a tiny bit jealous."

"Are you considering getting married?"

"I'm always *considering* it. Once you have the groom, you just need a date and time. Greg is awesome, but . . . I'm not ready." She paused for what appeared to be a moment of reflection before continuing. "I picked up a new wedding this morning, and I sent the couple to you for the cake. The couple will have a small ceremony in the middle of next week. Have they contacted you yet?"

Noticing the abrupt change of subject, Simone waited a beat and considered commenting about Cassie's love life. Instead, she took her phone out of her purse to check for messages and ignored the situation. Cassie would wait until she was ready. "If anyone tried to contact me this morning, I would have missed them." Simone scrolled through her phone and found the text. "Twenty-five guests. That's a simple two-tiered cake." She continued reading. "Next Wednesday at 3:00 p.m." Simone looked over at Cassie. "That's an odd time to have a wedding."

"It's the same date and time her grandparents were married. That year, the thirtieth fell on a Saturday. The grandmother was so excited when they first suggested the date that they chose it, even when they found out they'd ended up with a Wednesday."

"That is so sweet. I love those kinds of clients. She doesn't say what kind of cake she wants, so maybe I'll be able to talk her into one of the varieties I can make in a home kitchen. I sure hate to make a mess in your kitchen, though, but I doubt I can move into anything in the next few days."

"That's something I can talk about before Bella gets here." Cassie paused for a moment. "At least I think I can." She shrugged. "No matter what, we're going to do some house tours. I have multiple options for you. There's one I'm especially excited to show you." Cassie checked the time on the phone she held in her hands.

Simone sensed that Cassie would rather wait until they were all here. "Will Bella arrive soon?"

"She had to finish up with the bride, and she didn't know if her client would be a complicated or an easy bride. Based on the passage of time, I think I'm going with complicated."

Cassie's phone sounded with a ding. "It's from Bella. She says she'll be another half hour or so, and, as much as this pains her, she can't make us wait on her for everything." Cassie replied then stood. "I'm going to show you one place now in the hope that this solves everything."

They went back out the gate after Cassie put Romeo in the house. When Simone went toward her car, Cassie said, "We don't need that. We can walk over."

That was music to Simone's ears. One thing she loved about a small town was the proximity of everything. "How far is it?"

Cassie pointed to the left as they went down the driveway. Without saying anything else, she went right to the house next door and started up that driveway.

"This is the one?" The robin's egg blue Victorian house in front of her had charming bones. The yellow shutters and door added bright pops of color.

"I think the square footage is about the same as my house."

Simone nodded. She'd always liked Cassie's house. And this

place should be quiet. She knew that because of the number of times she'd been at Cassie's house.

"I know I'm taking a chance with this one because . . . well, let's go inside," Cassie said as she unlocked the door.

Simone didn't know what she'd find inside after that introduction.

Cassie stepped back and waited for Simone to enter in front of her. "We used this house for some of the wedding guests. Mrs. Brantley knew the owner who has moved to Denver to live near her son, and the proximity made it a great choice.

The forest green living room had wide white trim molding at the baseboard and crown molding where the walls met the ceiling added a historic touch. A brick fireplace would put out welcome heat on a cold winter day.

"I like this room."

Cassie seemed about to say something, then changed her mind. "Follow me." As they stepped through the arched entrance to a kitchen, Cassie added, "You will either love or hate this room."

When Simone stepped through the doorway, angels sang. The kitchen before her had clearly been owned by a woman who enjoyed cooking. She walked over to the countertops and ran her hand over them. "Marble."

"They're a little worn from years of use."

Simone shook her head. "They're gorgeous. I love the wear. And marble is the absolute best for pastry and chocolate." White kitchen cabinets rose to the ceiling, with smaller cabinets on top of large ones. The room must have been renovated at some point because the decor looked both modern and antique. She didn't think a historic Victorian kitchen would be like this.

A wall oven appeared about a decade old, so she had every hope it would work well. The gray and white marble met a tiled backsplash in blue and white.

"Turn around."

"Why?" As soon as Simone did, she laughed. "I focused on the cabinets and countertops so much that I didn't notice the paint color." Deep cobalt blue covered the walls. Simone's gaze moved up. "They painted the ceiling the same?"

"Is the blue a deal breaker? Mrs. Brantley's guests weren't enamored with the colors."

"Colors? Plural?"

"There are more."

"Well, I've always liked the classic look of a blue and white kitchen. I'll admit that this is more blue than I've ever seen in one, but—" She considered the color for a moment, turning to face the cabinets again. "I love this room. Is it unusual? Absolutely. But it's also pretty. I even like that old dining table in the corner. It has chairs for six, and that's more than would fit at my current table." She turned to Cassie. "Show me more. You may not be able to talk me out of this house."

Cassie grinned. "I hoped you'd say that. I'd like having you next door."

They left that room and went down a hallway with a series of doors. One opened to an antiquated but charming bathroom with tiny black and white tile on the floor and white tile up the walls to black tile trim. The next one revealed a small lemon-yellow bedroom she could use for an office.

Just past the last door on this floor, a staircase went upward. Opening the door, she found a generously-sized bedroom with large windows facing the backyard. The pink on the walls more closely resembled her favorite lipstick than a paint color she'd choose.

"And the paint?"

"You can't miss the fact that this is pink. Very, very pink. But I like the color more the longer I'm here. Besides, the light pouring in makes me smile. Admittedly, sunshine brightens the pink, but . . ." Simone parted the sheer drapes at the window to look outside. "The backyard looks about the same as yours."

"They're mirror images."

And then she knew. This place was too good to be true. She turned to face Cassie and put her hands on her hips. "I can't afford this. I've been sharing an apartment in Nashville because of the expense. I can't get something this nice, even if I'm in a small town."

Disappointment smacked into her.

"Don't panic. Yes, you can. This is Two Hearts. The house has been empty for years. The owner and her family would be thrilled if you wanted to move in and take care of it."

"For a price I can afford?"

"For any price. They would like to be able to cover taxes and utilities."

Simone took another glance into the backyard before heading into the hallway and up the stairs. She peered into each of the two bedrooms and the bathroom there. Every room was a different color, but all were in good shape.

Downstairs again, she peered into the rooms as she passed them, ending up in the kitchen. The color choices may be strange, but she liked them in spite of that. Maybe because she'd left a cookie-cutter apartment that looked exactly like the one next door, and she hadn't been allowed to paint or change anything else. "If I can get this for the figure that we talked about, I'm in."

"Do you want to see the other houses? I have some good options for you."

Simone stood at the kitchen sink and watched a bird land in the backyard. The setting felt peaceful. Idly thinking about the move, she opened the cupboard to the right, finding it clean and lined with pink rose-covered shelf paper.

When she opened the one on the left, she noticed a box about the size of a toaster on the highest shelf. "I think they forgot something."

Cassie came over to see. "I'm sure the box is filled with treasure."

Simone grinned. "Gold and jewels?"

Cassie shrugged. "Of course. What other kind of treasure would an old house in Two Hearts, Tennessee, have?"

"Well, the secret will have to remain hidden for now because I'm not climbing up and standing on the counter to pull that down."

When Cassie opened her mouth to speak, Simone added, "And neither are you. I want happy memories in my new kitchen, not a mental image of you flying backward off the counter with a box in your hands."

Cassie's eyes lit up. "You're renting the house?"

Simone closed the cupboard door and leaned back against the kitchen counter. Picturing herself working in the space, she knew she'd found a new home. "I love this. Where do I sign?"

Cassie clapped her hands together with glee. "I hoped you'd say that." She produced papers from her purse and set them on the counter. "I had Micah draw this up."

"What if I didn't want this one?"

"I had him make an agreement for each of them. He said that would be easy because they were all similar. I didn't want you to leave Two Hearts without a contract and change your mind about moving before you returned."

Simone happily signed them, pleased at the small amount of rent, and officially made this house and Two Hearts her home.

"Hello?" Bella spoke from the front room. "I got your message to meet you here."

"We're in the kitchen," Cassie called.

Bella walked in. "This is nicer than I would have expected. What do we have to do to talk you into joining us in Two Hearts?"

Everything had happened so fast that she'd forgotten she'd

only told one person—the person she thought she was going to spend the night with—that she was coming. No one else knew.

"I just signed the papers. This is mine."

Bella rushed at her and pulled her into a hug. "I'm glad to have you here. You're going to be so happy! And this is coming from someone who didn't think she could ever survive without city life."

Simone grinned when she thought about the rent. She could do a lot with the extra she used to pay.

Bella added, "We can get the guys together to move your stuff out this weekend. Are you ready to move in?"

"I just gave my apartment to my roommate." The emptiness of the house made her realize she had a problem. "But until my stuff is out here, I won't have anywhere to sleep."

Cassie said, "You can stay with me."

"Or with me," Bella added.

"First, I'd really like to be in my own space for the first time in years."

Cassie frowned. "We have air mattresses we used for guests. They weren't as good as actual beds, but everyone was happy to have a place to stay, and it worked out fine. If you're willing to sleep on one, you can spend the night here."

"Sold! If I can fall asleep with peace and quiet and no explosions and wake up to the sound of birds singing, I'm thrilled."

Cassie and Bella stared at her with the same stunned expression on their faces.

Bella said, "Explosions?"

"The short version of the story is that my roommate's fiancé loves movies with things that go boom. He likes to play them loud enough to hear them do that in a big way."

Cassie grimaced. "I think we can avoid that here." Then an alarm went off on her phone. As she tapped the off button, she said, "I have an appointment in a half hour."

Bella walked toward the door. "And I should get back to work. We're finishing a dress today. But we can all meet later for lunch." Bella looked down at the bag in her hand, then handed the paper sack to Simone. "I forgot I brought this. Pie and coffee for everyone. I guess everything's yours."

Cassie stared at the bag. "What kind of pie did you get?"

Bella grinned. "Does that change the amount of time before your appointment?"

"I eat quickly."

"There's blueberry, chocolate, and something that had caramel in its name. I know Michelle added whipped cream too."

Simone reached into the bag. "I'd love the chocolate." Dinah's rich chocolate pie was not-to-be-missed.

Cassie said, "I'll take whichever one the pregnant lady doesn't want."

Simone pulled her hand back out. "Oh, you're right."

Bella peered into the bag. "I think the baby and I would like blueberry."

Cassie grinned. "I really wanted whatever that caramel thing was, so thank you."

Simone went toward the back door. "I saw a table and chairs outside. They should be reasonably clean since people recently used them."

The three friends sat in old metal chairs in the backyard. They were painted black and had rusted flecks, but Simone could see them in bright shades of pink, blue, and green. "Do you think the owner would mind if I painted the chairs and did some other things to the house?"

Cassie slid a bite of the pie into her mouth, sighing as she did. "Oh, my goodness. This is so good." A few seconds later, she added, "I did hear your question. I just needed a moment with the pie."

Simone and Bella chuckled.

Simone asked, "Do you want us to leave you alone with your pie?"

Cassie dug in with her fork for another bite. "We're fine. Before I devour the rest of this, I'll say that you can ask the owners about changes, but I suspect that anything that doesn't take away from the value of the house would be perfectly fine with them. Until last year, they didn't have any hope of selling or even renting this property and weren't sure what they were going to do."

Simone started in on the chocolate pie, which was every bit as good as she remembered from the last time she'd eaten at Dinah's. Being out here would be wonderful for many reasons, the endless supply of pie being one of them.

"The crust on Dinah's pies is heavenly." Simone continued eating. "A slice of pie makes every day sweeter."

Cassie set down her empty container. "I can't argue with that."

Simone pictured not just the outdoor furniture repainted to her taste, but the whole house as she'd like it to be. The kitchen wouldn't have wallpaper but would have a fresh coat of paint. She could picture old-fashioned shelf liner in the cupboards to brighten them up every time she looked inside. Her bedroom could use a fresh coat of paint. She liked the color, though, so she might use the same one.

She hoped that Two Hearts lived up to the potential she thought it had.

# CHAPTER SEVENTEEN

*S*imone sat down on her couch for the first time in days, relieved that all of her things were now here in her new home and that her apartment in Nashville was now completely Chrissy's.

Boxes piled in every room said she hadn't fully moved in, but she could ignore them for a few minutes. Because she needed them for work, all of her baking supplies had been unpacked first and put on shelves in her new kitchen or stored in her yellow office. Her commercial oven waited in that room's corner for a new space—she hoped the one on Main Street—to be installed in.

She took a sip of the hot chocolate she'd made and closed her eyes to drink in the silence. She didn't think she'd ever get tired of that.

Then she heard scuffling sounds and the doorbell rang. Simone set her mug down and went over to the door, wondering who would be there. Anyone she knew would have called or texted first. In the city, she'd be tempted to ignore the sound, but here . . .

She looked out the peephole and found an older woman standing there.

As soon as she opened the door, the woman extended her arms with what appeared to be a casserole dish in them. "Here you are, my dear. It's so good to have you here. We had wondered if Nick would ever find someone, and now we know he has because he's even brought you here to Two Hearts."

"But—"

The woman interrupted. "There's no need to thank me. This is one of the wonderful things about living in a small town." The woman winked at her before turning and walking away.

Was she saying it was wonderful that people surprised you at your door? That they brought you food? Or that they were happy you finally found someone?

Or that she had finally taken their man off the shelf? She checked inside the container as she walked. Poppy seed chicken, one of her favorite southern meals. She tucked that in the fridge, earmarking the casserole for dinner. Then she picked up her mug and settled back onto the couch again.

*Ding dong.*

This time, she found a man with a foil-covered plate.

"My wife had me bring this by for you. Her triple chocolate chip cookies are the best."

He turned and walked away without a word from her.

She'd grown up in a town that was not big and not small. She'd never experienced anything like this. After flipping back the foil and grabbing a cookie, she called Cassie.

"Cassie! I have people bringing me food." Simone bit into the cookie in her hand, enjoying the dark, milk, and white chocolate.

There was a slight pause before her friend started laughing. "I forgot to warn you about that. My kitchen was loaded with food a day after I moved in. I think the chicken salad was one of my favorite things. Has that arrived yet?"

"Why do you think I'll get chicken salad? Does someone schedule what they want to bring?"

"I don't think so. From what I understand, everyone has a thing they bring over. The triple chocolate chip cookies were really good."

"I just discovered that." Simone took a second bite. "Melts in your mouth," she said around the cookie.

"How many dishes have arrived?"

"I have poppy seed casserole and a plate of cookies. Should I clear room in my fridge?"

Cassie laughed again. "You aren't done. Yes to making space there and on your counters because you're about to be inundated with food. But I would be happy to help you eat it."

"That's a relief. There's no way I could plow through this volume of food. And I hate having things go to waste. You know how I am about that."

"Now that you've got furniture, should I drop by at dinnertime?" There was amusement in her friend's voice.

"I think that's probably—"

Her doorbell rang again. "More is here. I'll see you at six o'clock."

Simone hung up the phone to Cassie's laughter. In the next hour—an hour in which she did not have a moment to sit down —she received seven main courses, including one of her favorites—chicken and dumplings. The chicken salad Cassie mentioned had arrived, along with what seemed like more desserts than she could count.

That evening, Cassie arrived with Greg. "I thought you could use another mouth to feed. I remembered that your table had room for six. Am I right?"

"You are. Are there more people coming? If so, I'm going to put a couple more casseroles in the oven to heat."

"I invited CJ and Paige, who are always up for a good meal. But that left you alone, so I also invited—"

"Please tell me you didn't." More time with Nick would not help her heart that teetered toward falling for him.

"I couldn't ask a man other than Nick, considering that the town sees the two of you as engaged. That would start a scandal that would rock Two Hearts."

"I see your point, but I hate to feed this fire." This could make things harder. She liked him. More than she should.

CJ and Paige knocked on the door a couple of minutes later, and they came in and sat down in the living room. When Nick arrived, she stepped outside to greet him, pulling the door mostly closed behind her so they could have privacy.

"I want you to know that I didn't come up with this idea. I'm not trying to make you do things you don't want to do."

"I was in town to spend the afternoon with my grandmother. I'm trying to do that as much as I can just in case . . ."

She hated seeing him so sad. "Then I think we have some of the town's finest meals."

"Did you get poppy seed chicken?"

"Is that a good one?"

He leaned closer, sending warmth through her. *Ignore that, Simone. You aren't really engaged to the man. You aren't even dating him.*

"*Terrible.* Mrs. Chambers makes that every time. I learned a long time ago not to eat the poppy seed chicken. On the other hand, Cassie's learned how to make a really good version from Mrs. Brantley."

"Duly noted. I had that heating in the oven. I think I'll warm up something else."

He gave a very serious nod. "Wise choice." Then he grinned.

Even with the warmth of being near him, the cold air made her shiver. Simone rubbed her hands on her arms. "The temperature seems to have dropped. Let's go inside."

As they went inside, Nick said, "I saw snow in the forecast for later in the week. I certainly hope not."

"Why not?"

Greg answered before Nick could. "Everything shuts down out here. If you thought winter storms made life harder in the city, it's even worse out here. Especially when we get more than an inch. This storm is forecast to give us two or three, possibly more."

"So I need to make sure I'm stocked up on groceries. With all this food, I was just going to eat hearty this week and not shop."

"You know how winter storm preparation in Tennessee is. If there's a forecast for snow, you need to buy milk, bread, and eggs. I'm not sure if anyone is certain why that's the emergency stores for your house, but it's a tradition."

The doorbell rang one more time. The door opened to Bella and Micah before Simone got there. "We could come after all," Bella said.

"Welcome." Simone meant that, but wondered where she was going to put them.

"We had something to go to tonight, but that was canceled. Can you squeeze us in?"

Instead of feeling stressed, Simone decided to roll with it. "If you don't mind scooting up to the edge of the table in a chair that doesn't match, I'm happy to have you here."

"As long as I don't have to cook. And I bet you got that lasagna, didn't you? It's almost as good as my grandmother's recipe. And we've been really enjoying Italian food." She patted her belly.

"Then I'm putting that one in the oven right now. Everyone relax. Today's so chilly that I made some hot spiced apple cider to warm everyone up. Does that sound okay?"

After everyone agreed, Simone poured the drinks and passed them out. Then she added plates and silverware to the table for everyone. Her new house had already filled with laughter. "I would have invited everyone earlier if I'd known about meal delivery."

Cassie took a sip of her cider. "This is good!"

Several others murmured appreciation.

"And meal delivery will be like this when Bella has her baby."

Bella clapped her hands. "Oh good. I was wondering how I was going to feed him—" she pointed to Micah "—right after the baby's born. We could, of course, get everything we needed from Dinah's Place."

"Hey, I fed myself for years before you," Micah defended himself.

Bella stared at him. "How often did you eat at Dinah's?"

"But I can scramble eggs and make pancakes."

Bella nodded. "Good point. Breakfast is taken care of. And notice how he avoided my question about Dinah's."

Everyone grinned at their exchange.

Greg leaned over closer to Micah and said, "Just remember not to eat the—"

"Poppy seed chicken. I learned that years ago."

Laughter filled the room. When Simone looked over at Nick, her eyes drawn to him, she found him with a wide smile and his eyes lit with laughter. Her heart felt full at that moment.

Everyone filtered out the door, with Nick the last one.

Halfway down the driveway, Cassie called, "Don't forget the treasure." Then she laughed.

Nick stopped. "Treasure?"

"Maybe. Or I could have a box filled with lids for containers lost decades ago."

At his puzzled expression, she motioned him back inside. Bella and Micah were already backing down the driveway in Micah's car, and Cassie and Greg had gone around the corner to her house. If she wanted to see in the box tonight, it looked like she'd be asking only Nick to help her.

"In here." Simone went into the kitchen with Nick behind her, stopping in front of the cupboard to the left of the sink. "It's just a box the previous owner left behind. Cassie and I came up with the many things that could be in there. Her favorite was—"

"Treasure."

She turned to him with a grin. "That's my favorite too."

His expression right now reminded her of a little boy's. "And there's a reason you didn't pull the package out to see inside?"

She pointed at herself. "Have you noticed I'm *not* six feet tall?"

Nick reached up and easily grabbed the box with one hand, quickly shifting it to both as he slid it off the shelf. "Cassie's treasure theory may be correct. This weighs more than I expected." He set what she could now see was a cardboard box with flaps folded in. Probably not the way actual treasure would be stored.

"Whatever this is, I hope I can display it. A house this old should have a history, and this one is a blank slate right now."

"A colorful one.'"

She laughed. "There is that." She'd like to postpone opening this so she could spend more time with him. But the last thing she should want was to feel more of a connection to Nick. She needed to remind herself why they had any relationship. *Fake engagement.*

"It's yours to open. Should I add an *arrgh* to sound like a pirate? If there's possible treasure, that seems appropriate."

This side of Nick surprised her. He was serious about work, but he had an unexpected playful side. And she fell a little more. *Ignore that, Simone.*

She lifted the tucked-in flaps and peered inside. "Ooh! This is treasure." The box was packed with antique blue and green glass Mason canning jars.

"What?" He leaned over to see. "Mom loves those too."

"These are great!"

He pulled one out. "This jar looks old." To her surprise, he reached around her to set it on her window ledge. "It will catch the morning light here."

She turned to thank him and came face to face with her fiancé.

"Simone." He hesitated for a moment, then, looking into her eyes, put a hand on each side of her face.

They inched toward each other, and his breath whispered across her face.

Simone leaned in and gently pressed her lips to his.

Nick returned the kiss, deepening it. She wrapped her arms around him, pulling him close. The countertop pressed against her back, but she didn't care. She only cared about this man.

He broke away and stepped back, staring at her with panic-filled eyes.

What had they done?

He said, "I'm sorry." Then he turned and raced out of the room, her front door closing moments later.

Had she just kissed Nick Barton?

She put her hand to her lips. Yes, she had.

He'd run away, but that didn't change the facts.

That had been a fabulous kiss. One for the record books.

Her shaking legs wouldn't support her. Sliding down the cupboards to the floor, Simone realized she wouldn't be the same again. Not after that kiss.

Just as soon as she recovered, she would pull out ingredients to make muffins. There was no way she'd be sleeping anytime soon.

# CHAPTER EIGHTEEN

$\mathcal{T}$he birds were singing when Simone opened her eyes. A few seconds passed before she knew where she was, then another minute for her groggy mind to remember why she was sleeping on the floor on an air mattress. *Two Hearts*. Reaching out her hand, she found her phone on the wood floor beside her instead of a nightstand.

Her last thought as she closed her eyes last night had been of Nick and *that kiss*. And what a kiss it had been. They'd crossed from fake everything to maybe something. But what?

As she made her way to the bathroom, she heard footsteps on the front path. Peering out the corner of the front window so no one would see her in her sleep shirt, she saw a man leaving and carrying a stack of something in his arms. Must be some sort of flyer. This wasn't the political season, so she was pretty sure she wouldn't find a request for a vote on her step.

After a long shower, she put on a warm sweater and jeans. Stepping out into the hallway made her happy. After years of apartment living, she had a house. The smile continued until she went into the kitchen.

Nick had been in here last night. They'd kissed. But more

than that, she'd enjoyed his company before then. No matter. She needed to go to work. Baking always made her forget problems.

She and Cassie had made an arrangement yesterday; Simone would bake something for breakfast and Cassie would scramble some eggs. Simone was leaning toward a coffee cake based on the items she had brought with her.

She knew her friend's cooking skills were developing, so the scrambled eggs were guaranteed to be okay. A baked good wasn't. After a leisurely cup of coffee while her portion of breakfast cooked, Simone wrapped up the warm coffee cake.

All the while, the peace and quiet worked its magic on her. Being at home had gotten to be stressful. She'd been wary every time she walked up to her door, and even when she left, she would wonder what she'd find when she returned. Now, she knew everything would be exactly as she'd left it.

When she opened the front door, she found a copy of the *Two Hearts Times* newspaper on her front step. "So that's what he'd been bringing."

She shifted the coffee cake to her left arm, grabbed the paper, tossed it on top of the stack, and continued on to Cassie's.

Cassie answered the door when Simone knocked with the one available hand. "I'm glad you moved here, not the least because of breakfast service." She smiled. "I could get used to deliveries of warm baked goods."

Simone set the coffee cake on the kitchen counter. "Is Bella coming too?"

"She thinks so. She says mornings have returned to normal, but not to be concerned if she doesn't show."

Bella's voice announced her before they could see her. "Hello, everyone! Isn't this a glorious day?"

Simone sighed. "This glowing thing that pregnant women do is a little weird." She made a deep sigh.

WAITING FOR A WEDDING

Cassie nodded seriously. "I know. I'd heard about the phenomenon, but experiencing this firsthand does give me chills."

Simone and Cassie both grinned.

Bella rolled her eyes. "*Funny.* I'm not going to let you guys take down my joy. And I am definitely ready for breakfast."

Over breakfast, they discussed the upcoming weddings, offering suggestions and ideas. Being part of this step in the process instead of sitting in Nashville and hearing about it in bits and pieces was more fun.

When Cassie described the wedding dress a bride wanted in depth for Bella, Simone's attention wandered back to Nick. Should she contact him about getting together? She already knew she had feelings for him that she shouldn't have.

"Hello? Simone?"

Startled, Simone focused on her two friends who both stared at her. "Did I miss something?"

Bella picked up her mug of tea. "Where were you? And before you answer, don't tell us you were thinking about business. You had a big smile."

Simone grinned. "I may have kissed Nick after everyone left last night. Or he kissed me. I'm not sure which."

Cassie's eyebrows shot up. "And that's good?"

Simone nodded. "Oh, yeah."

"But your engagement isn't real."

Some of Simone's joy faded. "You're right." Then the kiss came to mind again. "But that doesn't change what happened."

Bella leaned forward. "Was it an awesome kiss?"

Simone sighed. "Definitely."

"We don't want you hurt. But I'm sure you know what you're doing." Bella patted Simone's shoulder.

Did she? They continued with the wedding discussion, Simone alternating between joy from the memory of the kiss and confusion about what it meant. *If anything.*

Bella picked up the newspaper. "Micah's grandmother said the town had a paper years ago, but publication ended when the town's prosperity did. Someone new recently bought the business. This is the third or fourth issue. It's weekly, so you get a lot of what happened six days ago and a little of what just happened." She tossed the paper on the table in front of Simone. "But it's nice to have something like this. A newspaper makes Two Hearts feel more like a real town."

Simone said, "Look at you. You've become a native in just a short number of months."

"I know. It's the strangest thing, but there's something about this place that gets into you, and you want the town to succeed."

Simone picked up the paper and paged through, starting at the back as she usually did for some unknown reason. "Here's a farm report. And a small article about Paige and her new photo studio on Main Street. She's calling her business Two Hearts Photography."

"That's nice." Cassie paused. "I was about to say that a newspaper will help people know she's there. But her studio is on Main Street, so everyone has to drive by. Still, the article may be helpful so everyone knows more about her."

Simone kept reading. "There are only about ten pages here. I see an ad for each of you."

Cassie said, "Just trying to help them get started. And you never know when somebody may send the paper to a friend or loved one."

Simone flipped the newspaper over so she could see the front page. "Here's one that looks interesting about a wedding." And then the photo caught her eye. She gasped. "Ah, Cassie, Bella?"

They both leaned closer.

Bella said, "Is something wrong? There can't be anything important in there. It's only small-town news."

Simone turned the newspaper so they could see the front

page. "Nick Barton and Simone Mills engagement announced. Well-known Nashville restaurateur and Two Hearts native Nick is officially engaged to wedding cake designer Simone, owner of the bakery Delicious Weddings. No date for the nuptials has been announced." The photo had to be the one of the two of them that Nick had asked Neve to take with his phone.

With each word she read, Simone felt fainter. When she finished, Cassie pushed a glass of what turned out to be cold water into her hands, and she gulped some back. The room buzzed around her.

Someone said, "Head between your knees."

Simone did as told, and in a few minutes, she started to feel better.

"Please tell me that I made a mistake, and the words didn't say that. I was hallucinating based on the fact that I'm fake engaged to Nick. *Please*." She sat up slowly and leaned back in her chair with her eyes closed.

Silence greeted her. She opened her eyes and looked from one woman to the other.

"You read the article exactly as it's written, Simone. But how would anyone at the newspaper have caught a whiff of your fake engagement?"

Simone went through the list of people who knew about their relationship. More than she would like. "My list of those who know is you two and your guys, along with CJ and Paige. Oh, and Nick's mother and grandmother."

"I'm sure none of us told a reporter. And you said Nick's mom wouldn't. Would his grandmother have contacted the newspaper?"

Would she? "She's been so sick in bed that I can't picture her even picking up a phone. But if not one of the people that we know about, then who?"

"Do you think Nick did this? Maybe he thought I would

stick to our agreement if he announced our engagement in Two Hearts."

"I don't know, Simone. That seems rather farfetched and maybe out of character for Nick. He seems to be a very personal man. He doesn't share things with other people."

Bella added, "But then . . . we don't have a lot of options as to who leaked the story."

Simone slammed her fist on the table, making their mugs jump. "You're right. I'm going to call him right now. He can't kiss me when he knows a tell-all article is about to be published." She reached into her pocket for her phone.

"Hardly a tell-all," Bella muttered before putting her hand on Simone's arm and gently prying it off her phone. "Nick's in Two Hearts right now. At least he was a half hour ago. I saw him on Main Street with CJ this morning."

Simone stood, drank the rest of the glass of water, and headed for the door. "If you hear any screaming, you'll know I found Mr. Barton."

Simone marched down the sidewalk toward Nick's truck and the store he'd parked in front of, smacking the newspaper on her thigh as she marched. How dare he do this to her! Somehow, and for some reason she did not understand, he must have told the newspaper about their fake engagement. The why is what she couldn't figure out.

Barely registering a second vehicle at the curb, she pulled open the door and stomped inside, finding Nick in the back talking to CJ.

He looked up at her with a smile. "Simone!" He actually seemed happy to see her, which had her hesitating in her tracks. Would he be happy if he had actually done something like this?

She continued on. None of her friends would have and no

one else fit. He had to be guilty. Wasn't Sherlock Holmes the one who said if you eliminate everything it could not be, you ended up with the only thing it could be? Or something like that.

"Nick!" Her voice contained less joy than his had.

He frowned and CJ stepped back.

"Why did you do this?" She held up the paper.

His furrowed brow said volumes.

Before he could answer, though, CJ said, "I just remembered somewhere I need to be. Yes. I'm supposed to check on something in Paige's photo studio." He turned and raced out of there like his feet were on fire. She didn't really blame him, either.

Simone thumped Nick in the chest with the newspaper. When she hit him a second time, he grabbed it out of her hand. "What's going on?"

She pointed at the offending paper. "Don't pretend you don't know what I'm talking about."

He looked baffled. "Pretending? I have absolutely no idea what you're talking about."

This wasn't going the way she'd expected. Maybe there was somebody else who had leaked their story. But who?

"Please tell me."

She shrugged. "Front page."

He stared at her for a moment before opening the paper. A few seconds later, his jaw dropped. "You think *I* did this?" He looked up at her. "Simone, this is the last thing I would do. This was supposed to be a secret."

He seemed genuinely surprised.

"But if you didn't do this, who did? And I'm sorry I jumped to the wrong conclusion. I know none of our immediate friends would contact the paper. And I can't see your mother calling them."

He shook his head vigorously from side to side. "Absolutely

not. She knows not to say anything." Then his eyes narrowed. "But my grandmother would."

Simone pictured the little old lady lying in bed, so feeble she could barely lift a hand. "That doesn't seem likely in her condition."

He blew out a breath. "You're right. But I don't see a lot of options beyond that."

The air whooshed out of her, taking her anger with it. "Nick, I have had so many changes in the last couple of weeks. I've gotten tangled up in this thing with you and moved to Two Hearts. On top of that, I don't want to be a laughingstock in my new home."

He reached out and took her hand in his. "You won't be a laughingstock, no matter what. I'll just go over to the newspaper office and explain what happened. They can print a retraction next week."

Hope flickered inside her. "Do you think the solution will be that easy?"

He shrugged. "Two Hearts is a small town. I probably know whoever the newspaper editor is." He opened the paper again and searched for the name of the publisher, which she knew was usually inside the paper near the front. "I take that back. I don't know Amelia Marchant. But I'm sure I know someone who does. I'll go to the office to see what we need to do to fix this."

She threw her arms around him and pulled him in for a hug. "Thank you! I'm so relieved. I thought I was going to have to leave town after looking like such an idiot." When she tried to step back, his arms closed around her waist.

His phone rang, saving her from doing something stupid like trying to kiss him again.

They were engaged, but not really. They were just pretending.

While he was on the call, which she could tell was from CJ

based on the bits and pieces she picked up, she struggled to come up with a topic for after the call ended. Then she realized that this building had been transformed since the last time she'd been here.

"Nick, this is starting to look like a real kitchen. I didn't notice when I came in here."

He raised an eyebrow. "You mean when you stomped in here?"

"Yeah, sorry about that. But you seem to have accomplished a lot in a short amount of time."

"I learned that is one of the beautiful things about being in a small town. We were able to schedule all the subcontractors quickly. The building has been rewired and replumbed. New flooring will be installed on Monday, something that meets state codes. And then all the equipment arrives on Tuesday. I'll have a fully-operational kitchen then."

"There's a Wednesday wedding. Are you catering for that one?"

"They're a small group, so I'm using them as my test."

He would have a full catering kitchen next week. If only she could get started on the place next door. Maybe in six months, if business continued to be good. "Are you going to be driving out here to cater the event?"

He rubbed his hand across his face. "I am. For now."

"That's a lot of driving."

"Tell me about it. I chose not to live out here in the first place because of the long commute, and now I've ended up making the drive, anyway. But until I get someone in Two Hearts I can trust . . ." He looked at her for a moment too long. "You could help."

She waved her hands in front of herself in a stop motion. "Get rid of that idea right away, Nick. I bake now. I chose not to do savory and especially not in a busy kitchen."

"But you know how."

"Sure. I can also paint a room, mow the lawn, and balance my checkbook. But I don't want to do any of those things full-time, either. I want to bake."

He sighed. "Well, you can't blame a guy for trying."

CJ opened the door and peered around it.

"It's safe to come inside." Simone said. To Nick, she added, "I can help with anything sweet. If you have desserts, I'm on board."

As she left, Nick added, "And I'll let you know what I find out over at the newspaper office."

Her head whipped around to look at CJ, thinking that Nick had blown the situation, when he added, "CJ knows. I needed advice from the guys in the beginning, and CJ and Micah were both there."

Keeping their situation from others didn't matter, anyway. Not with the story being in the town's paper. "Our secret isn't a secret anymore."

CJ said, "You mean the fake engagement?"

She handed him the newspaper on her way out. And she heard the word "Whoa" as the door closed behind her.

After the door closed behind Simone, CJ said, "You've ended up with quite a mess."

"That's an understatement. I visited my grandmother, and one sentence exploded into this."

CJ went over to the side wall, pointing to a spot there. "I want to verify that this is where you want the vent hood for the stove placed."

Nick studied the area for a moment. "That should be perfect." He could see the function of the kitchen. Much of the layout as Simone had suggested earlier. He chuckled. "She was right."

CJ smiled. "By *she*, my guess is you mean Simone?"

"I hadn't realized I'd said that out loud. Yes. She'd told me how I should lay out the kitchen. I argued, but she was right."

"You sound a little happier about having her around than you used to."

He had to admit he was. "We definitely did not get along in the beginning, but I've come to appreciate the fact that she's passionate about everything she does. If that woman says she's going to bake you a cake, I have no doubt that it's going to be the most delicious and most beautiful cake you have ever known."

"I'm glad she didn't decide to get the store next door and renovate. Between your kitchen and my wife's photo studio, I've definitely been busy."

Nick had forgotten about Simone and the building next door. She'd clearly wanted the space.

"Why didn't she move in?"

"What?" CJ stopped mid-sentence.

"What changed Simone's mind? She clearly liked that place next door."

"She told me she couldn't afford to renovate the building to meet codes. She'd have to redo the bathroom, electrical, and everything else. I don't blame her for holding off."

Nick considered CJ's words. He'd feel guilty about fulfilling his dreams when Simone didn't get to bring hers to life too.

"But she's still considering it?"

"From what I understand."

The happiness that filled him at the thought of her being his Main Street neighbor startled him. He just enjoyed seeing everyone's business thrive. Yes. That's all.

CJ didn't seem to notice Nick's silence. "Watching this town come back to life is the best thing that's ever happened to me. Taking part in it? Even better."

Nick walked over to the deep stainless steel sink. "I'm happy with the progress so far. Is everything on schedule?"

"Yes. We're on track."

At least this felt under control. Now he needed to talk to whoever this Amelia was about their engagement announcement.

# CHAPTER NINETEEN

The newspaper office was located in a building down the street from the courthouse. Nick wasn't sure why, but Two Hearts didn't have a town square like so many towns in Tennessee built in this era. They had a street that intersected Main Street with a courthouse flanked by businesses.

He found a parking space in front of the newspaper office and looked up at the *Two Hearts Times* sign. This little paper probably wouldn't bring in much money, so he wondered who the current publisher might be.

Inside, he expected to find a receptionist and others working, but in true small-town form, he found one woman seated at a desk in an otherwise empty room. His cousin.

"Amy? What are you doing here? The last I heard, you were working on a newspaper in Wyoming." He hadn't seen her since her mother remarried after a divorce, and the family had moved away. But the Barton grapevine had kept him informed about her accomplishments.

"North Dakota. Further north and colder." She shuddered. "Winter was hard for a southern girl like me. To answer your question, though, I moved here a couple of months ago. Both my brother and I have come home to Two Hearts. He's a blogger who writes about small towns. He started doing that while in Denver."

"From memory?"

"He traveled to them."

"You're now working at this paper?" Nick hoped his words didn't show the surprise he felt. Amy had won awards for her journalism. This had to be a demotion.

"In spite of what you're thinking, the *Two Hearts Times* isn't a step back. It's a step forward. I'm not an employee this time. I bought the newspaper when it went up for sale."

"That's awesome! I'm sure you're glad to be back home." Nick wished he could make a similar jump and follow his heart as easily. Then he realized that made her Amelia Marchant, the publisher. "I haven't seen you in a long time, but I don't remember hearing about a marriage."

"You must have missed a piece of family gossip." Amy smiled. "My stepdad adopted us when we were still kids. I love him, but I chose to write using my original name of Barton. It's shorter and people usually spell it right." She laughed. "When it came to being a newspaper publisher, I thought I should choose my real name."

"And you're enjoying being back here after so long?"

"I am. I'm not fully settled, though. I'm currently sharing a house with my brother."

Nick winced. "I can't see myself living with a sibling. I hope that's going well."

Amy chuckled. "Our situation has its moments. I'm sure you didn't stop by to chat since you didn't know I was here. Do you want to place an ad?" Her hopeful tone said she could use more ad revenue.

That wasn't why he'd come, but he'd become an advertiser in

order to support family. "I would like to do that. But I'm here to discuss the article about my engagement."

"I knew readers would be excited about your news. Nick Barton getting married. I still haven't found the right person to share my life with." Amelia reached for a clipboard.

"Neither have I."

"Excuse me?" She stopped what she was doing and stared at him blankly.

"Where did you get your story?"

Amelia held up her hands and scooted away from him. "From a reliable source."

Nick hated the scoffing sound he made. His cousin should be treated nicer than that, but the noise had slipped out. "Who was this *reliable* source?"

"Your grandmother."

Nick's anger rose. One look at Amelia told him he needed to drop it. She'd only reported what she'd thought was fact. "If you can print a retraction in the next issue, that will take care of the situation."

"Did you break up with her?"

Did he dare trust the truth to a newspaperwoman? "If I tell you something and ask you to keep it confidential, a secret, would you be able to do that or do you feel the need to print all the news?"

"I can be trusted. You wouldn't believe the stories I haven't printed. Juicy stuff."

"I don't know how juicy this is, but we aren't really engaged. I said that to my grandmother because I thought she was dying and she wanted me to have someone in my life."

His cousin stared at him with a dumbfounded expression, not moving a muscle for so long that Nick wondered if she was okay. "You aren't in love with your fiancée?"

Nick rolled his eyes. "I've never even gone out with her." But he had kissed her. And he'd had trouble forgetting anything about that moment, a time when their relationship had seemed real.

"I could print a retraction—"

His taut nerves relaxed. "That's great! Thank you!"

"But Nick, I just bought this newspaper. These people don't know me or trust me yet. Sure, I'm from here, but I was a kid when I left. That's who they remember. I can see this in the way they talk to me. If I tell them that story isn't true when every word must be spreading like lightning through town, I'm going to lose whatever trust I've started to build. Aren't I?"

Nick thought through Amelia's words. This wouldn't just be the case in Two Hearts. Anywhere a new editor came in, printed an article that covered half the front page, then said oops, we're sorry, could be damaging. "As much as I hate to do this, and I really do, don't write a retraction. Maybe the story will die down in time if no one ever sees us together. They'd conclude we'd had an argument, but not want to say anything because they'd seem nosy."

The relief on his cousin's face told him he'd said the right thing. "Thank you. Whenever you do meet the right lady, let me know, and I'll run a full-page article about you two. They'll know the story's true then."

Nick chuckled. "Don't hold the space. There is no one in my life I'm interested in." He needed to keep telling himself that because he kept thinking about Simone. Especially after that kiss.

And now, he had to call her to help straighten out this problem.

After a quick call to Simone, he stopped to pick her up at Cassie's house. They drove in silence for a few minutes before she said, "I don't understand what's going on. You told me you were going to the newspaper office earlier. Then you called and said we needed to go to visit your grandmother."

He wanted to crawl under a rock and hide so he didn't have

to confront her, but he didn't have a choice. "We have to talk to her."

"Why? Not that she isn't a sweet old lady."

"She did it." He was both angry and concerned at the same time. "My grandmother did it."

"What, Nick?"

"The newspaper. My grandmother called the newspaper office."

Simone gasped. "How?"

He couldn't figure that out either. "Good question."

"Did you talk to your mother?"

"No. I wanted to be able to see Nana's expression when I asked her about the story. Besides, Mom might accidentally tell her I found out."

She nodded. "That makes sense. Are you sure you want me to be there, though?" she muttered under her breath. "Because I don't really want to be."

Even with all of this, she managed to make him laugh. "She's always sweet. You don't have to worry about that."

"Her? It's you. Your beloved grandmother seems to have betrayed you."

He sucked in his breath. "Betrayed is a rather harsh word."

"But one that fits, doesn't it?"

He thought for a moment. "No. We told her we were getting married."

"That we were engaged." Simone quickly corrected him.

"Engaged. We didn't tell her we were pretending. To her, this is a real engagement that should be shared with everyone, and by everyone, I mean the entire population of Two Hearts. What better way to do that than with the newspaper? Isn't it a good thing the publication came back to life just in time to print our story?"

They drove in silence for a while, perhaps the longest silence he had experienced with Simone since the silent drive with her damaged cake.

Finally, Simone spoke. "You're right, Nick. But a logical reason for her call doesn't make me love this anymore. At least after the newspaper prints the retraction—"

"No retraction."

"What!" She tried to keep her voice down and failed.

"The editor turned out to be my cousin, Amelia. I didn't recognize her name because her stepfather had adopted her. I didn't know that."

"And retractions aren't printed for family members?"

He glanced over at her, checking to see if she was being sarcastic. He found her with a sincere and confused expression.

Focusing on the road again, he said, "She's brand new to the job. Just bought the paper a month or two ago. If she prints a retraction, people will think she's unreliable and won't trust or buy the paper."

"As a businesswoman, that makes perfect sense to me. But how will talking to your grandmother help?"

"That's the million-dollar question. Do you have any other ideas? Because I don't want this getting any more out of hand than it already is. I hope to get Nana to back down from spreading the news."

She started laughing and leaned back in her seat. "Nick, our story was in the *newspaper*. How much more out of control can this get? Every single person in this town has now heard that we are engaged."

"Maybe we can get her to believe we don't have plans to get married anytime soon." As soon as he said the words, he knew that wouldn't work. "I know! We'll tell her that we both want a long engagement."

"How long? Because my best years for finding a spouse are right now."

He glanced at her, suddenly concerned. "You're looking for someone?"

"Of course I am! My closest friends are either married or engaged. I'm over thirty, and I would like to have a family of my own. My clock is ticking, Nick."

He gulped. "This whole situation is new to me. Do other women your age feel that way?"

"I can't speak for them, but I can say that as someone who works in the wedding industry and spends almost every waking hour focused either on weddings, baby cakes, or children's birthdays, it's a big part of my life."

"I can see that. But I would think that someone as awesome as you are would be able to find a man whenever she wanted."

The cab of his vehicle filled with an emotion he couldn't quite peg. But he knew he had said the wrong thing.

"What I mean is—"

"Do you mean that you think that I'm okay?" She smiled at him.

"Okay? You're amazing! You're great at your job, you're nice, and you're pretty. You have the whole package! Don't worry about this. When our fake engagement is over, you'll be able to find a great guy."

They drove in silence for a moment. "Thank you, Nick. That's the nicest thing anyone has ever said to me."

When he thought over his words, he wondered if he'd gone too far. Oh, she was everything he'd said she was, but he had never considered saying those things about anyone else. Maybe he shouldn't begin with a single woman who might think he was interested in her. But she didn't seem to be interested in him.

Other than when she'd kissed him. They'd both forgotten for a moment that they weren't really a couple.

They turned off the highway and toward his parents' house. Now, they just had to sort through the situation with his

179

grandmother. He wasn't looking forward to this conversation. He stepped out of the truck and went around to help Simone down, but she was already standing next to it when he arrived.

"Ready to go in to beard the lion?" she asked.

He'd never been on this side of his grandmother. They'd always been together on everything. "Since there's nothing we can do about the newspaper article, I guess we're just here for a visit. We'll gently encourage her to let the story quiet down."

Simone seemed to be waiting for him to add something to that.

"What?"

"Don't you think it's odd that a bedridden woman would somehow get to a phone and find the phone number for the newspaper—something that has only been around for a short time—just to tell them you're engaged?"

"Now we're on the same page. I haven't been able to figure that out myself."

His mother was in the kitchen when they walked in the door.

"Nick, I'm so glad to see you. Your grandmother has been in bed all day. Today and yesterday."

"Is that my Nicky?" a frail voice called from the bedroom.

His heart clenched when he heard her. Then he remembered what Simone had just outlined that Nana had done. The two weren't matching up, but he didn't know what that meant yet.

"It's me, Nana! I'll be there in a couple of minutes."

"Thank you, Nicky. It's so good to hear your voice."

He'd always been able to count on his grandmother. She'd been a vibrant and healthy woman who was ready for anything. Much like Simone. He glanced over at her. Maybe he shouldn't compare his grandmother to the woman he was engaged to. That might not go over well with either of them.

"How did she get to the newspaper person?"

His mother's brow furrowed. "I don't know what you're talking about. She hasn't left that bed except to go to the bathroom and only then with help."

He studied the doorway for a second as he considered his mother's words. "You don't know about the newspaper?"

"I know your cousin Amy started the newspaper again. We hadn't had one for decades."

"Have you seen the current issue?"

"She isn't going to deliver papers all the way out here, so I'd have to pick one up from the grocery store in town. I haven't been away from your grandmother that long." She put her hands on her hips. "What could be so important about the newspaper that you've delayed going in to see your grandmother?"

He leaned closer and Simone moved in beside him so she could hear. "Mom, there's an article on the front page of the paper about our engagement."

She gasped. "No! How did that happen? Your engagement was a secret. Wasn't it?"

"Such a big secret, Mom. I went to the newspaper thinking they'd printed a rumor from somewhere. Amy told me she had the facts on good authority."

"But whose facts were those?"

Nick pointed in the direction of his grandmother.

"No way! Like I said, she's barely been moving."

"Does she have a phone of her own?"

"She does, but she doesn't keep it with her. It's probably still in the living room where she normally sits and watches TV."

He went in there to look and sure enough, there on the end table next to his grandmother's favorite recliner sat her phone. Returning, he said, "You're right about the phone's location, Mom. She called the newspaper. I got that directly from Amelia."

"I thought there was something fishy going on here." She hurried toward his grandmother's room. "Mother!"

"How dare you speak to me in that manner? You know I've been unwell."

Nick hurried in, with Simone at his side.

"You somehow got out of your sickbed and called the newspaper." His mother paused for a moment, then snapped her fingers. "I know! I went to the grocery store two days ago and was gone for an hour. Maybe longer. Is that when you called?"

His grandmother sank further under the covers and pulled the blanket under her chin. In a wobbly voice, she said, "But I'm your dear old mom. Nick's Nana. How can you imagine such a thing?"

Now he was starting to see. "Nana—" he said softly.

She turned toward him. "Yes, Nicky? You believe your Nana, don't you?"

"Of course I do. I know you would never lie to me. You've always been completely honest with me. So I'll be honest with you. Simone and I have decided to elope. I'm sure that you won't mind."

His grandmother's eyes narrowed. "What do you mean by elope, Nicky?"

"The usual. The two of us go off somewhere alone, get married, and, in this case, we move to the city. We'll visit Two Hearts when we can, but you just never know about those things."

He felt Simone tense next to him when he mentioned the word *elope*.

"That isn't acceptable, Nicky."

He grinned. "I'm just kidding. But I need you to stop butting into our lives. We aren't going to get married for a long time."

He couldn't hide his smile when Simone muttered "Maybe never" close to his ear.

"You won't get us to the altar faster than we want to go. Is that clear?"

His grandmother sputtered in response. "But . . . but . . ."

Her gaze narrowed at him again.

"Crystal clear. I still haven't seen a ring on that girl's finger."

Simone fumbled around in her purse and pulled out the packet that had the ring, tilting her new piece of jewelry—the one he'd bought—out into her hand. Then she slipped that ring onto her finger. She stood up and went over beside his grandmother to show her. "I think it's beautiful."

His grandmother said, "Nicky, that's a gorgeous ring!"

"I bake cakes, so I have my hands in a lot of things. I always mean to take rings off, but I don't always manage to do that. I wanted something simple."

"But it is gorgeous," his mother added. "I would have thought Nicky would be the traditional type with a single diamond set in the middle. Not that there's anything wrong with that design. It's quite beautiful, but not unique like this one." She looked from one to the other. "But Simone is unique, isn't she?"

He agreed. "She definitely is that."

"What are your plans for the next few days?" his mother asked.

Simone answered. "I need to get settled into my house."

His mother asked, "You moved?"

Simone smiled. "Right, I forgot that not everybody knows. I moved to Two Hearts a few days ago."

"Oh my! A friend told me we had a new resident, so I sent food over with her. I'm so glad it's you! And I'm sure Nick is thrilled that you'll be living close to his family."

He gulped. She would be close to his grandmother. Having Simone nearby could offer his grandmother more ways to push them together. They'd have to be even more careful about their fake relationship.

On their way back to town, he said, "I was so focused on the article that I didn't think about where I picked you up today. Why Cassie's house when you have a place of your own now?"

"We were going over wedding plans for a client. And she's going to stop by my house soon to test cake samples. Then we'll offer her favorites to the client. It's handy having her next door."

He could get on board with helping. "I'm available for cake testing."

Simone grinned. "I tried a new cake for weddings. This one was orange cream."

"That sounds delicious." He couldn't keep the hopeful sound out of his voice.

She laughed. "I can get you a slice when we go in. I'm testing some dairy-free frostings and fillings so I can bake out of my home kitchen for a while. Nothing that's perishable according to the law."

"I wish I could do that. That would have been so much simpler, but almost everything I make is considered perishable. Guess that means there isn't actual cream in orange cream? I'm not sure how I feel about that." He said the last words in a sarcastic manner.

She laughed. "No cream, but still delicious. I'm impressed with what you can do without dairy."

They arrived at her house, and she climbed out. "Aren't you coming in?"

He hadn't really been serious about testing the cake, but when he saw her staring up at him with an earnest expression, he couldn't resist. "I'm right behind you." Nick turned off the truck and jumped out. "Are you sure I won't be in the way?"

"A handsome man is never in the way as far as Cassie is concerned."

He was glad she was ahead of him and couldn't see the expression on his face because he was grinning like a fool. He'd accidentally told her she was pretty earlier, but now he found out she thought he was handsome.

They were quite a pair.

And that was a thought he didn't want to contemplate for very long. That he and Simone made a great pair. But that truth grew stronger every day.

# CHAPTER TWENTY

$\mathcal{N}$ ick's phone rang as he prepped some vegetables for the evening service. He grabbed a towel to dry off his hands and looked to see who was calling. Staring at his phone, he considered ignoring the intrusion, but with everything that had been going on, he figured he'd better answer. They were probably trying to sell him a car warranty.

"Barton."

"Nick Barton?"

"Yes. May I ask who's calling?" His mother had taught him to say that when a stranger called, and those words somehow poured out at odd times.

"Yes, this is Caroline Fulbright. I'm a reporter with the *Nashville News*."

Nick hurried into the restaurant and away from the sounds of people, equipment, and cooking that were happening around him. The last time the *Nashville News* had done an article about his restaurant, it had truly put him on the map.

Putting a professional but enthusiastic tone in his voice, he asked, "What can I help you with today? I've enjoyed working with your newspaper in the past."

He hoped they wanted to do another review. Business was good, but business could always be better.

"You probably spoke with someone from our entertainment section then. I'm a society reporter."

He was just about as far away from society, country club, and all those things as you could get. Before he could ask any questions, she continued. "It has come to my attention that you're engaged. Your restaurant is so popular, and since you made our list of the top ten single men in Nashville last year, I felt like an article was in order."

He sucked in air. Engaged? What hole could he crawl into? When the paper had printed that article—without telling him in advance—there had been a rush of single women dining in his restaurant. He'd had to stay in the back for weeks and barely venture out. If he made even a brief appearance, he'd have phone numbers slipped to him. A few women did things to get his attention that were far more bold.

He thought he'd kept all of that under wraps, but apparently not because her next words were, "I know you had some . . . unusual experiences after you made that list."

"Ha. You're probably referring to the woman who came to my restaurant dressed as a steak because the article said it was my favorite food. It was actually quite a remarkable costume—"

"That's what I heard, too." Her voice held amusement. "I guess you weren't interested?"

"No. I don't know if I want to go down this route again of allowing my personal life to be public." Not to mention the fact that he wasn't really engaged. "And where did you hear about this, anyway?"

"We get all the newspapers from around the state and some of the counties in surrounding states to see if there's anything interesting. This time there was." She paused. "Someone's going to write this story. I'll do a good job and be respectful."

Silence followed her words. She'd put the ball in his court.

Did he pretend this would go away? Because it really needed to go away. Or should he come up with a good story and then later just break the engagement? He'd look like less of a fool that way. If the story would be widely known—and her words led him to believe it would be—then he should control it. He knew Simone would rather it be downplayed, but what choice did they have?

One simple sentence to his grandmother had started a storm.

"Okay. I can speak with you. When did you want to do that?"

"Excellent. But I really need to speak to both of you. We can do that together or separately." Simone was always nice and generally polite. She smiled a lot. And she did have a beautiful smile. She'd been kind to his grandmother. But could she give a good, discreet interview?

"Okay. Let me contact Simone and see how she wants to handle this. I really need to speak with her before I set anything up."

"Nice. You're a gentleman on top of everything else. Too bad I didn't get to you first." She sighed. "I'll call you later, Mr. Barton, to see what you've decided. I could interview you later today, if you're available. Have a good day."

Nick stared at his phone. He had a feeling that a good day was the last thing he was going to be having. Not if it involved a call to Simone to explain this and then a conversation with a reporter. He continued to stare at his phone, but for some reason, it did not dial Simone on its own—probably because he still did not have her phone number. He pulled in a deep breath.

Then he dialed Micah. "Did I catch you in the middle of anything?"

"I'm going into court in about five minutes. What can I help you with?"

"I need Simone's phone number. I know you guys have just

been forwarding my questions to her, but I really do need to speak to her this time."

"Well, I guess since you guys are engaged, it would be okay." Micah chuckled.

"So not funny."

"I wish I had more time to talk. Because it sounds like there's a story here."

Yeah, there will be a story. In the newspaper. "I'll be out there again this weekend. Maybe you, Greg, CJ, and I can get together for a pizza or something."

"Guy talk. This does sound serious."

"Definitely. Well, I'll see you then, and I'm going to have to send you over to Bella for Simone's number. Sorry, but I purposefully do not keep the women's phone numbers in my phone."

Nick dialed Bella's number after Micah gave it to him. This would be so much easier if he was in Two Hearts. He could just knock on Simone's door.

"Bella, I'd like to have Simone's phone number. Please."

Silence greeted him. Then, without asking any more questions, she said, "Okay. I've sent it over to you. Be kind, Nick."

That was odd. More oddness in a very odd day. He took a deep breath and steeled himself for the big call. Well, the big call other than speaking with a reporter about his love life.

"Simone? It's Nick."

"Give me a sec." He heard water running. It turned off before she spoke again. "I was rinsing out a bowl."

He dove right into the problem. "We have a situation." He explained the call from the reporter.

She sighed. "This would be really funny if it wasn't my life."

"I completely agree. And I truly am sorry for shouting your name to my grandmother. I never imagined anything like this."

"Fortunately, I wasn't dating anyone, so nothing got messed up in my life. You definitely want to talk to her?"

"Honestly, not really."

When she sputtered protest, he added, "I don't want *either* of us to talk to her. But she had a good point that our story is interesting, and somebody will run it. I'd much rather have a serious journalist write this versus someone who does paparazzi-style articles."

"Then let's do this. I don't think I can get away today to talk to her. I can't get to town today. I'm working on a cake."

"And I can have my interview today, but I'm slammed tomorrow."

"Then we're doing this separately. At least that question was easily answered. And we need to get our stories straight, Nick. Where did we meet? Where did we go on our first date? How did you propose?"

He groaned. "You're right, of course. But I'm not sure where to start."

Simone giggled. She was so cute when she did that. *No, Barton, don't go there.*

"I work with brides all the time. It's my business. If you knew how many cute meeting and proposal stories I have heard." He could picture her rolling her eyes. "Give me just a second to think about this. It needs to sound incredibly romantic."

Definitely not his strong suit. Although a couple of the women he had dated said he'd been romantic.

"I ate at your restaurant a lot in Nashville. I thought you were handsome every time I saw you. You'd interact with the customers. Once you stopped at our table. You weren't just handsome. You were also nice."

She sounded so convincing that he believed the story. Had she thought that?

Then she laughed. "That sounds good, doesn't it?"

No. She hadn't.

"When our paths crossed here in Two Hearts at the weddings we were working on, we naturally started talking, and everything took off from there."

"That's amazing. It's a good thing you didn't go into that much detail with Nana, or this would be even harder to get out of later." Then he realized what would happen next. "But Nana's going to read this article, isn't she? We keep getting in deeper and deeper."

"Don't worry, Nick. We'll find a way out of this mess you created." He wanted to argue that it wasn't a mess *he* had created. But this was actually 100 percent his fault.

Simone continued. "Let's call it a 'whirlwind romance.' Maybe that way it'll be easier to break things off later. We didn't know each other well before all of this happened—yadda, yadda, yadda."

"That's excellent. You've done so well with the falling. Please tell me how I proposed."

"Oh, no. That one's all on you. How would you propose to someone?" She added, "And the setting should probably be in Two Hearts. Let's keep everything centralized around here."

Okay. What would work? His mind froze up every time he tried to picture himself proposing. "I think I need some help here. Nothing—and I do mean nothing—is coming to mind."

Her deep sigh showed her frustration with his lack of romantic spirit.

"Start with the place. Options include downtown and the town's park. Your family's farm. Feel free to stop me if one of these sounds possible." She paused, probably waiting for him to spout forth the ultimate proposal any second. When he didn't, she continued. "The lake park. Cherry and Levi's farm. The Christmas Tree—"

An image came to mind. "Stop! I have an idea. I can see the two of us in a rowboat on the lake. I'm slowly rowing to the center. Then I stop and kneel. Awkwardly. I hand you a bouquet of wildflowers I picked, take a box with a ring out of my pocket, and propose." The strange thing was that he could actually picture the scene. He'd gotten caught up in their farce.

This time, her sigh sounded sweet. "That's wonderfully romantic! No girl would be able to turn you down."

"I'll call her back and set up a time for myself today and give her your phone number. If that's okay?"

"It really isn't." He thought she'd changed her mind about the interview until she added, "But I'll do what I need to do."

They hung up with Nick feeling everything was under control. He did his best to hold on to that thought because he knew everything was actually far from that. He was about to lie to a reporter from one of the largest newspapers in the country. Their simple, small-town fake engagement had traveled far beyond Two Hearts.

Nick sent a text to the reporter, and they set up a time to talk in two hours. He'd have to tell his staff he had an important meeting and not to disturb him. Everyone would eventually know about this supposed engagement, but he didn't plan for that to happen today.

He had trouble focusing on the rest of the prep work that needed to be done, finally turning it over to his staff. He grabbed a cup of coffee and took the mug outside to think while he drank. Right before his appointment, he went back inside, choosing a table near the front windows and watching for a woman he thought would be a reporter.

A well-dressed woman in her midthirties came down the sidewalk toward his restaurant at the right time. He opened the door to greet her. "Ms. Fulbright?"

"Caroline."

"Let's meet in here. Can I have someone bring you a cup of coffee or tea?"

She sat at the table. "If you have unsweet iced tea, I wouldn't say no."

Nick went to the kitchen, returning with her drink.

She dove right into the questions he'd expected her to ask and was thankful Simone had given him great answers. Then they got to one that hadn't been planned or discussed previously.

"So, when is the big day?"

He shifted in his seat. "We haven't set a date." That sounded good.

"Do you believe in long or short engagements?"

He believed in no engagements—at least not an engagement with Simone—but here he was. "Um, somewhere in between running away to Vegas to get married and waiting until I turn forty."

She laughed. "That's fair. Is there anything I need to know beyond what I've asked?"

"You haven't asked about Two Hearts."

"Your restaurant's website mentioned you're from there. Is there anything more to add?"

Was there? He'd like to bring people to town with this article. "Yes, there is. Two Hearts was a dying town—like so many other small towns in America. But in the past year, the town has been reborn with things for weddings."

"*Things for weddings*? What do you mean?"

"I guess that's bachelor-speak for everything related to weddings. We have a wedding planner, a wedding dress designer, and Simone makes cakes. I'm building a catering kitchen to simplify my work there."

She tapped her pen on the table. "So people from the surrounding small towns are getting married there." Her dismissive tone did not sit well with him.

"No. Country music stars like Carly Daniels and Nicki Lane

have gotten married in Two Hearts, along with many other couples."

The pen stopped. "Interesting. Would Simone have more information on this? She makes the wedding cakes?"

"She will probably know a lot more about it than I do. She's good friends with the women who have started the ball rolling on everything."

"Then I'm looking forward to meeting her." She stood and extended her hand to him. "I enjoyed our interview." With that, she left.

~

Simone called Bella and Cassie, asking them to meet her. Cassie agreed to be at Wedding Bella in an hour.

Comfortably seated in the wedding dress store, Simone told them what had happened.

Cassie said, "That isn't the kind of publicity Nick wants."

"The reporter asked to talk to me, and he thinks I should." She rushed her next words. "And I agreed. I'm going to call her as soon as I leave here." She sat back in her seat, waiting for her friends' response. She'd sounded bold, but she wondered if she'd made the right choice.

Cassie shook her head. "Do you really want to be in the *Nashville News* for an engagement you have no intention of following through with?"

Bella said, "I agree. Nick started this. Let him be in the focus. So far, you've been able to stay outside of the mess he's created. For the most part, at least."

"But am I really on the outside? When our happy news stayed in Two Hearts, it really didn't matter. But now?" Simone shrugged.

Cassie and Bella looked at each other.

Bella said, "I see what you're saying. I'm honestly not sure which is worse. You let Nick be the only one the story is about with the exception of your name as his wife-to-be."

Simone's heart did a little flutter at the word "wife." That wasn't something she'd even come close to in the past. One seemingly serious boyfriend had disappeared from her life when she'd hinted at a future.

With Nick, it sounded appealing. Maybe it was like a biological clock only ticking for weddings instead of babies.

"But, on the other hand, I can see why you want to get your voice out there." Cassie let her words hang in the air as though waiting to see what someone else said.

"So, what am I supposed to do? You told me it's good and bad if I talk to the reporter. I'm not sure where that leaves me."

Cassie explained. "Let me put it this way. You're going to tell a story the two of you have made up to a respected reporter from a big city newspaper?"

"It sounds so much worse when you say those words, Cassie."

Cassie jumped to her feet. "That's because it is bad! What are you two thinking?"

"We both knew it was a bad idea. Nick freely admits that. But would you have acted differently when you were helping a dying woman? A beloved grandmother?"

The two women said, "No."

Cassie sat down. "You're right. It's hard for me to put judgment on something that's already happened, and I wasn't there when the decision had to be made. Lies tend to get out of control, though. That's one of the many reasons they're bad."

"Point taken." Simone looked over at Bella. "Is this how you feel too?"

"I'm not as passionate about it as Cassie is. Your story is unconventional, but so is mine. Micah and I had a marriage of convenience."

Simone sighed. "That doesn't really count. The two of you decided that you loved each other and wanted to stay married."

Bella shrugged. "Theoretically, it could have gone the other direction pretty easily. There were times . . ."

The front bell on the store chimed. Simone looked over and saw Paige entering with Daisy beside her.

"Are there any customers in here, Bella? I was taking Daisy for a walk, and she seemed to want to come this way today."

Bella waved her over. "I'm glad you're here. I think we could use another opinion. I don't have another customer scheduled for an hour, and I know Daisy's a very neat and tidy dog."

Simone looked at Paige. "What would you do, Paige, if you were caught in the middle of a problem—a problem of your own making—and a reporter wanted to know all the details?"

Paige said, "This is about the fake engagement, isn't it? I knew that was going to be a bad idea."

Simone explained the situation with the reporter.

Paige considered her words for a moment before speaking. "I don't think you have a choice."

Simone stared at her.

"I mean, she's going to write the story with only Nick's interview. Who knows what a man's perspective on this might be?"

Simone blew out a breath. "You're right. His version will probably be straightforward and unromantic."

Cassie nodded. "Most likely."

Bella said, "Your story *needs* a woman's touch. Good work, Paige."

"Then I'll do it."

"If that's decided, I came here to deliver good news." Paige grinned. "My photography studio will open in two weeks."

"It's done?" Simone wished she'd been able to move forward with her own store.

"Almost. CJ put in late hours after working in Nick's place.

He told me he'd finish everything in a couple of days. I'm giving myself time to get my studio organized, though, before I announce the grand opening to the world. But I'll be there soon if you want to send clients my way."

"Congratulations!" Cassie stood and hugged Paige. Simone was about to do the same thing when she remembered Daisy was between them.

"Are you excited?" she asked the corgi.

"Woof!"

They all laughed.

Simone stood. "My decision is made. I'll tell her that I'll do the interview. I'm glad that's settled." Having a plan felt good. "I wouldn't mind getting a piece of pie and a cup of hot cocoa to warm me on this cool day. Anyone want to join me?"

Bella checked her watch. "I have plenty of time before my next client gets here."

Cassie said, "And I don't have any more appointments scheduled today. I have work to do. But I can go home directly from Dinah's as well as from here."

On their way out the door, Simone's phone rang. A woman named Caroline Fulbright introduced herself. "I'm with *Nashville News*. Nick Barton, your fiancé, gave me your contact information."

Simone froze halfway out the door. Panicking, she looked over at Bella and mouthed "reporter" as she pointed to her phone.

"You've already interviewed Nick?"

"I just left his restaurant. I must admit that I'm intrigued with the small town and big city connection. Nick gave me a lot of the details about how you met. You often go to his restaurant?"

This felt like a safe subject. "Yes, I have eaten there many times."

"And you noticed him then?"

Simone laughed easily. She had noticed him whenever he entered the room. "He's easy on the eyes."

The reporter laughed in response. "He is that. And he said you would be the better one to tell me about his proposal. Do you know why?"

Simone relaxed. She could handle these questions. "Nick is a guy. He's a caring man, but he doesn't like talking about emotions and romantic moments. I, on the other hand, work in the wedding industry and will be more than happy to share all the details with you."

"Perfect. Go ahead."

Simone described what they had come up with earlier. "And, in the middle of the lake with only the birds singing and a light breeze over the water, he knelt and pulled out a ring."

"You said 'yes'?"

"Before he finished his sentence."

"That's so sweet. I'd love to see the ring."

Simone looked at her bare left hand, then at her purse. "It's with me, of course, and I'm in Two Hearts."

"You're there for the day?"

"I moved here."

"Hmm. I don't have any notes about that."

"Probably because I've only been here a few days. I loved being in this town, and so much of my business had moved out here that I took the leap."

"One last question: when is the wedding? I couldn't get a date out of Nick."

She'd hoped they wouldn't get to that, but knew she had no choice now. What was an engagement story without a wedding date?

"That part is still undecided and in discussions that would be worthy of NATO. The only difference is we don't have to bring in a translator. Well, maybe we should. I speak wedding, and he definitely does not."

The reporter laughed again. "Tell me about this town. I've never been out there. As a newcomer, you must see it with different eyes than Nick would. He told me he was from Two Hearts."

"It's charming." Simone looked out the windows onto Main Street. "It was a dying and essentially dead town until earlier this year. It's being revived by weddings."

"Now that's a story. Maybe I should come out there to see it for myself." The reporter had a wistful tone in her voice that said she probably wouldn't do it, even though she wanted to. She confirmed that with her next words. "This story is due to my editor today, though, so a visit will have to wait."

With promises to tell them when the article published, they ended the call.

# CHAPTER TWENTY-ONE

*D*uring the long drive to Two Hearts, Nick had plenty of time to think about the newspaper article, Simone, his grandmother, and everything else going on in his life. By the time he arrived in town, he was glad he could focus on his new kitchen.

A couple of hours after he'd arrived, he had everything organized and ready to go. Pans were hanging from hooks on an overhead rack, spices had been arranged in a cupboard, and utensils sat in a drawer.

Now, he had three hours for him and his assistant—one of his top sous chefs—to prepare food for a wedding. It was only twenty-five guests, but the full meal included an appetizer, a salad, a main course, and dessert. Each of those things took time.

He tapped his fingers on his new stainless steel counter as he waited for Neve to arrive from Nashville. When she was five minutes late, he pulled out the food he had brought—some of the long-lasting onions, celery, and carrots he kept in abundant supply in his restaurant—and started prepping.

If Neve wasn't here in the next half hour, he was going to be in deep trouble. He'd had his usual suppliers bring the meats, other supplies, and the rest of the produce to his restaurant today with her bringing them out.

When he had everything chopped, the small amount of product in front of him concerned him even more. The clock was ticking. Loudly.

And dessert had not been started. Why someone wanted a dessert along with a wedding cake—which should be the dessert —he wasn't sure. But Neve made many of the desserts for the restaurant. Her skills in that area topped his. Pastry had never been his strong suit.

His phone rang, and he quickly answered.

"Boss, I am so sorry."

"It's no problem, as long as you're here soon." He tried to keep a patient tone in his voice.

"That's just it. My daughter was injured in gym class. I had to pick her up and take her to the doctor. I'm not going to make it."

He wanted to scream at her, but he knew this wasn't her fault. Take a deep breath, Barton. Inhale and exhale. After doing that for a moment, he spoke again. "That's okay. We'll get by. I hope your daughter is okay."

"Thank you! She's going to be, but she broke her arm. They're setting it for her now."

"I'm so sorry to hear that. Well, don't worry about this. We'll get you out here another time." He thought he'd done an admirable job of keeping the panic out of his voice.

They ended the call with her thanking him again, and then he stared at his counter, wondering what on earth he was going to do. It was early on Wednesday, so he knew the grocery store was open, but he also knew he had a finite amount of time to get this ready.

He did the only thing he could think to do at that moment. He picked up the phone and dialed the only available chef in town. At least, he hoped she was. Dinah may have been able to step in, but she had a restaurant to run.

"Simone?"

She sounded confused when she replied. "May I ask who's calling?"

Simone hadn't programmed his number into her phone or she'd know. And she hadn't recognized his voice, but he knew he would know her voice. That bothered him more than it should.

"This is Nick. If you aren't busy right now, I could really use you in my catering kitchen. Neve had to take care of her daughter, who will be fine. I'm stuck alone. I've barely started prep for this wedding."

"Oh my goodness, Nick! Everything should be half done by now."

At least she understood the situation. That put her light years ahead of anybody else he could ask. "Can I give you a list of things to pick up at the grocery store and then have you come over to help? I know it's a lot to ask with zero notice." He knew she had his ring because she'd been forced into the situation, but he hoped she thought enough of him to help.

It seemed like she had to think about it, though, because a full ten or twenty seconds passed before she spoke again. "Text me your list, and I'll do whatever I can to make this wedding's food a success. We don't want the bride and groom to know there was ever a hiccup."

"You're the best. I'll get it right to you." And he realized he did think she was the best. He liked her more than he had any business doing.

After the call ended, he thought about what she'd said. She agreed to help for the sake of the couple more than to help him. Sometimes they felt like engaged strangers, but he felt more and more attracted to her.

Simone loaded the bags into the back of her vehicle and headed for Nick's new kitchen. Three minutes later, she took one of those bags back out and walked toward the door with it.

As she neared his freshly painted red door, she took a moment to look longingly at the space next door. Each time she saw it, the picture became clearer in her mind of a place where she could bake and sell cakes.

Brides could come in and consult with her. She'd also have an orderly system in place for the other cakes she made. She didn't want to have to staff a front counter all day long. She wanted to stay a custom, specialty business. But that place would be lovely. She could almost see her way to doing it.

She opened the door and went into Two Hearts's newest business, a finished building with great details. Paige had the right idea. Marry the carpenter. With a grin, she said, "The cavalry's here."

Nick looked up from where he was working at a new wide stainless steel countertop in the center of the room. Everything had transformed since she'd been in here just a few days earlier.

A giant commercial stove with a hood above it was off to the side. She could see sinks in the back. And some pots on the stove, with a scent of garlic in the air. The amazing thing was, though, that it still looked like a wonderful historic building. He'd managed to preserve that and still make it what he needed.

"I don't think I've ever been happier to see anyone in my life." He hurried over, and when she thought he was going to hug her, he grabbed the bag and took it back to the countertop. "Please tell me the rest of this from the list is in your SUV."

So much for the hug. But she'd take his gratitude. "I was able to get everything except the beets."

She could see his mind working as he recalculated the menu.

"That was definitely in the list of things they wanted for the appetizer, but we'll make it work."

"I got leeks instead. They might be lovely roasted."

This time, he scooped her up into a bear hug and lifted her off the ground. Leaning down, he gave her a quick kiss. "You're wonderful, Simone Mills!" Then he set her back on her feet and hurried toward the front door. About halfway there, he glanced over his shoulder, stared at her for a few seconds, then kept going.

Somewhere between the fake engagement and today, she might have fallen for Nick Barton. And maybe he'd fallen for her too. She had a feeling he just didn't know it. At least, she hoped that was the case because she knew her heart would take a beating if he told her he didn't care for her.

When he returned with his arms loaded with groceries, she realized she'd been standing there doing nothing. She hurried around him, out the door, and grabbed the rest of the bags from the car. Inside again, she said, "Tell me your schedule."

"Ha! Like I could ever tell you what to do."

She grinned. "You'd be surprised. In a kitchen, I'm an excellent employee."

He stared at her for just a moment. "I believe that. Let's get started on the meal from beginning to end." He handed her his printout with the menu items.

Simone considered options as she read.

"They were only specific about the recipe for the dessert. We have more freedom with the other parts of the meal."

"What part do you want to do?"

"If you want to take the appetizer, I'll take the main course. I'm leaving the dessert until last, because I think it's odd that they want dessert and wedding cake."

"I'm in agreement with you on that one. But we always want a happy couple."

They went to work side by side at the stainless steel

worktable. Her arm might have brushed against his a time or two. Purely by accident, of course. Every time they touched, she felt warmth wash over her. If she described her day to Cassie and Bella, they would tell her she had it bad.

When Nick reached across her for garlic, leaning against her as he did, she wondered if he cared too. Her senses alive from his touch, she continued working, grinning as she did. When he reached around her back for a bundle of herbs, his arm resting on her back for a beat longer than it should, her heart sang.

She never had trouble concentrating on her work. Until today. *Focus, Simone.*

Almost two hours later, she stepped back. "The appetizer and salad are done. Where do we stand?" Her years of training had come into play because her thoughts had been more on being in Nick's arms than on the food.

He rubbed his arm over his forehead. His obvious stress about the situation brought her back to the present. "I think we're in good shape. The main course is in the oven. That just leaves dessert. Do you want to take that on? You're my pastry chef today." He handed her another printout, this one with a recipe on it.

Now, she was in her favorite place. She read through the recipe the couple had chosen, and her heart sank to the ground. "Uh, Nick? This is supposed to be individual apple pies. We don't have time for me to prep and bake over two dozen pies."

He blew out a breath in obvious frustration. "I know we joked about not having dessert, but I really hate disappointing the couple. Maybe having an apple dessert was something grandma did at her wedding. Bella told me she'd altered the grandmother's wedding dress for the bride to wear, so they're going to great lengths to mimic her wedding."

Nick stepped behind her and looked over her shoulder at the card. When she closed her eyes and leaned back, he rested his head on her shoulder.

And he did not move. When he spoke, his mouth was right next to her ear. "Any suggestions?"

So many, including turning around and kissing him. Focus, Simone. "We don't have time for a conventional apple pie, but if we chop up all the apples, I can cook that on the stove top and speed things up. While the apple mixture cooks, I can make the pie crust for the tops. Once that's cut in circles, we can bake them separately and assemble at the end. I think we can get this job done pretty quickly. It won't be exactly what they asked for—"

"It will be better. You found a way to save the day and give it an elegant flare. Let's get going."

Simone picked up her phone and found one of her favorite work-in-a-hurry sounds, water rushing over rocks in a stream. She started the background music.

"I don't know why you did that, but if that's your happy music, I can live with it." She felt his gaze on her as she collected everything she needed.

"What should I do first to help you?"

"Peel apples as fast as you can."

"Yes ma'am." Nick had excellent knife skills, so before long, he'd not only peeled, but also sliced the apples, which were now resting in a bowl of lemon water to prevent them from turning brown.

"This is a great-looking recipe. I love the dates for sweetness and cinnamon is a favorite of mine no matter what."

"Mine too. The scent of cinnamon rolls is one of my favorite things."

That reminded Simone of that first morning with Paige and CJ. "So you liked the cinnamon rolls I made at Paige and CJ's house?"

He chuckled. "Liked them? When I said those were some of the best cinnamon rolls I'd ever had, I meant it. I don't know how you managed to do all of that in the time you had."

In record time, both parts of the desserts were done. She scooped the apple filling into each of the ramekins and topped them with now-finished crusts.

Nick walked over to see the results. "That's gorgeous, Simone! I was thinking we'd have something more rustic, but this is beautiful."

She was pleased with how it had come out, especially under the circumstances.

Nick took a load of the prepared food to his SUV. When he returned for a second batch, he asked, "Do you have time to go with me over to the wedding today? Neve would have cooked and helped serve. I know that's a lot to ask of someone who isn't an employee."

Simone disliked working as a server. She'd done the job at different times to support herself in her travels and at others when she wanted to be part of a restaurant's staff to see how it worked. "Sure." She blew out a breath. "I can do that."

He chuckled. "I'm not going to argue with your lack of enthusiasm."

Grinning, Simone looked over at him. "That wasn't my best moment, was it? I'm happy to help however I can."

Then she remembered her actual role for the day. "I was able to drop the cake off before I came over here. That's the beauty of a cold day when I don't have to worry about arriving too soon because of possible melting cakes or insects. But I need to go home first and change into something more appropriate and server-ish."

Nick looked down at himself and his spattered apron. He took that off and set it to the side. "Sorry, I didn't tell you that earlier, or maybe I left it out because my subconscious knew I needed to wait and beg."

Simone laughed. Today had been far more fun than she would have imagined. They worked well together. That surprised her more than anything had in a long time.

As if his thoughts had mirrored her own, he said, "I couldn't have done this with anybody but you, Simone. Thank you." They stared into each other's eyes for a moment, but she broke the connection and walked away.

"I'll meet you over at the wedding in a half hour. Does that work?"

"See you there." His voice held more than the usual amount of interest in seeing her again.

It turned out to be a day full of surprises. But everything about her life and Two Hearts contained surprises.

# CHAPTER TWENTY-TWO

$\mathcal{T}$he next Saturday started with a surprise. He hoped it was the only one for the day, but considering it had to do with his grandmother, he doubted that would be true.

This time, the summons to visit her had come with an invitation for Simone. She'd apparently already spoken with her, which seemed odd.

"I had a request for the girl. Someone I know needed a cake. I knew Simone would be perfect for the job, so I asked her to bring it with her when you visit." So now Nana was selling Simone's cakes? That seemed odd too.

On top of that, today's weather forecast included the possibility of snow, something that brought both glee and concern, depending on whether you were a child or an adult. A few flakes would be pretty, but heavier snowfall could quickly make driving back to Nashville a challenge.

He'd called Simone right away and suggested a stop at Dinah's Place on the way. They needed to get their stories straight before seeing his grandmother again.

When he pulled into Simone's driveway an hour before they had to be at his parents' house, she stepped out of the door with a large cake box in her arms. He got out and went around to the passenger side to help her. "It will be hard to balance that and step up into the vehicle."

"True." She held the box out. "But if you hold this, I can climb in." As she did so, she added, "Your grandmother said the cake needed to feed thirty. And she said to be generous with those slices."

Nick chuckled. "That sounds like Nana. She loves dessert."

As they drove, they chatted about his new kitchen and her new house. He asked, "Have you made any decisions for or against the Main Street building?"

She stared straight ahead and didn't say anything for so long that Nick wondered if he'd said the wrong thing. As he opened his mouth to tell her it wasn't any of his business, she said, "It boils down to my wanting the building but not wanting to spend the money to fix it up. Getting everything up to code for a restaurant will cost quite a bit. The good news is that there's no rush in Two Hearts. Everything on the block has been empty for decades."

He didn't mention that several places that had been empty now weren't. That meant others could be interested in the place she wanted.

When they pulled up at Dinah's, Simone unbuckled her seatbelt and reached for the door handle. "I'm always ready for pie, but what made you want to go here today?"

He turned to answer, and her smile caught his heart. Avoiding falling in love only worked if you didn't spend time with the one person you could fall for.

"Nick? Did you change your mind about going inside?"

He shook himself. "No. I'd like some coffee before I find out whatever Nana has planned."

Inside, Simone asked, "Why do you think she's done anything special?"

Nick laughed. "With Nana, there are always surprises." His

grandmother had summoned both of them to the house. He knew there had to be a surprise.

They placed orders for coffee and pie, both of them choosing pecan. Who could turn down Dinah's pecan pie?

They chatted about the last couple of days. He found himself making a bad joke for no reason other than to see her smile. What had happened to him?

He came back to Earth when she said, "Ready to go?"

"Can I say 'no?'"

Simone stood. "She's a feeble little old lady. Don't worry."

"Mark my words. Nana is up to something."

Simone didn't know his grandmother, but he hoped she was right.

When they arrived at his parents' house, there were a dozen or more cars, some parked in the driveway, some on the grass.

Simone gasped. "You may be right about her. Does she do good surprises?"

"If you'd asked me a couple of months ago, I would have said 'yes.'" He glanced around at the vehicles.

As they walked toward the house, he wanted to reach for Simone's hand, but she was holding the cake. The one his grandmother wanted. That, combined with what appeared to be a party, made him want to comfort Simone in advance of whatever they were about to face.

When they reached the door, she said, "It can't be too bad."

Without confirming her words—because recent events said otherwise—he opened the door, and they went inside. The house was buzzing with activity. People were crowded around on all the chairs and every chair in the room was filled except, Nick noticed, two. They were off to the side and had pink ribbons tied on them. He had a bad feeling that those were for him and Simone.

For a moment, he wondered if he could escape and spend the day with his father who was nowhere to be seen. The last time his mother had a large gathering of her friends, his wily father had escaped with some of his buddies to his favorite barbeque restaurant in Memphis. A loaded car was probably heading east right now.

His grandmother sat in the thick of the group, looking completely healthy. She got up and bounded over to him, pulling him into a hug, something she did every time she'd seen him for as long as he could remember.

Until recently, when she'd been too sick to get out of bed.

"Nana, I'm so glad to see you feeling good and perfectly *healthy*." He said each word with enthusiasm and a special emphasis on the word healthy.

His grandmother stared for a second with her eyes wide, and then she leaned over and put her hand on her back. "It's a miracle, Nicky, but it still catches me every once in a while." The feeble tone was back in her voice. And now, he wasn't buying it for a second. Simone seemed to understand too, because she hadn't said a word.

His grandmother added, "Those seats over there are for the two of you. But oh, that's right. I see you have the cake, Simone. It looks beautiful. Thank you for bringing it. You can set it on that table." His grandmother pointed to a square table that had been set up with a tablecloth, a cake slicer, and small plates.

As Simone carried it over, after a long look at his grandmother—probably as she realized she'd made the dessert for a party she was attending—Nick also noticed the words "Congratulations Nick and Simone" on a heart-covered banner hanging from the side of the room.

And his heart almost stopped beating.

He leaned forward and said, in a low voice, "What have you done, Nana?"

She squinted up at him and frowned. "Why, I'm just giving my grandson a bridal shower. Isn't that wonderful?"

The innocence in her voice didn't sway him.

When Simone returned, he put his hand on her elbow and steered her to the side of the room, where he could talk to her a little more privately. When they got there, he said, "Simone, I am very sorry about this." When he looked at her, he found her grinning. "Doesn't this upset you?"

She laughed. "Nick, she pulled one over on us. She was never sick. Don't you understand? It was just to get you engaged."

He whipped around and stared at his grandmother. "You're right. I hadn't thought of that, and I should have. All I could think is that she had tried to tell me she'd been sick and she wasn't."

He wanted to shout his grandmother's name across the room and reprimand her, but he couldn't with all these people here. That was probably part of her plan. She could reveal that she was healthy, and he would have time to get over her lies before he said anything he'd regret.

Simone leaned over to him, and he put his arm around her shoulder to make it look like they were having an ordinary conversation between two engaged people. As soon as he did that, he regretted it, but he couldn't jerk his arm away without attracting attention.

He had to remember not to get too close to her. Not unless he was willing to start actually dating her, and he still wasn't convinced that he was ready to date anyone in a serious way. And something about Simone said that it should be serious, not just a night out for pizza every couple of weeks. More of a commitment.

"We're going to play into her hands here. Are you willing to be the giddy fiancée?"

"Giddy? I don't think I do giddy. Other than when I'm entertaining children."

"Let me rephrase. *Happy*. Can you pretend to be happily engaged to me in front of all of these people?"

She looked up at him, staring into his eyes for so long that he wondered if she'd forgotten the question. "I can look happy about being here with you, Nick."

His grandmother clapped her hands together to get everyone's attention—again, strong and healthy. "Everyone! We have food, and we have ridiculous games. Which do you want first?"

Some voices shouted "Food!" And others said "Games!"

The possible games terrified him. Whatever she had come up with, he hoped it wasn't too embarrassing.

"Why don't we eat first, Nana? Then the food won't dry out."

He thought that would appeal to her practical side. They were soon seated—he and Simone in the places of honor—and munching on sandwich triangles, fruit, and chips.

His mother said, "I know it's not as fancy as you would have made, Nick—"

"It's all fine, Mom. It doesn't have to be fancy to taste good. Besides, this is quite a crowd you had to cook for. When did you learn about the party?"

He was really asking how long she'd known that his grandmother was okay.

"First thing this morning. She told me she'd invited everyone and that we needed to clean the house and get ready. This was the only thing I could think to make."

Simone took a bite. "Are you the one who makes the amazing chicken salad?"

Nick's mother laughed. "I make chicken salad. I don't know if it's amazing."

"When I moved in, someone brought me chicken salad. Was that you?"

"Oh, yes, I always bring chicken salad to newcomers and shut-ins."

Simone leaned toward her. "Will you give me the recipe? Please."

His mother beamed.

But then someone else said, "She won't share that recipe with anyone. We've been trying to get her to do that for years."

"Ah, but I do share it with family. And Simone is almost family." She directed a secret smile at the other woman.

An "Aw" went around the room as everyone sighed.

Nick panicked. Was Simone getting so into her role that she wouldn't say anything about that?

Simone whispered, "Don't worry. But before we break this thing off, I want the recipe."

"It's all for a recipe?" he said, tongue in cheek.

"I'd do a lot for that chicken salad recipe."

The games turned out to be even more embarrassing than he had anticipated. They tied them together at one point, made them guess things about the other one. Thankfully, he'd spent enough time with Simone in the last couple of weeks that he could answer most of the questions.

When they asked how many years he'd been a chef, Simone gave the answer without hesitation, so she must have studied him at some point. That pleased him. But when one of his grandmother's friends asked how long she'd been making wedding cakes, he'd had no idea, guessing three years. It turned out to be four.

His grandmother clapped again to get attention when everybody booed his error. "Okay, we have just one more game. This is one where we get to help the happy couple."

After assuring everyone's silence, she asked, "Where should they go on their honeymoon?"

*Honeymoon?*

"Beach or mountains?" his grandmother added. "Nick's mother will pass out little strips of paper and everyone can vote."

As she did that, Simone leaned over and again whispered to Nick. "Is this as embarrassing for you as it is for me?"

"Maybe more. She is my grandmother."

Simone nudged him with her elbow. "You can't control what other people do. Oh, and by the way, between the two, I prefer the beach. But I'm also open to other places like the Midwest or Paris, France."

"I'm glad you mentioned the word France after that, because Paris, Tennessee, isn't very far away."

She grinned. "I found that out when I first arrived in Tennessee and someone mentioned going to Paris. Where would you go?"

He thought about it for a moment. "I don't think I really have a preference. But going to France does sound fabulous. I'd probably only be able to get away for a week, though. Would that be long enough?"

As soon as he said the words, he realized what he had done. "Not that we're really, you know . . ."

She shook her head vigorously from side to side. "No. I can see that. You just got caught up in the moment."

"Right."

Simone watched the women talk about the choice, the noise in the room growing louder as everyone argued their reasoning for the potential honeymoon destination and then made a note on their piece of paper. His grandmother, who had now given up any pretense of being less than in excellent health, went from person to person and collected their entries in a bowl.

When she had them, she and a friend Simone didn't recognize counted them. A couple of minutes later, they announced, "Fifteen for the beach and ten for the mountains. What do you think, Nicky?"

"Simone and I discussed it, and we actually like the idea of Paris, France."

His grandmother's face fell, and he hated to disappoint her.

When he was about to add to his comment, Mrs. Brantley—the last person on earth that he would expect to do something like this—said, "The city of love" and sighed.

Simone stared at her. Maybe she'd found a romantic side since getting married. "We've both spent time there, so we'd like to go back. I lived there, so I can show Nick the sights in Paris."

Everyone oohed and awed over their selection.

His grandmother stared at him, the shrewd expression back on her face. "I can see we encouraged you to choose where you'll honeymoon."

Simone turned to Nick. And she found the same dumbfounded expression on his face. They had indeed chosen their honeymoon location. And there was nothing they could say right now because everyone in the room believed they were getting married.

"Then I believe it's time to serve the cake." To everyone in the room, she said, "And for those of you who don't know, Simone is a wonderful baker. She made Mrs. Brantley's wedding cake."

More oohs and awes ensued.

"And she made this, too." She waved them over. "Nicky and Simone, why don't you come over here and cut the cake together?"

Simone's jaw dropped, and Nick reeled backward in his chair. Before she could come up with a reply, he did. "Grandma, I believe that's best left for a wedding day. Not a bridal—" He choked on that word "—shower. Why don't you slice it? Or maybe someone else would like to do it." He had managed to keep his voice in an even, happy tone.

She wasn't sure how he'd done that, because everything about this moment was causing her to panic. Most of what had happened earlier had passed without stressing her out. But this time, his grandmother had pushed them too far.

As Nick's mother passed out the cake, someone looked out the window and said, "It's starting to snow."

Still holding a slice on a plate, Mrs. Brantley went over and looked out. "Oh my, it's really coming down. Everyone, eat quickly and let's get out of here. They were forecasting a winter storm. It looks like they may have gotten it right."

Simone jumped up to help distribute the cake and get everyone on their way. She didn't want these ladies on the road in bad weather. People shoveled it in but did offer her compliments. "This is wonderful," one woman said before booking a cake for her 50th anniversary. That would be a fun one to make.

And soon everybody was hustling out the door. This was no calm departure. When everyone had left, Nick marched over to his grandmother. "Nana! I think an explanation is due. You're obviously quite healthy. What's going on?" He glared at her. When Simone was getting concerned that he was being too hard on her, the older woman put her hands on her hips and glared back. Now she saw where he had gotten part of his personality.

"You be careful how you talk to your elders, Nick Barton."

He looked sheepish for a moment. Then he said, "Nana, you scared me. I thought I was about to lose you. Do you know how much that upset me? I've lost sleep over this. Why on earth would you do this to me?"

This time, she did look ashamed. "Nick, you weren't getting any younger. I wanted you to find someone to share your life with. All you ever do is work."

"But Simone and I aren't really dating! I barely know her. Sometimes we don't even get along very well. We did this for you because we thought that we were about to lose you. I never would have chosen her if I hadn't been pushed."

With every word, Simone felt her heart clench tighter and tighter. These words rushed out of him. They were what he felt in his heart, which was nothing good for her. Kissing her. Holding her hand. The sweet things he'd said and done had all been an act.

Simone called to Nick across the room. "I think it's time for us to go." It was long past time for her to walk away from him. He looked up at her and seemed to realize for the first time since he started speaking to his grandmother that she was in the room.

"Simone, I—"

Simone held up one hand in a stop motion. "Don't bother to explain. Let's leave before we get trapped at your parents' house."

He looked out the window and winced. "We'd better get going right now." He shook his finger at his grandmother. "Enough of this nonsense. No more matchmaking. Okay?"

She shrugged. "It was worth a shot. And for what it is worth, Simone, I really like you. I think the two of you are wonderful together. Don't let him tell you otherwise."

Simone and Nick hurried to the door. His mother waited there with a pair of boots she handed him as they left. She glared at her son but said nothing.

Outside, their feet sank in several inches of freshly fallen snow. She slipped and slid on her way to the car, grateful when she grabbed the door handle that she had something to hold on to.

"Please tell me you have four-wheel drive on your vehicle."

Nick shook his head. "We so rarely need that here and I'm mostly in the city, so I didn't pay extra for it. We're going to drive slowly and hope that the snow doesn't get any worse."

She really hoped that, because she did not want to spend any more time in this vehicle with him than she had to and sitting there waiting to be rescued could take a long time. He crept down the driveway, which was gravel and had excellent traction. On the highway, she saw that very few cars had left tracks in the snow. It seemed like everyone was staying home because of the inclement weather.

"I'm going to drive as quickly as I can, because I'm actually getting concerned about the amount of snow that's coming down. I don't remember seeing inches adding up this quickly. "

His words echoed her thoughts. By the time they arrived at the outskirts of Two Hearts, the snow had doubled in depth and was coming down so fast she could barely see the road.

"Nick, I'm getting worried."

"I am too. I slowed down to twenty miles an hour, but I'm wondering if that's too fast. I'm afraid I'm going to slide off the road, and then we'll be stuck."

"At least we'd be in town at this point."

"But I don't want to walk in this much snow. That would take a while to slog through."

By the time they inched up her road and he pulled into the driveway, they had more snow on the ground than she had ever seen in Tennessee. Simone opened the door and grabbed her purse. "Thank you for the lift. I don't imagine we'll be seeing each other around much anymore."

Then she remembered she still wore his ring. Simone peeled off her glove and slid the ring off her finger. She hadn't expected to keep it when he'd given it to her, anyway. "Here." She dropped it in a cup holder between their seats.

"Simone, I'm sorry. I was upset and words just came out."

"But you weren't filtering what you said, so you said what you meant. That's okay. It's not like either of us expected this to be real, did we?" She looked at him and thought she saw something in his eyes that mirrored her own emotions earlier today. Probably not, considering what he'd said.

She climbed out, stepping in snow that went most of the way to her knees. "Drive carefully."

Then she closed the door and dragged her feet through the snow to her door. Before she reached her front step, tears were running down her cheeks. She heard Nick's vehicle leaving and then nothing but silence. She'd be alone in the storm and in life.

Inside, she grabbed a tissue and wiped away her tears. She would not cry over Nick Barton. If she'd foolishly fallen in love, she'd have to learn to live with that pain. Maybe this was all an illusion, anyway. She'd been waiting for her own wedding. Helping to make other weddings wonderful put ideas in her head that shouldn't have been there.

She started a fire in the fireplace, grateful she had thought to order in some wood when she heard the storm was coming. Then she went to work on a cup of hot chocolate. It would warm her insides, but it would take a while for anything to warm her heart.

# CHAPTER TWENTY-THREE

Simone looked over at the fire and wondered what she was going to do during the storm. She'd be alone for as long as it went on. Hopefully, the power wouldn't go out to make her more alone and isolated. At least Cassie was next door.

A knock on the door surprised her.

She found Nick wrestling with the screen door. She pushed it from her side, the inches of snow adding up so quickly that it took force to move it. "Are you okay?"

He kicked the snow off of his boots and stepped inside. "Remember how we were concerned that my vehicle might slide off the road, but at least we were in town so we wouldn't have to walk far?"

Gasping, Simone put her hand over her mouth. "Did you go into a ditch?" She checked him out, not seeing any cuts or bruises. "Where did you go off the road?"

He pointed down the street. "I made it a block and gently slid into the yard of an abandoned house. I may need to stay here until the roads clear."

He looked her in the eye, and she realized the gravity of this situation. They were supposedly engaged and would be sharing the house during a snowstorm. That would appear incredibly romantic to everyone in this town.

"I can't turn you out of here. But you could stay with the man on the other side of Cassie's. I know that house is occupied."

He shuddered. "Please don't make me spend a snowstorm with old Mr. Haslip. He makes the former mayor—you know, the one who fell asleep in his soup—look young. And he has some eccentricities about cleanliness or the lack thereof that I'm not sure I could handle."

Would she rather be alone?

He watched her long enough to make her uncomfortable. "I'd rather stay here. In case the power goes out." He rushed to add, "Which is likely."

Did he want to be with her? The words he'd said to his grandmother told her otherwise. A gust of wind shook the house, and she jumped. Yes, she was a strong woman, but she didn't like storms. Alone with wind, snow, and who knew what else? Or would it be worse to spend the storm with Nick?

She couldn't turn him away. "I have a guest room with a bathroom upstairs you can use."

His shoulders relaxed. Smiling, he said, "We'll be the best-fed people in Two Hearts. I cook to ease stress."

She did that too. An image of them in his kitchen came to mind. She'd thought then that they had connected, but it seemed she'd been wrong. Seeing him here again, she knew why his words had cut so deeply. She may have wondered before, but now she knew without any doubts. She'd fallen in love with him. Their fake relationship had become real in her mind.

Simone swallowed hard and did her best to hold herself together. "Take off your coat and relax." Simone stepped into the living room. "I have the fire going, so you can warm up here."

He went straight to it and held his hands close to the heat. "This is great. It may not have been a long walk, but snow wedged into my shoes and everything else I had on. I can stand here to dry my clothes—unless you have men's clothing somewhere."

"Other than big socks I like to wear around the house, no."

"I'll take them."

Simone went to her room and returned with a pair of red-and-white-striped wool socks, which he immediately exchanged for his damp ones.

She sat on the couch and tried to relax, but her stress level increased every time she glanced at Nick. "We'll take a few photos and share them on social media so people know the actual situation. We can't let anyone assume there's more of a relationship than there is, can we?" She knew it sounded bitter and petty, but she couldn't help herself. Sure, people thought they were engaged. But she didn't want to prolong that belief with gossip. They'd soon have an official breakup.

Nick stayed silent in front of the fireplace. It was beyond strange that he was the first guest in her furnished house. The first one since it had become her home.

She had to do something because she couldn't stay this tense for days. Maybe conversation would help. "I've never been in a small town in a storm like this. Is there anything special we should do?"

He shook his head. "Nothing at this point. If I'd known I was going to stay here, I would have planned ahead and bought enough groceries to last several days. How are we set?"

"I stocked up on everything. I needed to do that anyway—to make this house have everything I wanted. Especially now that I can't just run to the grocery store any day I want or go out to eat if I'm in a hurry."

"It's less convenient, but you will probably eat better. I am relieved to know, though, that we'll be eating well while we're stuck here."

Simone turned to look out the window, and Nick's gaze followed hers.

"It snowed like this once when I was a kid. At least there isn't any ice."

Simone pulled out her phone, more for something to do than anything else. She and Nick had been reduced to an in-depth conversation about the weather. When she found the forecast, her heart raced. "Nick, it looks like an ice storm is about here."

He chuckled. "Don't even joke about something like that."

She walked over to him and held the phone in front of his face so he could read it.

"That isn't good. I had hoped to go home tomorrow. If we get a layer of ice on top of all this snow . . ."

She pointed to her fireplace. "Remember that I've got a stack of wood out back."

He stared at her for a moment. "I thought you did everything on a whim, but you have firewood and groceries. You didn't seem to like to plan for anything."

"I like adventures. I don't like to do the same thing day in and day out. That's why cakes are amazing because each one is different. It's like a new piece of art. But I'm a planner at heart. I wouldn't have been able to travel the world years ago if I hadn't planned enough financially and worked in various places to earn my way. It may sound like everything was off the cuff, but it wasn't."

He looked at her with admiration in his eyes. "It looks like we have something in common, after all. I love a good plan." He grinned.

Something about Nick Barton's smile worked magic on her. "You must remember, though, that I like excitement and adventure. You don't."

She waited for his response, wondering what he'd say to that.

He moved away from the fireplace and sat on the chair facing her. "Owning a restaurant is the most complicated thing imaginable. I had to learn management skills, which included planning and structure. But I actually love an adventure." His boyish grin had her focusing on his oh-so-kissable mouth.

*Ignore his charm, Simone.* "I think this is an adventure. Do you know what the odds are that the power will go out?"

He wavered his hand back and forth. "Sometimes yes. Sometimes no."

Simone jumped when her phone rang. Answering, she put it on speaker without thinking about it. "Cassie? Did you make it home from wherever you were today?" Simone kept her voice calm, even when that was the last thing she felt.

"I'm stuck in Nashville. I'm here for a wedding and didn't know the storm would be this bad. Greg sent me a text a few minutes ago in capital letters that said, *DO NOT TRY TO DRIVE HOME TONIGHT.*"

"Are you okay, then?"

"We arrived at the hotel for the reception before the storm kicked in, so I got a room here. And I always have a change of clothes in case something happens to what I'm wearing. That, along with everything in my wedding-planner tote, means I can take care of myself and everyone else on this floor." She laughed. "I'll be fine."

Simone was grateful that she'd made it back to her home. Even with her guest here.

"You must have been smart and stayed home today."

She wished she hadn't left the house today. If Nick weren't here, she'd tell her friend all about her day. "Are Bella and Paige with you?"

"I think they're both in Two Hearts. I know Bella had a client who canceled due to weather. Micah's been protective of her, so he would have driven her home when the first snowflake hit the ground. Paige didn't mention anything special when I talked to her a couple of days ago."

"Just a sec." Simone muted the phone and spoke to Nick. "Bella and Paige were available. Why weren't my friends at the shower?"

Nick frowned. "I think the actual reason is twofold. One, my grandmother wanted to have her friends in on all of it. Two, if she had told your friends, they probably would have let you know what was happening. You would have run as far and as fast as you could away from there."

"You're looking through this with the eyes of someone who knew he wasn't really engaged. But if she thought we were . . ."

Nick opened his mouth to speak, then closed it. After a moment, he spoke. "You're right. She had to suspect or know this was a fake engagement. Otherwise, she would have invited everyone you knew too."

Simone tapped the mute button again. "Nick's grandmother threw us a surprise bridal shower. I just asked him why she didn't invite you guys. It seems that you would have ratted on her and let me know what was about to happen."

"You're right about that. Hold it. Did you say *bridal shower?*"

Simone shuddered involuntarily. "It was horrible." She looked over at Nick, remembering what had happened when it ended. That made it even worse. "On the upside, I have three new crock pots and two blenders."

Cassie burst into laughter and Nick grinned.

"I can't even imagine someone doing that to *me*. And Greg and I have been engaged for months. I actually plan to marry him soon."

"Everyone's wondering about when that's going to happen, probably including Greg."

Cassie sighed. "I know. I'm getting close. It hasn't been a year since my almost wedding."

"You need a year? I didn't know there was a required waiting period."

"You've probably got the cake already baked and in the freezer waiting, don't you?"

"I was thinking more in the line of cupcakes. You seem more like a cupcake person than a traditional cake because you've seen so many of them over the years."

"Hmm. I do like that idea. I'll consider that. For the future, which isn't now. But we were talking about your wedding, Simone."

Simone's eyes went to Nick's and locked. "It's a fake engagement. Remember?"

"But—"

Simone interrupted her. Cassie had been about to mention Simone's mistaken belief that Nick cared for her. His words from today continued to sting. She wiped at suddenly moist eyes. "I can't talk more about that now. I have a houseguest."

Another gust hit the house, making her almost glad she had company.

"Who's with you? Someone waiting out the storm?"

Nick crossed his arms and smiled—almost encouraging her to get through the explanation of their situation.

"Nick dropped me off. His vehicle went off the road after he left here." She stated it as matter-of-factly as she could.

"Oh no! Is he okay?"

"He's fine." Simone looked at him and he shrugged. There wasn't another way to say this. "And he's here."

Silence greeted her. "He's there, as in your houseguest?" Cassie said the words slowly and deliberately.

Simone sighed. "He is. I can't kick him out, can I?"

He shook his head from side to side.

"He can stay in my house."

Nick's eyes widened.

Did she want him to go? If the weather forecasts were

correct, ice would be here soon. Growing up in a warm climate meant she had limited winter skills, so having him here to help might be good.

On the other hand, he'd been using her for his own purposes. But she'd known that all along, hadn't she? That had been their arrangement from day one.

"I think I'll leave him here for now." She looked over at Nick and cocked her head to the side. "You don't snore loudly, do you? I want to make sure I get a good night's sleep." Her smile told him she was being sarcastic.

"I'm sure my mother would have let me know years ago if I snored. If not her, definitely my grandmother."

Simone snorted. "Your mother and grandmother think you're the most amazing thing that ever walked the earth. I don't think so."

She heard laughter coming through the phone from her friend. "I'll let you two work that one out. Your chaos made me forget that I called for a reason. I can't get home to feed Romeo."

Something to do would be great. "I'd be happy to feed Romeo. Should I bring him here?"

"He'll be fine as long as he has food. There's a spare key under a rock by the back door. It's cliché in a small town to hide a key like that, but Two Hearts does seem to be safe."

Simone couldn't agree more.

"I'll send you a text with his feeding directions, but if you could go over in the morning and the evening, that would be wonderful. And if you wanted to stay and talk to him for a little while, I know he would appreciate it." Her friend added, "I know that sounded a little strange, but he really does like people."

Right after they ended the call, a text came in with Romeo's dining directions. The cat seemed to live pretty well. It was a good thing Cassie had been there to save him when he was a kitten.

Nick stood. "We should probably get started on dinner. I noticed before that you had an electric stove, so we can't cook if the power goes out."

In the kitchen, Simone watched while Nick went from the freezer to the fridge, and finally the cupboards. "You said you had stocked up . . . I just couldn't envision this. There's enough food in the cupboards alone to last months. And it's a chef's dream. Fresh basil in the fridge, capers and saffron in the cupboard."

Simone shrugged. "I may have gotten a little excessive. The idea of not having a grocery store handy made me—*perhaps*—overbuy on my last trip to Nashville."

"You have a whole chicken in the fridge. Do you want to make baked chicken for dinner? We can stuff it with a wild rice and brown rice pilaf. And have roasted green beans on the side."

Simone's mouth began watering as he spoke. "It isn't that I can't cook those things, but if you're here, I don't have to. Maybe it won't be bad having you here after all."

He stared at her, looking as though he wanted to say something. Then he pulled his gaze away. A moment later, he pointed at the stand mixer on the kitchen counter and said, "Dessert is on you. If you can help me with the main course."

They had worked well together when they were in his kitchen the other day.

The kiss they'd shared came to mind, and she felt her face heat. Then her eyes drifted over to the place they'd kissed in the kitchen. Push those thoughts out of your head, Simone. He's made his position quite clear. *Not interested in you.*

# CHAPTER TWENTY-FOUR

*S*imone peered outside past the lace curtains, which would eventually be changed and weren't in any way her style, to a morning that sparkled in the sunlight. A thick layer of ice covered the snow, adding a shiny gloss to the white. It may be beautiful, but she knew Nick wouldn't be able to drive anywhere today.

"At least the power is still on."

She jumped and put her hand on her chest. Turning around, she faced her houseguest. "You scared me."

He started for the kitchen doorway. "I shouldn't have. That upstairs floor is creaky."

She loved all the historical details. "Isn't it wonderful?" She followed him into the kitchen.

"Excuse me?" he asked as he checked out the coffeemaker.

"I love old houses. They come with squeaks and doors that are bigger or smaller than the stock ones today. Fabulous things may be tucked behind cupboards, like that ironing board over there." She pointed toward a narrow cupboard on the wall on the opposite side of the room, where she'd discovered a built-in ironing board a couple of days ago.

When Nick continued to stare at the coffeemaker as though he was willing the appliance to produce hot brew to wake him up, she nudged him out of the way. "Let me do it."

"Thank you! I'm one of those people who needs coffee before his brain begins working." When she started to speak, he added, "And no snide comments about it not working, anyway."

She laughed. He may not be able to think clearly, but he was funny in the morning. She added the water and fresh-ground coffee and turned it on. "What do you want for breakfast?"

"My first answer is, let's make something fabulous because we have nothing else to do. My second answer is, I wonder if the power's going to cut out and ruin it all."

"I always go for fabulous."

He gave a weak, pre-coffee smile. "Why am I not surprised? Now to choose. You have almost every food substance known to man in your home. The choices are endless."

After going back and forth, they decided on coffee cake, an egg, bacon, and potato frittata, and a fresh fruit salad. By the time they were done preparing everything, Nick had consumed two cups of coffee and was working on his third. With each one, he'd gotten a little more spring in his step.

"You're coffee-powered."

"Told you so."

They filled their plates and ate, but barely made a dent in the food.

Nick stood at the counter in front of the bounty they'd made. "I think we may have created more food than we need for two people."

Simone had been thinking the exact same thing. "If we eat like this at every meal, I'm going to need exercise. I'm already going a little stir-crazy."

Before she could say anything, Nick was at the door, pulling on his coat and the boots his mom had thrust at him as they were leaving his family home yesterday. He opened the door and stepped into the pile of frozen weather on the front step. Calling over his shoulder, he said, "It's a little slippery, but the ice breaks when you step on it, and the snow underneath should give us traction. We just have to walk very, very slowly."

Hope rose in her. "Does that mean you can drive out of here?"

He stomped his feet together to knock off the snow and came back inside, closing the door behind himself. "Are you trying to get rid of me, Simone?"

She had been. "I know you were anxious to get back to town."

He frowned. "And I know I'm inconveniencing you by being here. But remember that my SUV is in a ditch. It's going to be a while before mine and all the other vehicles in ditches are pulled out. Leo's the only one in town who owns a tow truck. A couple of people in outlying farms might have the ability to tow if they can get out."

Maybe there was a chance he'd leave today.

"Besides, it's one thing to walk on something that's slippery, and it's another thing to need to hit the brakes on it. No, I think you're stuck with me until the temps are above freezing."

Or not. But that's what she'd been expecting, so it wasn't a surprise. The thought of living this close to Nick for a couple of days was daunting. Once she'd realized that everything good between them had been a lie, she'd wanted to stay far away from him.

Her phone rang, and she answered the call from Mrs. Brantley. "Dear, I heard you got saddled with Nick for the storm." She made tsk-tsk sounds. "That's certainly an unusual circumstance, but I'd like to put it to good use."

Cassie must have told her future mother-in-law, who hopefully hadn't spread this all over town. Not when they needed to make a public breakup next week.

"There are some people in this town who rely heavily on

Dinah's Place for food. I just talked to Dinah. She can get to her restaurant, and Michelle might be able to find her way over there too—all on foot, of course—but the people she's concerned about are the elderly who cannot take the chance of walking on ice to get to her restaurant for their next meal. One of those people is just two houses away from you on the other side of Cassie. Would you be able to take him food today?"

Simone grinned. She had something to do. "Two chefs are locked up. We would be more than happy to do that. Anyone else?"

"Two chefs? I thought just Nick was with you."

She'd let that slip out without realizing it. The town may as well know the real Simone. "I'm also a trained chef."

"That's even better! I happen to have a list of people who could use help with meals during the storm." The sound of papers rustling told Simone that Mrs. Brantley was more than prepared as usual. She read off a list that Simone hurried to write down. When she was done, there were nine names on the list.

"I don't know where all these people are. Do you have directions for them?"

"Nick should know. If he doesn't or if he doesn't remember after all these years—" Her tone of voice said he would remember if he hadn't been away so long "—give me a call back." After promising to do that, they ended the call.

She glanced over at Nick. "What do you think?"

"This is great. It gives us something to do instead of just sitting here."

"Let's package up what we have from breakfast. We made a lot, but not enough of anything but the coffee cake for nine more people. We'd better get to work."

Before long, they had made nine omelets and added to the fruit salad. Once they had each portion on foil-covered paper plates, Simone felt a sense of accomplishment. "I guess we're the winter weather meal delivery service. How are we going to do this?"

Nick was staring out the back window of the kitchen. "Have you been in that shed?"

Simone shuddered. "I pictured it as a den of spiders and snakes."

"It's winter. You might be right in the summer. I'd suggest you clean it and close up any holes before warm weather comes." He pulled open the back door.

"What are you thinking?"

"I have an idea. This house had children and then grandchildren and possibly even great-grandchildren in it." Before Simone could ask what that could mean for delivering meals, Nick was halfway across the snow-covered lawn.

Simone put her boots and coat on and went out after him. If he'd opened the shed door, she should probably see what was in there in case she needed something later. After slipping and sliding, she managed to get there. Barely.

Peering inside, she found a surprisingly well-lit storage unit, due in large part to a hole that something must have whittled in the back wall. Nick pointed at the light source. "You probably want to fix that. Looks like some squirrels got in here. And before you start thinking you don't want to take away a warm home for squirrels, they're happy outside and don't need you to provide that. They like to chew."

Nick moved a tricycle, a rake, and an old wooden rocking chair. "I found what I thought I would." A wooden sled with the corner nibbled off came into view, proving his point about the squirrels. "We can load everything on here and tie it down, then pull it behind us while we deliver."

*Us?* "I pictured us each going in different directions." Please let it work out that way. The last thing she wanted to do was have more reinforcement for the town about their relationship as a couple.

"Did you slip and slide on your way out here?"

"Some." She'd actually had a hard time staying on her feet, but she wasn't going to admit that.

"Did you fall?"

So he had been watching. "Only once. But I see your point. It's going to take two of us to get through this. Then let's get going." They had to stage a public breakup already. Being together now would make a more spectacular breakup.

Before long, they were going down the driveway, with Nick pulling the sled and Simone walking beside him. Maybe being outside would relieve some of the tension between them that he felt in her house. She didn't want him to be there, and he couldn't blame her. He had to find a way to talk to her, though. To try to tell her again that his words to his grandmother had been about the past.

Simone turned right at the end of the driveway. "We need to make a quick stop at Cassie's house to feed Romeo. Help me remember to come back tonight too. I'm not used to having a pet."

He parked the sled at Cassie's back door. The gray and white cat greeted them as soon as Simone opened the door, meowing as they went inside.

As Simone prepared his bowl of food, Romeo twined around Nick's legs. He crouched and petted the cat. "Cassie will be back as soon as she can," he told Romeo.

The cat meowed loudly at his words.

Simone put the bowl on the floor. "I think he's questioning why she isn't here now."

Romeo planted his face in the bowl as soon as it hit the floor. Nick felt guilty for leaving the cat so soon after they arrived, but they needed to deliver breakfast.

Simone must have felt the same way because she said, "I'll be back later," as they went out the door.

Back outside, Nick glanced over at her. He had to try again to tell her how he felt. "Simone, I wanted to talk to you about the party—"

"I don't want to talk about it. Not now. Maybe not ever. Just let the subject drop, Nick."

Did she mean they could go on as they had been before? Should he give her back her ring? "I know my grandmother can be pushy. Of course, I didn't realize exactly how pushy until recently."

This time, when he looked over at Simone, he saw a smile. "I have to admire her. She saw a problem—you being single—and decided she had a solution. I respect that." Her words surprised him.

This was going better than he'd hoped. "I'm glad you feel that way. I'm sorry about what I said."

"I don't want to talk about it, Nick. I just said that."

"I need you to understand. Can I at least apologize, or do you not want me to say even that much?"

They had stopped in front of their first breakfast delivery house before she spoke again. "It would be wrong of me not to allow someone to apologize, but I'm not ready to talk about it beyond that."

He'd take any opening he could get. "I was a thoughtless jerk yesterday."

That got him a nod of her head.

"I never should have said what I did. More than that, I didn't mean it."

"Nick, you just passed from apology to not allowed. And quite frankly, the strength of your voice when you were speaking to your grandmother tells me that you meant every word." She started up the driveway. "We've arrived at Mr.

Haslip's house. Let's just do our deliveries and get through the storm."

The look in her eyes broke his heart. Was it possible she had grown to care for him as much as he had for her?

As Mr. Haslip came to the door and Nick saw the shriveled-up old man he remembered as vibrant, he knew he had to do something to fix his own life so he didn't end up alone when he grew old. But he didn't want just anyone. He wanted Simone.

Simone nudged him.

He looked up to see the old man staring at him. "I haven't seen you in years, sir. But you were my fourth-grade teacher. I'm Nick Barton."

The old man nodded. "I remember you. Aren't you the one who's some fancy chef now in Nashville?"

Nick smiled for the man's sake, even though his brain couldn't focus on anything but Simone. "I don't know about fancy, sir, but I do have a restaurant there. My friend Simone here moved two houses down, and she's also a chef. We brought you some breakfast if you'd like. Since the diner's closed today."

The man beamed at their words. "Would I like that, young man? Thank you! I was going to be left to a piece of toast and butter because I don't keep breakfast things in my house. Dinah does such a good job that I don't need to."

Simone reached down and picked up one of their packets. Handing it to him, she said, "You have cinnamon coffee cake, a ham and cheese omelet, and some fresh fruit. Does that sound better than toast?"

The man moved faster than Nick would have guessed for someone his age. In ten seconds, he had taken the package from Simone. "Thank you so much! My niece will be happy to know I ate a good meal." He leaned closer to them and dropped his voice. "She worries."

Nick smiled genuinely at this. "We don't have anything to do while everything's shut down for the storm. Would you like it if we brought you something for dinner too?"

"That sounds great. Thank you again. All the heat's leaving the house, so I better let you go."

They were soon on their way to the next stop, which was about a block away.

Nick wanted to try to apologize again, but the last time hadn't gone well. When they returned to Simone's house, he'd call Micah to see if he had any advice. He and Bella had about the rockiest start to a happy marriage that he'd ever seen, but they were deeply in love now.

He stopped in the middle of the road. Simone turned back and said, "Aren't you coming?"

He had fallen so in love with this hard-to-pin-down, sometimes flighty, sometimes planning, probably-going-to-drive-him-crazy woman that he couldn't even think straight now. The question was, what was he going to do about it?

They made the rest of their deliveries and came back home. To her home, that is. She went into the living room and put logs into the fireplace.

"I can start that. Do you want to get us hot chocolate? I know I could use a warm drink right now."

She rubbed her hands together. "Me too." As she worked in the kitchen, she continued talking. "Nick, I enjoyed what we did today. We fed people and made them feel less lonely. At least Mrs. Randolph has her pet rabbit to keep her company."

He laughed.

"It made me feel useful. But a little cold." She laughed.

"That's the truth." He put a match to the newspaper he'd added to the fireplace. "Fire's going."

She brought him the hot drink she'd topped with a swirl of whipped cream, chocolate shavings, and chocolate sprinkles.

"You decorated our hot chocolate?" he asked as he took his mug from her.

"I like making things prettier." Simone sighed. "Sometimes there doesn't seem to be a way to make something better, though." She took a sip of her drink.

He hated being the one who had made her sad. Then he remembered he'd planned on calling Micah for advice. "I'm going upstairs to my room for a while. Do you want to eat dinner in about an hour?"

"Are we having the same meal we're going to deliver, or are we making everything different for us?"

"Good question." If they made two meals, they'd get to work side by side longer. And their dinner would feel more intimate because it would be just for the two of them. "Let's make something new."

He hoped Micah could help him come up with a plan to win her love.

# CHAPTER TWENTY-FIVE

*M*orning began in a normal way. But not. She got up and took a shower. If Nick hadn't been in the house, she would have put on her robe and trudged down the hall to the kitchen to put on a pot of coffee before doing that. There was no way she was going into a semi-public space with bed head.

As Simone stood in front of her open closet door debating what to wear—something she rarely did—Cassie called to share what she called "good news." The quick call ended before Simone had decided if her friend was right.

She sat on the end of her bed. Nick would be leaving today.

Knowing that, she went for easy. This needed to be a comfortable clothing day, not one with clothing that took a lot of thought. With faded jeans and a pink, yellow, and blue sweater on, she stepped out of her bedroom, ready for her day. Or as ready as she would be.

The smell of coffee and other good things greeted her. *Bacon.* As she entered her kitchen, she said, "I don't know what you're making, but I want whatever it is."

He turned around and grinned. "I didn't think you'd mind if

I got started on both our breakfast and what we're dropping off with everyone this morning."

"I'm definitely not complaining." Simone peered through the kitchen window to the backyard. "Cassie just called to check on Romeo. I told her I'd fed him twice yesterday and would be over there first thing this morning." She poured a mug of coffee and took a sip before continuing, her nerves getting the best of her. "Greg said she can come home in the middle of the day, so the roads will be clear enough for highway travel."

They both knew what her words meant. Nick would be able to drive back to Nashville safely. Away from here. Away from her.

Back to the life he loved.

*Focus on food, Simone. That's always happy.* "Bacon and a pastry in the oven?"

"Hash brown casserole. You know how much that's loved in the South. I've got eggs, grated potatoes, cheese, onions, and sausage in there." He opened the oven to check it. "As for pastries, you know I'm not a baker."

"I don't know what came over me." She laughed. "Any ideas for what I should make for the sweet side? Or not necessarily sweet, but some sort of baked good?"

"Muffins? Those travel well."

She browsed through her cupboards and the fridge. "Cinnamon apple?"

"Sounds delicious. I think it'll be a much easier walk for us today. The outside temperature is already approaching forty degrees."

Simone got to work on the muffins and soon slid them into the oven. While they baked, she sat down at the table in the corner of the room. The comforting breakfast scents filling the kitchen relaxed her to the point that she said something she probably shouldn't have. "How often will you be visiting Two Hearts?"

He stopped for a flash of a second, then continued his work. She'd caught him—and her—off guard with her question. "Nana may have made me angry, but she also taught me that family matters. I'll be here often." Potholder in his hand, he turned to face her. "I have other people here too. Friends. Those I care about."

The intensity of his gaze shook her. And then it was gone. Only necessary words were spoken as they put together the breakfast packs after eating their own meal. It didn't feel so much uncomfortable as . . . off.

She focused on the task at hand. "This time, let's start our route with Mrs. Randolph."

"Because?"

"I included some raw zucchini sticks and fresh basil for Nosey. I checked, and those are both good for rabbits. We'll be less likely to give it to someone else by accident if we go there first."

Nick started laughing. "We're doing door-to-door delivery for rabbits too?"

"He's a cute rabbit."

Nick couldn't argue with that point. At the first stop, Mrs. Randolph met them at the door, wobbly and leaning on her walker as she had yesterday. Also like yesterday, the rabbit waited beside her.

"I have something special here for you and for your friend there."

Simone set the separate packet of veggies on top of the human meal.

"You see, Nosey? Everyone loves you." The rabbit looked up at her as though it understood every word. Mrs. Randolph wobbled more, enough that her lack of stability concerned Simone.

"Nick and I have been away from my house for a while. Could I get a glass of water from you?"

The old lady smiled. "You come right in. And you too, young man. You don't need to be standing out in the cold while she's getting something to drink."

Nick glanced over at her with a questioning expression. Simone leaned over and whispered in his ear, "She looks like she needs a little assistance getting back to her chair. Let's walk in on either side of her. Then I'll get that glass of water I don't really want."

He gave a nod, and they went inside, helping her to what turned out to be a recliner in the living room. They got her set up with her breakfast on a tray, and then Simone went into the kitchen and ran water for a moment.

Mrs. Randolf called out, "Do you think the weather's improved so I can get out tomorrow?"

Simone certainly hoped the woman wasn't driving. She was past her prime for being behind the wheel. Simone came back to the living room and stood beside Nick.

"One of my neighbors stops by to pick me up and takes me over to Dinah's every morning. She also picks me up for church."

Now her words made sense.

"It's been a pleasure meeting the two of you."

Simone bent down and petted the rabbit, who was now in a round, padded bed next to her owner's chair. "I've never known a pet rabbit before."

"They make wonderful pets. Nosey is loving like a cat. He has his favorite places in this house to curl up just like that."

They left with Simone wondering if she needed to have a rabbit as a pet. About halfway home, she realized that as long as she was cooking out of a home kitchen, she probably didn't want any pets. If they were anything like a cat, they'd want to be in the middle of everything.

By the end of their deliveries, Simone was sure she would scream if one more person congratulated her and Nick on their upcoming nuptials. Unfortunately, their last stop was the Gerard house. Edna and Alberta Gerard had been her favorite people the previous day because they'd been so sunny and happy. But they must have congratulated the two of them three or four times. That was wearing pretty thin right now.

She just wanted this fake engagement to be over. She knew now that she needed him out of her house. The strain between good moments and knowing the reality of his feelings hurt too much.

Nick spoke. "If Greg decided that the love of his life can safely drive from Nashville to Two Hearts, I'll be able to leave midday."

Nick must have had the same thoughts she did. When they arrived at the Gerard House, they both stopped at the end of the driveway and stared at it.

Simone asked, "Do you think they're going to tell us what a great couple we are?"

"I'm sure of it."

She sighed. "Let's do this."

They walked up the driveway toward the door much more slowly than they had their other stops.

Alberta had the door open before they were halfway there. "I'm so glad to see the two of you. Aren't you the cutest things?"

Simone looked over at Nick and shrugged.

"Well, come on over here. What did you bring us this morning? Sister and I have loved the food so far. Are you sure we can't pay you anything for it?" Alberta paused for air.

"Absolutely not. We're just helping out neighbors during a storm," Nick said quite firmly. "And in answer to your question, we brought you hash brown casserole and bacon." And he added with a smile at Simone, "She made cinnamon apple muffins."

"Did I hear muffins?" The other lady came into view.

"I tucked a couple of extras in there because I knew you enjoyed sweets," Nick said.

Simone turned to him with surprise. He hadn't spent much time in this town in recent years, so these ladies must have quite the reputation for sweets.

"In my day, I was quite a baker," Alberta said. "Now I'm happy to let other people do it. Besides, if I make a pan of something, I'm going to eat the whole thing. My doctor doesn't approve of that." She shook her head as though the doctor had some strange ideas.

Simone stepped back from the door. "Well, we'll be on our way now." They had been spared well wishes, and she'd like to keep it that way.

The two of them started down the driveway. When they'd almost reached the street, one of the ladies—she couldn't tell from the voice which one—shouted, "I'm looking forward to going to your wedding!"

In unison, Simone and Nick turned and gave a little wave as they walked away.

He pulled out his phone and checked the weather report. "It has already climbed ten degrees. Soon, it will all be wet snow instead of ice."

Simone's foot slid as he said that, and Nick grabbed her arm before she fell. She wished that man's touch didn't warm her heart every time. As soon as she was stable, she continued walking, and they arrived home without more problems.

Of course, both of them sitting in her living room on a snowy day came with its own set of problems.

When she announced that she was going to her room to read for a while, Nick appeared much too gleeful. He must have been feeling the tension too.

# CHAPTER TWENTY-SIX

$\mathcal{W}$hen Simone left the room, Nick jumped to his feet and hurried into the kitchen. He threw meat and produce into a couple of bags, along with a few other essentials. Then he crouched in front of a cupboard and pulled out some items he'd stashed there last night.

Winter gear on, Nick went back outside, set the bags on the sled, and started down the road. As soon as he was far enough away that Simone couldn't see him through a window, he relaxed a notch.

This had to be a surprise to have even a chance of working. But he had a tight timeline to work with.

He stopped and made a call. When they'd been in the living room, he'd texted Micah to ask for Albert's number. Unfortunately, the hardware store owner didn't answer. Micah had guessed that he'd be out shoveling someone's snow, but now Nick had to find the man.

Towing the sled, he walked as quickly as he could in the softening snow toward the hardware store, hoping to find its owner along the way.

Within sight of the store, he spotted the gray-haired man not with a shovel but a snow blower. "Albert!" he called. When there wasn't a response, he yelled his name louder.

The man looked over his shoulder and turned off the machine when Nick pointed at it. "Can I help you?" He leaned down and brushed snow off his pants with gloved hands while waiting for a reply.

"I have a favor to ask. I need a couple of things from the hardware store. Could you open up for me?"

Albert shook his head. "I'm closed, just like every other store in town. Come back tomorrow." He reached for the switch to turn the equipment back on.

"Wait! I need to show her I care before too much time passes." Micah's words from yesterday flowed out of him.

"What?" Albert's brow furrowed.

Nick felt foolish, but he pressed on. "I said something stupid a couple of days ago. Simone and I will break up if I don't take action."

Albert stared at him.

"She won't talk about it, so I have to *show* her I care."

"With something I have in the hardware store? Isn't this the time for jewelry or flowers? Maybe chocolate?"

Nick shook his head. "I know she'll love this." And he hoped she'd love him too.

A half-hour later, Nick had added a can of paint, paintbrush, sandpaper, and other items Albert considered important for the job to his sled. He checked his watch when he finally reached Main Street.

Noon. Based on the road conditions here, he had a couple of hours to get this job done and bring Simone over to see it. He wouldn't put it past her to leave her own house when she could safely drive away. Anything to avoid him.

He hoped this would show her he cared or at least that he wanted to make her happy. He had to admit that his words to his grandmother had done the opposite.

Nick gave the door a quick sanding, wiped off the dust, and opened the can of paint. Just when he thought the town had more than enough pink, he was going to add more. But pink made him think of bakeries. He'd chosen a more intense shade than the color used on the park's picnic tables. More intense made him think of Simone.

When he had a coat of paint on the door, he propped it open to dry and went to work on their picnic. It turned out that he'd grabbed chicken breasts, lettuce, and other things that could be used for a salad, along with an assortment of foodstuffs that he put back in the bag because they didn't go together at all.

He poached the chicken, shredded it, and set it to the side. Once he had everything for the salad chopped and ready, he assembled the salads and knew he'd almost reached the time to get Simone. He spread the blanket from her hall linen closet on the floor and placed the bowl of salad, plates, and silverware on one corner. Then he switched on the flameless candles he'd spotted on a shelf in that same closet and placed them around the room.

Standing, he surveyed his work. Good food. Candlelight. He'd done all he could think of here.

Now he needed her.

Simone picked up the sweet romance novel she'd been reading and curled up on her couch with that and the cup of tea she'd just made. About halfway through the novel, her front door opened. The book flew into the air as she jumped to her feet.

A grinning Nick stood there. "Sorry to startle you."

"You were outside?"

He shifted on his feet. "For a while. Um, just wanted to stretch my legs. Yes, that's it! I went for a walk."

What was going on?

He continued before she could ask. "Would you mind coming with me?" When she stared at him without replying, he added, "It's pretty out here. Sunny and the snow is melting. I can see pavement on the street now."

She probably wouldn't be with him outside of weddings in the future. Maybe she should take advantage of this last time. "Let me get my coat." Simone picked up the book and set it on the couch. Then she put on her outdoor gear.

The snow volume had shrunk as it melted. The traction she found with her first tentative step surprised her. "This snow is *much* easier to walk in."

"We could make a snowman later. But it won't last long."

"We'll decide when we get back from wherever you're taking me." When she tried to turn right out of the driveway, he directed them left. "I, uh, saw something on my walk that you'd enjoy."

There he went again with hesitation. The normally confident Nick seemed to be nervous.

"I'll follow you."

He smiled at her words. About half a block from Main Street, Nick said, "I'd like you to check out a special project I did. Over on Main Street."

She silently walked beside him. He seemed so hopeful that she couldn't say no. Even though he didn't want her, he was still a decent guy. They were going to end up working together on future weddings whether she liked it or not. Especially now that she'd moved to town and he had the kitchen here.

To add a lighter note, she said, "Okay. But you're making the hot chocolate when we get back to my house."

"That works for me."

They continued on, side by side on the cut-through between buildings that led from this road to Main Street.

When they were on Main Street's sidewalk, she noticed a small sign over Nick's new kitchen across the street. The gold background on the oval sign had black lettering that read "Southern Somethings" with "Catering" in smaller letters beneath. "Is that it? I love your sign. It looks like a real business now."

Instead of appearing happy, he glanced over at her nervously. "There's something else. And I need you to promise you'll let me explain." He stopped and faced her. "Do you promise?"

She didn't want to promise him anything, but they were here, so she didn't have anything to lose. Besides, what would they do instead? Go back and sit in front of the fire where they could stare at each other? That wasn't uncomfortable at all, was it?

"I agree."

He slipped his arm around hers, and she tensed. "Over here." He tugged her gently down the sidewalk. When they were in front of Bella's Brides and opposite his new kitchen, he stopped. "There." He pointed across the street.

"I saw your sign. What else is there?"

"Not that." He sighed. "Let's move closer." He nudged her forward and over the road that had no traffic today. Instead of stopping in front of his business, he continued to the smaller one next door.

Her heart sank when he stopped in front of it, and she realized what had happened. "Someone took my store." The door had been painted bright pink, a color that would have been perfect for her business.

A tear slid down her cheek and then another. It was too much to take on top of everything that had happened in the last few days. She'd moved here with big dreams, but things weren't going well.

When Nick glanced over at her and saw the tears, he pulled his glove off and wiped them off her cheek. "Please don't be sad. This is a good thing. A surprise for you."

She knew it was good for the growth of the town if someone moved into another storefront, but that didn't change her life. "I think I'm missing something, Nick. Why is this good news for *me*?"

He let out a deep sigh. "I have done this completely wrong. I painted the door for you. I asked CJ to talk to the owner because he's been in contact with the owners of all these buildings. She's willing to make you a great deal just to have someone in there. You've got your oven in storage, so it can go in."

"But I won't meet all the health codes. I need to redo plumbing and so many other things in order to use it as a commercial bakery. It's really no better than the house I'm in."

"If CJ cut an opening between that store and mine, then you would be able to use my license, and you would be fine."

Hope blossomed in her heart. "That could work. But you don't want to be around me. We'd have to work together and coordinate."

"Simone, I was angry at my grandmother, and I didn't mean for the words to sound as they did."

She stomped her foot in anger, feeling like a petulant child but not able to help herself. "That's terrible, Nick. I heard you say we weren't compatible. You meant every word. I heard it in the strength of your voice."

"What I meant was that we didn't seem to be a good match. We *are* different kinds of people. That's true, wouldn't you agree?"

"Of course! But that didn't mean—"

He put his hand on her cheek and gently brushed across it with his thumb. "Exactly. My words didn't mean I didn't want you. Just that we're an unlikely pair." He looked into her eyes, and she could see how deeply he meant what he'd said. "I wanted to show you I did care, and I couldn't think of any other way to do it. You're pretty self-contained. You have everything you need."

He gestured with his shoulder toward the freshly painted door. "Except a pink door."

She threw her arms around him and pulled him in for a hug. "Thank you! For this, but more. Thank you for being you."

He leaned back and looked into her eyes. "For anything else?" He was back to nervousness.

"For everything. I can't imagine my life without you. It was breaking me in two."

"I felt the same way. I'm going to fix up the apartment over the kitchen and live there until..."

She felt like her grin would split her face. "Until we're married and you move into my place? Or did you want to get a different house?"

"That squeaky floorboard bothered me at first, but I've grown to like it. I think we can make a good life here, don't you, Simone?"

"What about your restaurant in Nashville?"

"I'm still going to have to go back and forth some. But I have a wonderful team in place. I can spend most of my time here. And you can come along with me when we're going to the city."

"I agree with your terms. Now I need you to kiss me immediately and then get us back home before I freeze to death."

"I have something better." He took her hand and pulled her toward his storefront. When he opened the door, she gasped. A blanket on the floor had a wicker picnic basket resting on it. Candles lit the perimeter of the room, casting a warm glow on the scene. The luscious scent of herbs and garlic filled the room.

"How? When?" she sputtered.

"Today."

"But I thought you were upstairs in your room."

"I snuck out the door as soon as we got back and have been

over here since then. Well, after a stop to get Albert to open up
and sell me paint."

She laughed. "You have been busy."

"Let's take off our coats and pretend it's a spring day we
could picnic outside in."

Simone felt warm to her core—without the addition of the
room's heating. "This is the nicest thing anyone has ever done
for me."

Nick pulled her in for a kiss, and the room became warmer
still. When he stepped back, he said, "Nothing is better than
holding you in my arms."

Simone agreed. She could spend a lifetime kissing Nick
Barton.

When he kneeled and took out the engagement ring she'd
returned to him, she knew she would have that lifetime
with him.

# EPILOGUE

*N*ick pushed the rowboat off the shore and jumped in, rocking it slightly.

"Careful!" Simone almost dropped the bouquet of wildflowers he'd handed her a moment ago to grip the sides of the boat.

"Don't worry." Nick sat on the bench facing her and reached for the oars. A few minutes later, they'd arrived at the center of the lake. "Simone, I can't believe I'm saying this, but I'm nervous."

She giggled as she set the flowers on the bench beside her. "Me too. We've been dating for months, but this . . ."

They both knew what she meant. When they'd realized they'd fallen for each other, they'd also decided to stay engaged as the world knew them to be. But also that they needed to date a while before they made their engagement real in their hearts.

Today was that day.

When Nick had mentioned this outing, she'd known he'd propose. But neither had said the word out loud. She'd known for quite a while that she'd spend her life with Nick Barton.

Winter weather had become springtime. Redbud and

dogwood trees bloomed on the shore. Temperatures had warmed up to the no-jacket-needed season. Now, with the natural beauty around them, he would ask her to marry him.

Or would he? What if he didn't bring her here for that? She glanced over at Nick. Maybe he just wanted a boat ride. No, he would ask. But if not—if they ended up with a boat ride—he'd ask another way. Or she would ask him. If he didn't propose to her soon, she'd buy a ring for him and get down on one knee.

Just when she thought nothing would happen, Nick cleared his throat and leaned forward on his right knee, wincing when it hit the rough wood plank floor. He pulled the familiar ring box out of his pocket. She had the ring on her finger, but she appreciated the symbolism of holding the box.

"Simone, would you do me the honor of marrying me?" He turned the box so she could see inside. A slender band that matched her engagement ring nestled inside. "I asked the jeweler to make a wedding band. I hope that's okay." His sweet, insecure expression made her smile.

"I hadn't thought about needing a ring for the wedding, but this is beautiful."

He slipped the ring out of the box and slid it on her finger. "I know we aren't married, but I wanted to put a ring on your finger today. You can take it off later."

She sighed. "It's so pretty."

Nick leaned forward for a kiss. The boat rocked again, but she ignored it. She looked forward to a lifetime of kisses and love with this man.

PERFECTING THE PROPOSAL is the next book in the Wedding Town Romance series. Amy's the new newspaper owner you met in Waiting for a Wedding, and Scott's in town to visit his friend Greg. One thing leads to another and Scott's soon doing pretend proposals with Amy as a way to help her newspaper. Plus Cassie and Greg get married in this book—but it isn't a simple event to plan.

Join Cathryn's newsletter to learn when the next book is coming out. And if you've missed it, HOW TO MARRY A COUNTRY MUSIC STAR is the prequel to the series. Carly was mentioned in Waiting for a Wedding. She's a down-on-her-luck country music star. Jake is the wealthy man who hires her to be his housekeeper. Get the ebook FREE at cathrynbrown.com/marry

# ABOUT CATHRYN

Writing books that are fun and touch your heart

Even though Cathryn Brown always loved to read, she didn't plan to be a writer. Cathryn felt pulled into a writing life, testing her wings with a novel and moving on to articles. She's now an award-winning journalist who has sold hundreds of articles to local, national, and regional publications.

*The Feather Chase*, written as Shannon L. Brown, was her first published book and begins the Crime-Solving Cousins Mystery series. The eight-to-twelve-year-olds in your life will enjoy this contemporary twist on a Nancy Drew–type mystery.

Cathryn's from Alaska and has two series of clean Alaska romances. You can start reading those books with *Falling for Alaska*, or with *Accidentally Matched* in the spin-off series which includes *Merrily Matched*.

Cathryn enjoys hiking, sometimes while dictating a book. She also unwinds by baking and reading. Cathryn lives in Tennessee with her professor husband and adorable calico cat.

For more books and updates, visit cathrynbrown.com